THE FINAL HITCH

Izzy Mistry loves her job planning weddings in Majorca, though she wasn't expecting any proposals herself — certainly not from two different men in one night! But now she's chosen the one she wants, old flame Harrisson, *and* fallen madly in love with a rustic house in the mountains. Izzy's life is looking a lot more romantic. Yet, as the happy couple wrestle with renovations and struggle to settle into village life, everything suddenly seems a little less rosy. Izzy's beginning to feel the heat. So is this normal pre-wedding nerves . . . or is she about to make a massive mistake?

SAMANTHA SCOTT-JEFFRIES

THE FINAL HITCH

Complete and Unabridged

ULVERSCROFT
Leicester

First published in Great Britain in 2010 by
Little Black Dress
An imprint of Headline Publishing Group
London

First Large Print Edition
published 2011
by arrangement with
Headline Publishing Group
London

British Library CIP Data

Scott-Jeffries, Samantha.
  The final hitch.
  1. British- -Spain- -Majorca- -Fiction.
  2. Love stories.
  3. Large type books.
  I. Title
  823.9′2–dc22

  ISBN 978–1–4448–0934–3

Published by
F. A. Thorpe (Publishing)
Anstey, Leicestershire

Set by Words & Graphics Ltd.
Anstey, Leicestershire
Printed and bound in Great Britain by
T. J. International Ltd., Padstow, Cornwall

This book is printed on acid-free paper

For Dad, with love

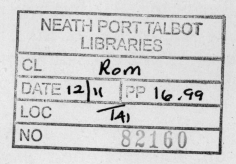

Acknowledgements

With enormous thanks to Robert Caskie for his unwavering support and to Grant for his endless encouragement and keen eye over my first draft. A huge thank you to Daisy and Norman 'Scottie' Scott, Wendy Alderman, Jack Jeffries, Alexa Newman and Poli Bautis. Finally, my gratitude to Claire Baldwin, Leah Woodburn, Maura Brickell and all at Little Black Dress Books.

1

I, Isabelle Mistry . . .

It had taken seven months of extreme dieting, four emotional bridesmaids, one overzealous Spanish seamstress and some incredibly stern words from two people who feared it might never happen to coax me into 'the dress' that day. As I finally wobbled atop a pair of impossibly high ivory silk Manolos and worried that one wrong move might dislodge the beautiful antique roses woven delicately through my up-do, I could see 'team wedding' resting up in the pews. I eyed them nervously and prepared myself to take the biggest step of my life — from the safety of the Spanish soil I'd grown to love, into the heady atmosphere of the Gothic cathedral in front of me and . . . gulp . . . married life.

The female sopranos' powerful voices began to fill the impressive cathedral from the walnut choir stalls, their a cappella resonating around the slender stone pillars, the decorative shrines and up to the almost never-ending sculpted ceiling. And at the very end of the sanctuary I could just make out Father

1

Cooper, smiling warmly. The guests rose on cue, as one. I took as deep a breath as I could manage beneath the constraints of my corset, and led the procession through the impressive wooden doors that towered above us.

This is it, I told myself, willing my feet to take each step and embark on the very long walk down the aisle. 'This . . . is . . . it!' I whispered the phrase to myself repeatedly.

Having waited months for this very moment with a mix of eager anticipation and sheer fear, it was almost impossible to believe that it was finally happening. It was a feeling that I could only describe as an out-of-body down-the-aisle experience.

I was floating, with an over-firm grip on Dad's arm, slowly passing row upon row of friends and family, remembering to smile back at the faces smiling at me. I felt light-headed, heavy-footed, self-conscious, and I regretted that final glass of pink champagne that was supposed to have steadied my nerves. As I carefully surveyed the scene, bathed in the jewel-coloured light filtered by the vast spherical stained-glass window, I carried out a mental audit, checking off each of the details, as if I was still the wedding planner, the planner who made the perfect choices and meticulous arrangements for other people's big days. It was a habit that I just couldn't break.

The church: romantic, imposing, majestic; Palma Cathedral more than delivered — tick. The flowers: English garden roses, in the palest lilacs and faded antique tones, teamed with the largest, softest creamy peonies, which looked natural but were large enough to make an impression — tick. Rows of lit candles leading from the aisle to the altar, a personal touch that had taken several heated conversations with the Spanish priest who ran the cathedral, and yet more to convince my mother that they wouldn't be a fire hazard — a well-deserved tick. I stopped myself there. It was finally my turn, and everything seemed just as I'd planned.

I took another deep breath and looked up at Dad for reassurance. His gaze was firmly fixed on the altar and his mind obviously focused on the one-foot-forward, feet-together walk he'd been so concerned about perfecting at the rehearsal. He kept careful time to the moving rendition of 'Ave Maria' as we drew ever closer to the altar. Everything *was* perfect, I told myself repeatedly. *Everything*!

Carmen, my formidable dress designer, crossed herself as we drew near. Having just gone ten rounds lacing my corset, her face, recently contorted by a mouthful of pins, was now soft and full of emotion as she fixated on the Virgin Mary beside the altar. A row of my fashionista friends let out a gasp as they eyed her creation — the intricate beading on the corset, the exquisite cut of the full, netted fifties-style skirt. Carmen's gaze fell to admire her own handiwork. I shot her a thankful smile.

I firmed up my grip on Dad's arm as the altar suddenly seemed close, and glanced forward a few rows to try and spot the rest of my family. A wonderful wide-brimmed hat in the palest lemon obscured my view. I focused on the slim, immaculately dressed figure it belonged to. It had to be Celia, my boss and mentor. The lady who had taught me all I'd come to know about weddings, who had insisted that I live in her sprawling finca whilst I did so, and who had used her sway to ensure that the cathedral was the venue for my wedding day. As if she knew I was watching, she slowly turned to face me, a wide smile in Chanel's Flamenco Red on her lips as her shimmering blue eyes filled with tears.

A few tentative steps later, I reached the worn stone steps in front of the altar. It was time. The sopranos fell silent, and the only sound was the quickening click of heels as the bridesmaids took their places. I looked up at Father Cooper, his warm round face framed by a shock of white hair. I reluctantly let go of Dad's arm as the priest welcomed our guests to the island in his friendly address. And now, for the first time, I looked up at *him*, the tall, handsome, strong man by my side, emanating confidence and warmth ... my future husband.

2

Flashback!

I had always wondered what went through a
bride's head as she stood at the altar. What it
felt like when the very moment she'd thought
about endlessly finally arrived. And now it
was my turn to find out if that moment lived
up to the dream. My turn to listen to the
priest and focus on the life-changing event
that I was about to enter into.

Yet focusing was the furthest thing from
my mind. I was so deliriously nervous and
emotional that I felt as though I wanted to
both laugh and cry. The heady smell of the
roses, the thought of a hundred pairs of eyes
watching my back, and the atmosphere of
the cathedral, heavy with incense, was a
sensual, intimidating cocktail that made me
feel giddy. I wanted to giggle. I wanted to
jump with pure glee. I watched Father
Cooper's lips move, but I failed to hear a
word he uttered. All I could think about was
the moment when both Harrisson and
Tomas had made their feelings so clear —
the moment that determined how I came to

be teetering on pin-thin heels at this very spot.

The day it had happened was supposed to have been someone else's big day. One of the biggest events of last season. Layla's wedding was a huge affair held at a stately vineyard finca overlooking the Tramuntana mountains, complete with media guest list and triple-barrelled gentry on the top tables.

Over weeks of steamy weather and an unrelenting sun that scorched the mountain-tops and cracked the treasured earth beneath the vines, stylists had lavishly decorated the finca at the bride's instruction. They had carefully constructed an abundance of chill-out areas, cocktail bars and cigar rooms for guests to explore amongst the traditional olive presses, wine cellars and grand court-yards. A team of chefs, wilting in their whites, conjured the very best banquet, prepared in specially created kitchens on site. And Layla had worn a couture wedding dress, the designer of which had flown out to make the final adjustments so that it would fit the bride's model frame absolutely perfectly on the day.

It was the kind of day that most girls dream of, a modern-day fairy-tale wedding. As the wedding planner, I couldn't deny that it had been fun spending innumerable euros on the firework display, organising industrial-strength light beams to illuminate the mountain behind the vineyard and attending the many tastings it took to perfect the invention of a 'Layla' cocktail. But it was also a day I'd been silently dreading, as the old Notting Hill life I'd run away from was destined to follow me to Majorca, via the stellar media guest list.

To make matters worse, I'd learnt that those attending included Harrisson, the ex I thought I'd left behind in London for ever, as well as his new fiancée. And if *that* wasn't enough to deal with, Layla's wedding was also the final event of the season, marking the end of my trial period with Celia. She was expecting great things of me; if I didn't deliver, she would send me packing back to London and my previously chaotic life. For all of Celia's kindness, she was also a tough, no-nonsense lady. A one-season trial had always been the agreement, and she'd given no indication of what lay beyond. Everything, it seemed, depended on how I executed my share of the meticulous planning, and how I fared as the perfect host. The pressure had almost matched the intensity of the heat that day.

On the morning of the wedding, I'd survived the embarrassment of bumping into the old boss who'd fired me, the ex I'd also hoped to hide from, and one of my best friends, the maid of honour, who'd been embroiled in a fashion disaster of what she considered to be epic proportions (but which actually equated to no more than a moth-munched hole in a Prada dress), all just hours before the ceremony. Undeterred, and still holding my nerve, I'd upheld my rather large side of the bargain with Celia — overseeing the reception at the finca.

Before the ceremony, I'd checked that the abundance of florists, designers, caterers and furniture hire companies were on schedule. I'd organised meetings with the live band, the barmen, the technicians and the maître d's, who were briefed and poised. I'd nervously counted and re-counted the names for the table plan, checked the stock of champagne and elegant glasses that had been ordered, the richly embellished cushions and the vintage Moroccan lanterns, crossing the details off a never-ending list and worrying about the strangely elusive wedding cake, a delayed flight carrying dancers from Brazil and a refrigerated delivery of the bride's favourite Manchego cheese from Menorca that had yet to arrive. It was an epic operation, and I was thankful to have the on-site help of my friend Marta.

Marta's family had owned and lived in part

of the finca for generations. Together, as a tightly knit team in which everyone played a crucial role, they had always worked hard to make the vineyard pay for itself, and the current inhabitants were no exception. Grandma kept a tight rein on the books with a pencil clasped between arthritic fingers and a keen eye on every euro. Francesca, Marta's effortlessly chic mother, and something of a Spanish domestic goddess, took care of the endlessly changing decoration. Her two sons ran the vineyard. Paco, who had inherited the family's strong good looks and impeccable manners, was in charge of production, wine ordering and tastings. Juan, the gentle dreamer of the family, tended the grounds, nurtured the vines and oversaw the gardeners. Being the lazier of the two, he would routinely sneak off on hot afternoons to sample the fruits of his labour or smoke beneath the shady pines, where he'd be artfully rumbled by Margalida, Marta's pretty teenage sister. Raul, Marta's revered but generous father, would set him back to work. Raul ran the whole operation to the highest standards, making it his business to oversee every detail, speaking frequently in his calm, mellow baritone about the honour of maintaining and bringing life to the family home.

Marta, although only in her early twenties, was in charge of scheduling, planning and co-ordinating the never-ending flurry of events at the finca. From Spanish society parties to grand weddings for couples and their guests from all over Europe, she charmed everyone she worked for. She enviably spoke three or four languages, and had a seemingly stress-free way of making big plans come together without breaking into even the mildest panic, shrugging gently and sighing '*poco a poco*' when things took a long time to conjure, or '*uno vez mas*' when a first attempt at a detail just wasn't good enough and she had to try again with a new supplier or technique. I was grateful for her diligence, but more than that, she had become a great friend. She'd been there for me when I'd wobbled a few days before the big event. She had got me back on track and had made sure that she took care of as many details as she could on the day itself, without hurting my pride by telling me that she'd done so.

I survived the wedding ceremony, keeping my composure despite the sight of the ex being dragged to a seat by his visibly stroppy fiancée and the grotesque consequences of what happens when you suggest to a distraught fashionista in moth-eaten Prada that she construct her own unique outfit. It was therefore a relief to escape the church before the ceremony had ended, and I was thankful to speed up to the finca in a taxi ahead of the guests. It had felt good to drive up through the mountains in silence. Watching the lush green pines flash past the window, I felt the cool of the car's air-conditioning prickle my skin as the sun beat down on the tarmac that wound like a helter-skelter around the mountain. It was an enforced moment of calm, but one that inevitably gave way to a knee-jerk sense of panic as we swept up the drive to the finca.

My hands felt clammy with nerves and my heart was in my throat as I walked through the main courtyard, but I found on tentative inspection that Marta had everything perfectly in place. So when the ice buckets were finally filled, the cocktail rooms had come alive with the bustle of waiters and the hordes of guests started to fill the lavishly decorated spaces, I could relax, just a little. I spent my time skilfully avoiding various ex-colleagues and the silver platters of canapés that endlessly circled at head-skimming height, whilst staying focused on the next stage of events. Ahead of schedule, with the reception in full swing and half an hour to go before seating almost two hundred people for dinner, I made the final checks to the dining tables on the vast terrace overlooking the mountains. The sun had begun to fade beyond them, bathing the olive trees and vines in pale pink light. I wandered out to the gardens, taking a sneaky glass of bubbly with me, to enjoy a few minutes' break.

The air that night was clean, sweetly scented with wild jasmine and just starting to drop to a deliciously cool temperature. I could hear the DJ mixing salsa beats in the distance, the bossa nova sounds distorting as they echoed around the mountains. I made my way to a rickety old wooden chair and table that had been placed in the shade of a leafy tree with views of the vines below. It was the most welcome sight of the evening, and with the knowledge that the party was going to plan, I enjoyed the sensation of a moment of quiet and the chance to rest my aching calves. I even felt enough mind space to start contemplating the next chapter of my life. How would I feel if Celia invited me to stay working with her? What, more to the point, would I do if she didn't? It was then that a tall, dark shadow unexpectedly appeared. It was Harrisson, the ex, and although I was determined not to listen, he'd come to talk.

I didn't want to hear his explanations as to why he'd treated me so badly in the past, or how he'd ended up with a fiancée, but he was persistent, his voice gentle and familiar, his scent warm and musky. I'd never seen him so keen to get my attention, so eager to explain and apologise. It was also an act so completely out of character that curiosity glued me to the spot. Harrisson, the guy who always seemed so unfazed and so in control, started to unravel the mess he had got himself into. I resisted my desire to race back to the party and lose myself in the crowd, and listened, despite myself, to the story of how his new girlfriend had suddenly turned into a self-appointed fiancée. I was sceptical, but I felt that at least he deserved a chance to elaborate, and besides, I really did want to hear all the juicy details.

Anastasia, or Stazi (an unfortunate but evidently accurate nickname that all of Notting Hill knew her by), was just a fling on the rebound, he pleaded, like so many other guilty men before him, a fling that had gone on too long. When he had told her that he was going to accept a job as an art director for an international fashion brand in New York, she'd assumed that he was inviting her along. She then chose to announce to her family at a Sunday lunch they'd both been invited to that they were not just going to be living together overseas, but planned to get married. It had been as much a revelation to

Harrisson as it was a horror to them. They had eyed him disapprovingly as he stood before them open-mouthed in his battered jeans, Converse trainers and bed-head hair.

'What wedding?' he'd pleaded after Stazi's carefully crafted speech had prompted a grilling from her rumbustious and scarily influential father, and a particularly awkward pushing of the Sunday roast around several plates with the family's best silver.

We stood under a star-lit Majorcan sky as he continued to pour out his heart, with the sound of the party I was supposed to be overseeing in the distance. Harrisson started to apologise for taking me for granted when we were together, his voice quiet and regretful, suddenly making me feel like the most important thing in his life. 'But why now, why after all this time?' I wanted to yell at him, had he not seemed so sincere.

For a fleeting moment I couldn't help but wonder if I still respected this guy who had turned out to be a puppy behind the cool exterior, before realising that of course it only made him seem more real, more vulnerable. More than that, he was finally saying all of the things that I'd always wanted to hear. He begged me to come back to him. To live with him in Manhattan: Start a new life with him. Whatever it took.

He looked to me for an answer, but I didn't have one. I wanted to say yes, but I was still cautious about trusting him. With my mind whirring I hesitated, and as everything seemed to fall silent, a voice softly but definitely said, 'Marry me.'

The voice wasn't Harrisson's, it was Tomas's. Sweet, kind, cerebral Tomas, Celia's son, who possessed gentlemanly manners and a passion for botany. When he had come to stay unannounced at the house that summer, I'd seen him as the antidote to all the bad boyfriend material I'd dated in London. The kind of guy I should give a try as part of my new life. He was thoughtful and considerate and I found him attractive in an earthy, understated way. But after a humiliating date where I'd totally embarrassed myself and later received a reality check from my best friend Ray, I had decided, in a panic, that though a man with corduroy patches on his jackets might be dependable, that didn't necessarily make us compatible, and it certainly didn't make him exciting. Yet deep down I knew that I hadn't given him a real chance. I'd been a coward. And I'd ensured that I didn't have the opportunity to explain that I was scared of getting hurt after Harrisson. It was easier to pretend that nothing had happened between us and never would, and I'd spent weeks avoiding him whilst both of us lived in Celia's house. I'd been an idiot. I'd presumed that he'd understood.

All three of us stood stunned. Tomas's face flushed red in the dusky light and Harrisson looked aghast. Then we all turned, startled by a loud and dramatic commotion on the stone steps nearby. It was Stazi.

'What the bloody hell . . . ?' she shrieked, her eyes ablaze at the sight of Harrisson's arm still resting territorially on my waist.

She was heading our way, wobbling precariously on vintage De Havilland snake-skin platforms that must have added at least six inches to her height, and spilling her Layla cocktail as she negotiated the steps down to the garden.

'H . . . I've been looking simply EVERY-WHERE for you. What on earth is going on?' she demanded in her public-schoolgirl voice.

Then, as quickly as she had appeared, she seemed to vanish, slipping down the worn stone steps as her skinny knees buckled beneath her. Her exotic Matthew Williamson dress flew over her hips, billowing like parachute silk, the cocktail glass shattering as it hit the steps, the shards twinkling like the diamonds from a broken engagement ring.

Instinctively Harrisson rushed to Stazi's

side before fishing his mobile from his suit pocket and pacing around the garden to find the best spot for a signal. I pulled her dress down over her ruby satin knickers and checked to see if her dramatic wails were those of real pain or just a side effect of a seriously battered ego, as she lay in an ungainly heap on the grass. When I looked up, Tomas had gone and Harrisson had made his way to the roof to call for an ambulance.

'Who the bloody hell are you?' Stazi screamed, between yelps reminiscent of a pedigree chihuahua, her eyes finally opened in a fuzzy, mascara-smudged state. It was at this moment that Harrisson returned from his rooftop phone call, chose to lean over her and inform her quite firmly, whilst looking deeply into my eyes, 'My bride . . . ' And as he did so, she fainted.

I left Harrisson clutching Stazi's limp, willowy frame, smoothing her hair away from her pinched features, and rushed off guiltily to help seat the guests for dinner. As I turned to climb the steps, Stazi opened her eyes to shoot me an evil, smug look, clutching desperately on to her man. But it was a small victory. Harrisson beamed a smile at me and gave me a 'What can I do?' shrug, and I knew that finally, if I wanted him, I had got my man.

* ★ ★

The rest of the night swept by in a haze. An endless flurry of beautiful, impeccably groomed people, platters of food piled high like delicate artworks, firework displays spectacularly timed to music, live bands, surprise acts and grand speeches all raced by like a film on fast forward, with me the outsider, watching in slow motion. My mind was with Harrisson. He'd taken Stazi discreetly to the hospital whilst Marta had stepped in to help keep an eye on the wedding with me. The party I'd so carefully planned flowed seamlessly at its own meticulously timed pace, as I floated above the scene, wondering if this parallel world that Harrisson had promised really existed, or if he was about to disappear in the way he'd always had a habit of doing.

Finally, at the end of the longest night I could ever remember, with the Brazilian dancers performing a final show-samba, the gentleman's cigar room abuzz and the Moroccan chill-out areas awash with ani-mated drinkers, there was little left to do but let events unfold. I scoured the finca for my fashionista friend Remi, but found her draped and giggling around the ample torso of an Arab billionaire at an otherwise deserted and seemingly endless dining table. I looked for my best friend Ray, but he had been seen leaving with Ramon, the spirited Spanish guitarist. With no one to share a heart-to-heart with, I decided that it was time to leave.

I battled my way through the casualties of hard-partying guests to find the taxi I'd ordered, looking for Marta to thank on my way. I found her politely trying to brush off a lecherous-looking older man breathing alcoholic advances in her direction, whilst maintaining her professional manner.

'So sorry to interrupt,' I said, putting my hand on her arm, gently leading her out of his reach.

'*Gracias, chica!*' she sighed in relief when he had turned to stagger away. 'How would you say in English? . . . Very gross!' She laughed.

'I should be thanking *you*,' I replied with sincerity. 'Really, thank you so much for everything, I couldn't have done it without your help. The party was a big success and the couple are ecstatic. Look . . . ' I pointed to Max and Layla, seemingly glued together on the dance floor.

'No, Izzy, it is my job,' Marta pleaded with her usual modesty. 'Did you see Tomas leave?' she asked. 'I did not get a chance to say goodbye.'

'Ah, well, no, not exactly.' I hesitated, feeling guilty. 'Look, lots of things happened tonight, it's a long story.' I suddenly felt exhausted and confused, not knowing where to start even if I'd wanted to. Although Marta was my usual and most understanding confidante, now was not the time, nor the place.

'Everything's OK, right?' she asked with enquiring brown eyes. '*Todo bien?*' she repeated in Spanish.

'Err, sure,' I answered unconvincingly. 'Look, I'll call you and explain everything later.'

'Everything?' she asked, her concern brightening into a look of intrigue, her brown eyes growing bigger with the exclamation, the whites shining out against her flawless brown skin.

'*Long* story!' I smiled, reaching out to hug her goodbye. 'You get on, there's so much I know you still have to take care of.'

I gave Marta a kiss on both cheeks and turned on my heels, heading out to find my cab. There was only one place to go. That was home. And home was Celia's, where Tomas, I presumed, would also be.

'*Adios, guapa!*' Marta called after me as I ran out into the darkness of the driveway. The air was cool and the sound of the party resonated from inside the finca, fading from earshot as I picked up pace. I realised that although relieved to leave the wedding behind for the expanse of star-sprinkled sky and the quietness of the mountain road, I felt even more nervous now than I had at the start of the day. I was dreading a confrontation with Tomas, but at the very least I owed him an explanation, and finally some honesty.

As I drifted in and out of sleep on the ride home, the taxi seemed to sway endlessly and without warning through the pitch-black mountain roads, headlights flooding the way. Each time I awoke at an unexpected bend or as my ear tuned into the commentary of superfast Spanish on the driver's radio, my stomach lurched in anticipation.

Finally we pulled up in the gravelled drive of Celia's house, and her one-eyed mutt Pepillo came running out to greet me, baring his teeth at the driver.

'Shhhh . . . ' I urged the small black dog as I rummaged through the contents of my handbag to find the keys that I knew had to be lurking somewhere at the bottom. He jumped up and clawed urgently at my bare legs, also keen to get inside. 'Get down!' I chided him in a loud whisper. Finally I turned the rusty old key in the lock and pushed open the heavy wooden door, willing the warped, creaking frame to slip silently over the worn and uneven terracotta tiles beneath it. Just inside, at Celia's farmhouse table, was a bottle of rough Spanish brandy and a heavy-bottomed half-filled glass. A single light had been left on, but there was no one to be seen.

I took a seat as Pepillo watched me intently from his blanket. I tried to play through the scene from that night and make sense of it. My feet too tired to move, I eyed the half-filled glass and eventually downed the contents, dragging myself to bed when my eyes felt too heavy to focus and anticipating a thumping head full of confusion the next day.

3

Great expectations

Palma airport, out of season, was deserted. A tiny Spanish woman in a pale blue uniform and slip-on shoes mopped the vacuous sea of pale grey marble that shimmered seamlessly under the harsh glare of fluorescent lighting. A businessman sat alone in the café, sipping a *cortado* coffee without taking his eyes from a copy of his *El Pais* newspaper. The arrival boards flickered, the banks of monitors relaying to no one details of recent touchdowns from other parts of Europe. I'd arrived early.

Having woken before the first chorus of cockerel crows that usually stirred me at Celia's, I'd resisted the urge to catnap and reached a bed-warm foot to the cold tiled floor as soon as I'd opened my eyes. Today was the day that Harrisson arrived; it was going to be our first weekend together on the island, and I could hardly wait.

After his marriage proposal, Tomas had flown back to England almost immediately and Harrisson had given up his big job offer

24

in Manhattan. We'd met up as soon as we could after he'd delivered a bandaged-up Stazi to the airport, replete with her pile of monogrammed LV luggage and a Louboutin wedge balanced on the end of her plastered leg as she teetered ridiculously on crutches. As we had strolled along an almost deserted beach that afternoon, I'd stood my ground (albeit in far more sensible footwear). As my Havaianas flipped up the warm golden sand at the back of my heels and the heat of the sun beat down on my bare shoulders, I knew that now was definitely not the time to be hopelessly girlie and give into his ideas for the future, when I knew, for perhaps the first time ever, exactly how I saw mine.

I made it clear that I wasn't going to drop everything I'd worked so hard for to join Harrisson in the States. I didn't want to be the quirky English girl who got dragged to work events and had to plaster on a fake smile when his colleagues told me they loved my accent. I couldn't see myself stuck in a tiny shoebox of a flat in New York, waiting for him to come home every night, making do with Facebook friends for company. In short, I wanted to carry on carving out a good life for myself. And if Harrisson had finally decided that he wanted to be a part of that life, then he had to make a commitment by

25

coming to join me in Majorca. As I had expected, when the words came firmly from my mouth, he was speechless.

Looking out to the mountains that towered above the sea like giant, familiar guardians, I was deliberately silent, waiting for him to respond, knowing that if I caught his eye, he could, as always, persuade me otherwise. I wanted to test his commitment. I wanted to see if the man who had promised me so much in the past but let me down was really ready to be with me for ever. And, most importantly, to see if he could finally put me first.

After a few moments' silence he had taken hold of my hand and given it a firm squeeze to get my attention. I reluctantly looked up at him, not quite knowing what he would say.

'Look, Izzy . . . ' he started, his voice soft and warm, 'you're the most important thing to me . . . really. Not some job,' he emphasised, squeezing my hand again. 'If I have to come here to show you that I'm serious, I will, and I'll make it work.'

With what felt like a toffee apple lodged in my throat, I wanted desperately to believe him.

'How will you make it work?' I asked eagerly, looking for reassurance and finally crumbling a little.

'I'll go freelance,' Harrisson announced. 'Art directors are needed all over the world . . . you know that,' he soothed, smiling, and we spoke no more of it. I believed him.

This weekend was the first step towards putting everything into practice. I had raced downstairs to the kitchen before even Pepillo had uncurled himself, and watched him for a moment whilst waiting impatiently for a pot of coffee to bubble on the stove. His legs twitched as he slept.

'Probably dreaming of chasing rabbits,' I'd muttered to myself, glancing from the sleeping dog to see how the weather was looking. Across the valley the sky was a pale winter blue against the green mountains, save for a few translucent white clouds that bobbed like airborne candyfloss above the pines, masking a pale, almost heatless, early-morning sun.

I'd got ready at record speed. Having laid out my clothes the night before, I'd put on my make-up between mouthfuls of buttery toast and strong Spanish coffee, the window ajar to let in the cool breeze and birdsong. And although Harrisson's flight wasn't due in until 10.30 a.m., I'd left the house just after seven, taking the small silver Seat I'd hired for my remaining time at Celia's, from a company who supplied her with bridal cars.

Now, at the airport, I paced. I paced along the shiny steel handrail that separated people greeting passengers from baggage collection. I paced past rows of empty leatherette seats and I paced past the flimsy white booths that belonged to a hundred different hire car companies. I sought out the news kiosk and indulged in a copy of *¡Hola!*, kidding myself that celebrity trash and photos of Spanish royalty on holiday was actually helping me get to grips with the language. In the middle of Penelope Cruz at home, the arrival lounge slowly started to fill. A British yachtie sidled up to wait beside me, his small white West Highland terrier lying patiently beside his worn deck shoes. Spanish families chatted in animated voices and a well-groomed lady stood alone, dressed in black leather trousers, a crisp white shirt and large diamond earrings beneath a glossy blond ponytail.

As the cleaning lady finally packed up her mop and bucket to head for another floor, passengers from the first domestic flight flooded the arrival area, their trolleys piled high with suitcases. The Majorcan grandpas wore their slippers and flat corduroy caps to travel; their wives in their most glamorous coats and neatly set hairdos clasped the hands of their grandchildren. They were met with joyful greetings and sloppy kisses on both cheeks that made me feel emotional just watching. When the bustle subsided, I shuffled over to the arrival monitors, craning my neck to see that Harrisson's flight had finally been announced as '*en tierra*', literally on the ground. I positioned myself so that I had a view of passengers pushing their trolleys to reach the luggage carousels, and waited.

It was easy to spot the easyJet flight arrival from Gatwick. There was a hen party of girls wearing silver wings on top of T-shirts emblazoned with the slogan 'Angi's Angels' squealing excitedly as they ran to claim their luggage. There were families on package holidays trailing trendy stroppy teens, and vibrant pensioners with already brown faces seeking winter sun. I returned a smile to three immaculate older men wearing Pringle tank tops and pulling golf clubs alongside their luggage. Just behind them was Harrisson.

His face broke into a warm smile as his eyes fixed on mine, and I itched for him to rush over and scoop me up, but of course, that wasn't his style. I resisted the very uncool urge to bounce up and down as I clutched hold of the shiny metal barrier I wanted to whiz by to reach him, and willed my feet to stand their ground. He looked good, his face handsome, his uniform of battered jeans, a box-fresh white T-shirt beneath a honey-coloured cashmere jumper, deliciously familiar. He carried a tan leather overnight bag that had been halfway around the world and looked as though it could tell some stories. His face was soon against mine, his fuzzy stubble rubbing my cheek, his warm, clean scent unmistakable and his bear hug enveloping. 'Hey!' he whispered soothingly into my ear as I closed my eyes for a moment and melted.

I pulled away to look at him again. 'So, welcome to Majorca!' I beamed.

That morning we headed straight from the airport and into the city. With the sky clear and blue, it was a winter's day to make the most of. We took the busy Cintura road, weaving through the three lanes of fast traffic, with an impressive view of the cathedral bathed in golden sunlight in the distance. As we gave each other an update on our news, we sped past the port, passing ambling cyclists, tanned, lythe rollerbladers and joggers, whilst taking in the view of the white masts of yachts and vast gleaming motorboats bobbing gently on the water. We headed through the historic part of town, past immaculate flower beds boasting neat rows of cherry-red flowers, and elegant buildings, sophisticated shops and well-dressed inhabitants going about their business before the shops closed at lunchtime.

'Coffee?' I asked, spotting a chance space to park the car.

Out on the street Harrisson took my hand in his and I led him through the back streets of the old town to my favourite café. His tales of fashion shoots and difficult models, photographers with inflated egos and stylists with attitude sounded like an alien world that was a million miles away. I'd got used to the slower pace that came after the end of the busy wedding season; the working days that drew in as autumn daylight hours dwindled, the site visits that diminished as even some of the most popular venues closed until the spring, the lack of urgency and luxury of time to lavish on existing brides. Harrisson's stories of Notting Hill gossip, parties and fall-outs were all part of a world and a lifestyle that I'd almost forgotten existed. Palma, even on a Saturday, was operating at its usual laid-back pace.

In the narrow stone streets, where the large wooden doors of grand historic houses nestled alongside the open shutters of small boutiques and hidden restaurants, there was a gentle buzz of activity. Workmen filled the bars with the laughter of their mid-morning break, shop girls grabbed a quick *café solo* and ladies queued to be served at a bakery renowned for its *ensaimadas*. We passed a beautiful jewellery shop and a row of shops selling contemporary furniture that looked like hidden gems. The road then widened and opened on to a square, a church at its centre, flanked by restaurants and bars and a view of the port beyond.

Outside Café La Lonja the waitress gave me a friendly acknowledging *hola* and eyed Harrisson with interest as she balanced a tray brimming with drinks on a cupped hand. She delivered them to a table of well-groomed Spanish girls wrapped in layers of scarves. We pulled up chairs to a neighbouring table, to take in the bright winter rays and the view. I eyed the tapas menu hungrily.

'So, babe,' Harrisson started with a twinkle in his eye, 'what have you got planned for us this weekend?'

Before I could answer, the waitress was at our side, flashing a friendly smile and a pen poised to her pad. We made our usual 'how are you?' exchanges in Spanish, and I blushed slightly, wondering if Harrisson would notice my bad accent and limited vocabulary.

'Pretty impressive.' He smiled as she walked away.

'Well, I should be able to order a coffee by now.' I blushed again.

'So!' I remembered excitedly. 'Houses!' I

exclaimed, rummaging in my handbag for a number of folded-up property details I'd printed out from the internet. 'I thought we'd spend this morning in the city, grab some lunch and then when everything shuts for a siesta, we can start to house-hunt.'

'House-hunt?' Harrisson quizzed.

'Yes, house-hunt,' I confirmed seriously. 'We discussed it . . . ' I nodded, having planned it for weeks.

'Babe, that sounds great, but look, I just didn't think we'd start so soon.' He noticed my obvious disappointment. 'I don't even know the place yet.'

The coffee arrived. I ripped open a sugar packet and tried to hide my disappointment as I stirred the contents into the cup.

'Yes, you're right,' I concluded, smiling at him. 'I didn't mean to bombard you as soon as you got here. It's just that we have so little time together, and now it's quiet in the office . . . well, I guess I just got carried away and started to make appointments,' I confessed, feeling a little guilty now that maybe I'd been too hasty in pushing things forward.

'Appointments?'

'Just a couple,' I confirmed, 'to give us an idea of what's out there.'

Harrisson picked up the details on the

table and started to thumb through them.

'Those are in Spanish, but I sent you web links in English, remember?'

'Yeah, course,' he muttered unconvincingly, frowning at a photograph of an overgrown garden that needed a serious overhaul. 'Well, if you've made appointments, best we keep them,' he concluded, giving me a big smile and resting a hand on my knee.

4

Houses, pigs and whisky

'This house has potential for seven bedrooms,' the estate agent told us as we stood outside a stone cottage in a neighbouring valley to Celia's. 'It is very good house.' It was our first viewing of the afternoon, and the estate agent appeared to be right. There was a gravel drive leading to the pretty entrance, dotted with ancient olive trees, and views across the valley to the distant town below.

Greta, the estate agent, was tall, blonde and smart. She spoke almost perfect English with a clipped German accent. The three of us stood in the milky light of the afternoon admiring the slightly crumbling stonework of the house, the handsome shutters with peeling emerald-green paint work at the windows and the canopy of vines that sheltered the path to the wooden front door. The air was fresh and the valley quiet, save for the sound of a bleating donkey and several cockerels with late body clocks, even by Majorcan standards.

'This is good country house.' Greta smiled

with a shake of her glossy ponytail before leading the way towards the front door. I glanced at Harrisson and he signalled for me to go before him. It was clear from his face that he was less than convinced by the whole situation. Looking up at the sturdy building, I imagined a country kitchen, roaring log fires and romantic nights in.

'So, there's no parking?' Harrisson asked Greta directly, his Converses crunching on the gravel and his voice cutting through my daydream with a reality check.

'No need. You can park on the roadside all of the time here. Just a hundred metres away,' answered Greta efficiently.

'And it shares a pathway to the garden and entrance with the neighbouring house?' Harrisson observed out loud.

'Yes, but these are friendly people, it is no problem. With these people you also share the well.'

'The well?' Harrisson repeated slowly, as if the concept was incomprehensible.

'Yes, for the water,' Greta replied. I couldn't help but giggle.

Harrisson looked at me in disbelief. I had yet to explain that many of the houses on the island didn't have mains water. I remembered that he'd been in London just that morning and the idea must seem prehistoric. I shrugged apologetically.

Inside, the house was in darkness. A damp, musty smell filled the building and the sound of Greta's flat, heavy boots echoed on the stone floor. She grappled to open the heavy wooden shutters to let in the daylight. The windows, with a few broken panes, revealed a beautiful view of the mountains, but as the now thin light streamed in and on to the thick whitewashed walls, it was clear that we had walked straight into a depressingly basic sitting room. There was a simple fireplace, with two worn wooden chairs positioned in front of it, and a television set from the 1970s in the corner.

I felt a damp chill come up from the cold stone floor and sighed.

'Original tiles . . . ' Greta remarked as I looked down at my shoes and the terracotta floor that hadn't seen a mop for some time. 'You see, it is simple and traditional,' she added. 'Ready for new owner to make their mark.'

Unconvinced, we followed her through the room to the back of the house as she continued her sales pitch.

'This is the kitchen!' she announced as we stood in a room with an old stone sink and another open fireplace, this time low to the ground and surrounded by concrete benches.

'This is the original fire for cooking,' she told Harrisson, who was eyeing it suspiciously. 'It is antique and this room is needing of some modernisation . . . as it says on the plans,' she added defensively, noting his expression.

I raised my eyebrows at the understatement. Bare wires hung against the walls, a single open shelf was fitted along the length of one yellowing wall and a large wooden cupboard seemed to be the only place for storage. I tugged gently at the handle of the warped open door to peer inside, and the round wooden knob came away in my hand. I quickly pushed the cupboard shut as Greta continued her tour oblivious and Harrisson gave me an amused smile.

'Of course this room has the benefit of opening to the garden at the back.' I nodded in polite agreement as Greta pointed to the door leading to the garden.

Next to the kitchen was another tiny room.

'Perfect for dining room or bedroom,' Greta remarked, pushing open another set of shutters.

Both rooms had views on to the neighbouring farm, where pigs, chickens and a tired-looking horse seemed to be at home and a towering pile of rubbish waited to become a bonfire. No sign of the now infamous well, I noted.

A small staircase rose from the sitting room up to three bedrooms, one of which led to the only bathroom, which had a grubby tub and no running water. The bedrooms were eerie. A heavy wooden single bed dominated every room, each one guarded by a simple wooden cross on the wall above it.

'Then we have top floor,' Greta announced with a smile.

An ancient wooden ladder from bedroom three rose up to an attic. As we climbed the rickety rungs to take a look, I noticed that a partition wall divided the two rooms.

'Here we have room where traditionally you would kill and prepare the pig . . . and here bedroom four . . .'

Harrisson and I looked at each other in horror.

'It is very cold,' I mentioned to Greta, feeling another chill whilst spotting the missing panes in the thin glass windows and the bare concrete floor underfoot.

'It is old house and has not had shutters open for air to come inside. When in use, it will not need heating. The open fires will heat the whole house,' she insisted.

Harrisson shook his head slightly at the thought and we followed Greta back down to the ground floor and outside.

'This is final room,' she told us, leading us

through the pretty but unkempt garden.

'Room?' queried Harrisson. 'I'm a little confused,' he grumped to Greta, as we took an old stone path past a large jasmine bush and flowering succulents, proving that the garden was definitely the house's best feature. 'You mentioned that there are seven bedrooms here.'

'Yes,' Greta confirmed. 'It is different the way we see houses here. I have heard this said before. Here, if a room might be able to be used as a bedroom, it is marked on the details as possible bedroom. So, in this house you have the room used to kill the pig, the other room on the top floor, dining room downstairs, plus three bedrooms and this room. All are bedroom!'

She was now standing next to a three-walled construction with no roof and a trough at one end.

'This is room once used to *keep* the pig. Or another bedroom, maybe for summer.'

I let out another giggle. It was an uncontrollable response to Greta's most ridiculous elaboration yet, as well as the pained expression on Harrisson's face.

'I'm not sure this is really quite what we're looking for.' I smiled at the estate agent, stifling a laughing fit as I watched the colour come back to Harrisson's cheeks.

'OK, no problem,' Greta offered, unfazed. 'I can show you more houses today?' she urged keenly. 'At the same price?'

'Yes, the price,' Harrisson managed inquisitively. 'Remind me again . . . '

'Of course. The house is three hundred thousand euros,' Greta answered with a poker-straight face.

'Three hundred . . . ' Harrisson mouthed in amazement.

'Yes, it comes with land and olive trees. The owners will hold out for the right buyer. They are in no hurry to sell.'

'And how long has it been on the market?' I asked, trying to keep up the interested and polite conversation in a very English way.

'Two years,' Greta confirmed, 'but in Majorca this is not so long. This is normal.' Harrisson shot me a look that seemed to say 'nonsense' and 'get me out of here' in one desperate glance. I wound up the tour and mumbled to Greta about emailing details and keeping in touch.

As we waved goodbye from the now seemingly plush interior of our car, we sighed in relief. Feet damp from spending just half an hour in the house, and feeling strangely uncomfortable in the driver's seat, I realised I was sitting on the doorknob I'd stuffed into my back pocket when I'd pulled it clean off the kitchen cupboard. We sat for a while and joked about growing old in armchairs in front of the fire, knitting. Then we considered the benefits of sleeping in the room once used to kill the pig and hang the meat, versus the idea of sleeping in the open-air pen used to keep the pig.

'Seriously, though, Izz,' Harrisson finally said with a straight face. 'If that house is so expensive *and* completely uninhabitable, how are we going to find something that works for us here?'

'Maybe it's a one-off,' I offered. 'We can't give up yet, we've only just started looking . . . and this *is* one of the most expensive areas on the island, after all,' I pleaded, not sure who I was trying to convince, him or myself.

We grabbed a quick drink in the warmth of a traditional tapas bar tucked away in the back streets of the local town of Andratx and waited for the next estate agent to arrive. Maria, a young Spanish girl with perfect English but less than perfect properties, showed us two townhouses that looked great on paper but on inspection didn't live up to the dream.

'The next,' she assured us, 'I think you will like. It is more modern.'

Harrisson's apartment in Notting Hill had

been what I called a 'man den'. It was a buy-to-let that a City boy he'd met at a party had bought with a bonus, and was the top floor of a mews house on one of the best streets off the Portobello Road. Harrisson had fallen for it the very moment he'd stepped through its opaque glass doors.

The place was full of high-tech lighting, with a state-of-the-art sound system wired to play in every room and an abundance of hard shiny surfaces. The charcoal marble bathroom, glass-encased en suite and glossy wooden floors continued the sophisticated, masculine look. Unlike my scruffy tiny flat, which was in perpetual disarray, his was decked with bespoke bookcases on which he kept his 'library' of art books and DVDs, and banks of concealed storage that merged so seamlessly with the walls that I could never find the broom cupboard or locate the wardrobe. It was possible to watch the plasma TV whilst you took a shower, get ice dropped straight into your drink from the front of the American fridge and admire large abstract artworks that looked like they should belong in the Tate Modern; ones that I quite liked to look at but wasn't sure why, let alone understand what they were about or of. It was also a place in which I never felt entirely comfortable.

Despite whole Sundays spent lounging on the oversized sofa, watching movies on the cinema-sized projector screen and eating calorific takeaways, I could never completely relax. To me, the flat felt like a film set that I, with my clumsy tendencies and naturally untidy ways, was just messing up. The kind where a beautiful leggy model wearing nothing but one of Harrisson's shirts should at any moment emerge casually from his bedroom. But I knew that girl wasn't me. I just didn't fit with the decor.

This, I told myself, wandering the streets of the small Spanish market town on the way back to the car as the light began to fade, was more my world. It was real and I wanted to be part of it.

Back in the car we followed Maria in her nippy, logo-ed Citroën as she sped her way artfully through the one-way system of narrow residential streets that mazed through the old town, just avoiding dogs out for an evening walk and a wizened old lady bent double over a walking stick. Her delicate hand flailed, signalling for all to stop, her pop socks ruched around the ankles of her slippered feet.

I'd chosen the next property thinking it might be more Harrisson's style, but had no idea of the precise location. All I knew was that it was an apartment with good-sized rooms and spectacular views of the sea, but that it looked a little dated, I warned him.

Harrisson brooded silently in the passenger seat. He looked tired from his journey and fed up with viewing properties that he had no intention of living in. I knew that so far, our first weekend together in Majorca hadn't been much fun or much of a success.

We negotiated a dual carriageway, avoiding the taxis that drifted across several lanes to their exit at the very last moment, cutting up everyone in their wake, and two tiny electric cars that struggled to keep up with kids on scooters in the slow lane.

Maria pulled off at the Santa Ponça exit and my heart sank. I let out a little disappointed groan.

'What is it, babe?' Harrisson asked in a deep, sweet tone.

'Oh, just that I've just realised where the next property is located.'

'No good?' he asked as we reached a roundabout that led down to a shopping centre, past a massive McDonald's, a scruffy supermarket and a Texaco garage.

'No, it's just, well, kinda touristy,' I offered, trying not to be too negative. It was an area that was popular with British holidaymakers, but I couldn't see myself living there.

'Loving the ironic names of the English bars,' he laughed. 'And how many Irish pubs does a Spanish resort need?' I was grateful that he'd kept his sense of humour.

'Well,' I said as we passed the first Chinese takeaway I'd seen in months, 'I guess you can get everything here if you need a Brit-fix . . . and the beach looks good.'

'Beach is *always* good,' Harrisson agreed.

Maria's car continued to speed through the town and to my relief parked up in a wooded area high above it. It was a residential street with two massive white concrete blocks of flats shaded by pines, facing the sea beyond.

'This isn't so bad,' I piped as we got out of the car, trying to muster some enthusiasm for the last visit of the day.

'I wanted to navigate this way,' Maria said, greeting us again with a smile, 'so you understand where the apartment is located, but if you drive one exit further and take the roundabout, you come straight here.' She pointed in the direction of the pine trees. 'This is very nice area, new houses, very expensive,' she added. 'Do you want to see inside first, or the pool?'

Harrisson's face seemed to instantly brighten with the mention of the word.

'Pool,' I confirmed with a giggle.

The apartment block was a whitewashed

bunker of a building, just six storeys tall.

'It is not possible to have high-rise in Majorca,' Maria explained. 'It ruins the landscape.'

'It's kind of modernist,' Harrisson noted, just as I was thinking it was kind of ugly.

'Yes,' Maria agreed. 'It was built in 1964.'

To the left of the building were communal lawned gardens parched from the sun, the grass thin and worn. A path led directly to a large pool area with a tuck-shop-style bar and shop at one end and a few plastic loungers shaded by Guinness logo-ed umbrellas at the other. The water itself looked murky, but the pool was vast and oval, large enough for a very good swim.

'This area and pool the apartment shares with three blocks,' Maria told us. 'It is good for families or if you want to swim in the summer and not go to the beach.'

Harrisson's step quickened as we followed her to the main entrance of the building. Inside it was indisputedly dark and tired. The walls, which appeared to be pebble-dashed, were slightly peeling with damp; the original, clunky lift was just large enough to take us, its steel doors closing to reveal a small mirrored interior.

The flat was on the top floor, but I had resisted calling it a penthouse, knowing

Harrisson's expectations of such a label. The lift doors opened and we stood at the front door.

'Please . . . ' Maria offered, deftly tackling two locks with a heavy set of keys on a loop before holding the door open so that we could step inside.

There was a narrow hallway leading to the living room, from which I heard Harrisson express a 'wow' before I'd even reached it. The room was large and the view from the glass doors that made up the end wall was purely of the sea.

'This is more like it,' he beamed.

As I looked around at the tired seventies furniture, the plastic plants and a damp patch on the wall, I couldn't seem to see what he saw.

He slid open the glass doors and stepped on to the vast balcony. 'This is great,' he proclaimed, gazing out to sea as the lights in the distance started to twinkle on the horizon.

'Check out the terrazzo floors in the living room!' he continued excitedly, rushing back inside to explore. 'They'd definitely be worth keeping.'

'They run throughout,' Maria confirmed. 'Although the plumbing . . . I am not sure, you might want to take out the kitchen and also put in a new bathroom, and to access the pipes, you must take the floor up.'

Harrisson seemed to ignore her as he raced around the apartment, checking out the rooms.

There was a large master bedroom, covered in an orange geometric-patterned sixties wallpaper that would once have been described as 'groovy'. The sun had faded both the pattern and its vintage appeal, but the room did have two double glass doors, similar to those in the living room, that opened on to a smaller terrace, just large enough to be a sunbathing spot for two. Back inside, there was an archaic yellow en suite that looked filthy, a separate chocolate-brown WC, and a second bedroom in an equally dreary decor. However, the rooms were all good sizes and the layout worked.

The kitchen was at the back of the apartment, and had a large rectangular window overlooking the pine trees beyond. A box room of a study faced the same way.

'This,' Harrisson noted, 'would be a great work base for me, so peaceful.'

I tried to hide my incomprehension. To me, the flat was fine, but it looked like a holiday home that needed a lot of money spent on it, not a house to live in full time and be integrated with the local community.

'Try to see past the bad wallpaper and wall tiles, Izz,' Harrisson urged. 'Imagine, we get someone to strip all of this back to a shell, paint it white, restore the floors, put in new appliances . . . it would be amazing. It could be the coolest retro pad, like the ones you see in *Wallpaper* magazine,' he continued. 'Just think what something like this would cost in Notting Hill, and that's without the view of the sea and your own pool,' he added, on a roll, still trying to convince me.

'I think he might like this one.' I smiled at Maria.

She grinned back.

'So, tell me,' Harrisson asked her, in a more businesslike tone, 'what's the deal here?' Maria looked confused. 'What's the situation with the owners?'

'It is an older lady who owns the property,' Maria told him in her pretty accent. 'From Denmark. She bought it with her husband when the block was built. But last year her husband died and now she lives back in Denmark with her daughter.'

'OK,' said Harrisson with a nod and thoughtfully pursed lips. 'What is the asking price? Does she need to sell quickly?'

Maria blushed. 'The asking price is two hundred and forty-five thousand euros, but I have never got to these other questions with this property.' She shot me an apologetic, embarrassed smile. 'But I wanted to show it, in case you like it.'

'No problem.' I beamed back. 'Do you want to find out?'

Maria was already dialling a number by the time I'd finished the sentence, and as she spoke in sing-song Spanish, I turned to a frowning Harrisson to explain.

'It's different here,' I whispered. 'Sometimes agents will take property details from another agent's site, show it, then contact the owner to say they have interest and ask if they want them to handle it!'

Harrisson raised an eyebrow. 'But that's so unpro — ' We turned as we both heard Maria's fliptop mobile click tightly shut.

'I am sorry, Mr Harrisson' Maria started, her eyes a little sad behind her rectangular specs. 'Now I hear from this lady owner that the apartment . . . is not for sale.'

* * *

Within the hour I had whisked Harrisson off to the coolest bar I could think of in the city, one with beautiful views of the boats bobbing gently on the water, a DJ playing chill-out beats and one of the best cocktail menus around. It was all I could think of doing to calm him down. He'd travelled several hundred miles to see three houses that were a definite no-go and made our budget seem like it might never stretch, and an apartment he'd fallen for that had been taken off the market.

Although the bar was almost deserted at such an early hour, save for a group of cool Spanish twenty-somethings drinking coffee and ignoring the smoking ban, I hoped that sipping a whisky sour in the laid-back atmosphere might help lighten Harrisson's mood.

I apologised humbly into my coffee and tried to make him see the funny side. He didn't. So I left him to brood and thumb through a pile of glossy Spanish art magazines.

'The whole thing stinks when you think about it,' he declared, as his second cocktail arrived and the stools at the endless gleaming bar started to fill with couples nibbling on bowls of tapas. 'How can it be so unprofessional that you're shown properties that don't match the details, or that are owned by people who're not even signed up to the agency?' he quizzed, still smouldering. 'In England, it's just not allowed!'

I looked at him square on, taking in his serious expression, his tightly furrowed brow, his fingers working at the stem of his glass. As he stared at the floor, I reminded myself to call Maria to explain that Harrisson just wasn't used to the way everything worked here, and to apologise for him losing his temper.

'It's just not going to work,' he said seriously, his eyes lifting slightly but not meeting mine. 'Already, it's crazy.'

My heart sank. I couldn't believe that he was going to give up so easily. And what did he think wasn't going to work? Everything? Us? Majorca? I half expected the subject of Manhattan to rear its ugly unwanted head.

'Babe,' he started after a pause that seemed to fill mounting minutes, 'I think it's just going to be best if you take care of the house-hunting . . . Show me a shortlist or something.'

I let out an audible sigh of relief and slowly smiled.

He met my eyes now with his, and they twinkled.

'I *love* this place,' he said with an excited smile. 'It's got everything for us here, I see that . . . but Izz, I'm just not ready for all the stuff that's going to drive me nuts.'

'A slow initiation.' I laughed. 'That's what you need.'

'Yeah,' he agreed, emptying his glass.

5

Hair today, gone tomorrow!

Monday morning came around with the kind of unexpected rude thud that I vaguely remembered it delivering when I was young and wanted the weekend to last for ever. Harrisson and I had spent Sunday night in Palma, at a jazz club that had opened its basement for a special party in honour of a trumpeter who'd played with Miles Davies in the sixties. We'd drunk bourbon, spoken in loud, animated voices to compete with the live music, chatted with an English-speaking couple on the next table, and sat with our hands entwined, marvelling at the complex trill of the trumpet solos as the old guys, in their seventies, showed that they could still wow a crowd with their improvised set. Harrisson loved it. Having filled Saturday with estate agents' appointments, I knew that Sunday was my day to make it up to him, to show him some of the things that the island had to offer. So I'd had the deceptively relaxed agenda organised to a T. Now, as I trawled sleepily through my inbox in the office, I ran the date back through my head.

We'd grabbed a strong, dark *café solo* on the way out of the house and headed down to Portixol, the renovated fishing port at the edge of the city. We strolled along the beach front, past the rows of candy-coloured fishermen's cottages now turned into million-pound homes, as pretty girls on rollerblades and men jogging with their dogs overtook our leisurely pace. The air felt salty and clean against our skin, the pale sun warm on our backs, and our route led us to a bar with tables outside and a big pile of international newspapers for sharing. We devoured crusty bread with local *jamon*, cheese, deliciously sour green olives and strong milky coffee.

Coaxing a very comfortable Harrisson out of his chair, I led him next through the grounds of the beautiful cathedral and on to Es Baluard, the city's contemporary art gallery. My fuzzy mind dwelled now on the airy modern spaces filled with beautiful paintings and the impeccable surroundings. The vast terrace that overlooked the bay, the permanent collection that was home to so many paintings and objects that spoke of the history of the island. We'd wandered around the vast interior, hardly seeing another soul, whizzing up to the terrace in the glass lift, kissing, with no one but the guards there to see us.

Now, as I deleted my junk mail, recalling the details of our late lunch overlooking the sea, and the siesta we'd taken before going back to the city that night, I realised that Harrisson had been gone just five hours. He had caught the first flight of the day to get him back for a fashion shoot in the East End of London by 9 a.m. I missed him already. My face lit up as my inbox displayed his name and I opened his message.

Hey, thanks for a great weekend, babe, it read. *Have just got on set to find that the photographer is running late . . . we could have stayed in bed for another hour!*

I blushed at the message, sent from his BlackBerry, and gazed dreamily out of the office window. The autumn day was bright, the familiar view across the valley bathed in a soft buttery light, and below I could hear the sound of Pep, Celia's gardener, tending the hibiscus shrubs in the garden and chatting away to Pepillo in the local dialect.

'Ah, good morning, Isabelle.' Celia's formal tone interrupted my daydreams, bringing me back to the room. 'You're in, marvellous!'

I looked up, startled. I'd almost forgotten that I was, in fact, sitting in Celia's office, working for her business. I put a hand up self-consciously to my still-rumpled bed-hair and wished I'd at least scraped it back. I glanced up at the clock on my computer screen: just gone 8.35. I'd been too preoccupied with the chance of getting a message from Harrisson to say he'd arrived back in London safely to worry how I looked, or to grab breakfast, and now, feeling hungry and scruffy, I regretted both.

'Good morning, Celia,' I chimed back, trying to shake the woolly feeling in my head and focus. 'Did you enjoy the weekend?'

'Yes, perfectly well, thank you,' Celia replied politely with a gentle smile as she wandered round to her desk. She bent down gracefully in her pale blue pencil skirt and matching cashmere twinset to turn on her computer. 'I did receive a telephone call from a somewhat urgent-sounding Maureen Silverstein,' she added, standing up again, her back finishing-school straight. 'I promised that you would call her first thing this morning.'

Maureen Silverstein. The name rang in my head with alarm bells. I'd almost, momentarily, forgotten. It was Maureen's wedding to Gavin that very Friday.

'Yes, of course, no problem,' I gulped.

She had called the office earlier that summer and we had arranged to meet at one of her favourite spots on the island to discuss her wedding plans — the pool of a five-star hotel that led down to the ocean. Maureen had turned up an hour late, dressed in the shortest white hotpants I'd ever seen on a lady in her fifties, a white vest draped in gold chains and a pair of oversized Chanel sunglasses with white frames to match. Her feet were pedicured with tiny diamanté motifs and slipped into high gold sandals, and her fingers were heavy with jewels, including a very impressive diamond-encrusted engagement ring that she couldn't wait to show me. She was quite a vision amidst the otherwise relaxed and understated Europeans occupying the sunloungers.

She was also enormous fun, a bubbly fifty-something from north London who spoke at a million miles an hour and was marrying a man in his thirties.

'He's the only one who can keep up with me,' she'd giggled, pulling out a supple white leather wallet to show me a photograph of him before I could comment. 'Here's my Gav,' she'd cooed. 'We met in Naples, Florida, have you been?' she asked me, before showing me photos of her children at every conceivable age.

'Now, do you have a good make-up artist?' she'd continued. 'Because Paris here, this one, she's sixteen and totally obsessed with how she looks and is *always* fighting over something or other with Natasha, she's fourteen, pretty, aren't they . . . and they will drive me crazy if I get ready with them on the day . . . And at my age, I'll need a bit of work! Isabelle, we'll need a team!' she decided. 'I'll need fake tan, hair, make-up and nails, and I have around fifteen friends who will need the same . . . we'll need a fleet of girls.'

It was in this endless, breathless stream of consciousness that our planning came together. Maureen didn't do email and preferred Olympic phone conversations in which she was definitely a triple gold medal winner. She excelled at conference calls with contractors and epic half-day meetings that she loved to nip over for, clutching a bulging file of magazine clippings of elaborate table decorations and towering cakes and celebrity wedding pages from *Hello!* that she hoped to emulate. I grew fond of her very quickly.

'So, why a winter wedding?' I'd asked at our third meeting that first month, noting how much Maureen seemed to love the sun. Her skin had already turned the darkest mocha against a black cashmere playsuit that was just a little too tight.

'It's always been a dream,' she offered, before bending the straw on her drink

59

between her long manicured nails in deep thought. 'My first two weddings were over here, in the sun, so really, to be fair to Gav, it seemed only right that we try and make this one really special, something different . . . And anyway,' she laughed, leaning in towards me, 'at my age, a little more make-up, a little more of a frock and a little less heat will help me feel more like a beautiful bride. It's just . . . you know, all a bit more forgiving.'

It was a concept I'd not even considered, as she seemed so vivacious and outgoing. But Maureen, as always, had everything sewn up.

'Besides,' she continued, throwing her head back with laughter, 'as I keep telling Gavin, I have no choice but to come over to the apartment throughout the summer to get things organised.'

For the wedding itself, I wasn't surprised to hear that Maureen had worked her magic on her local rabbi and persuaded him to give her the wedding of her dreams.

'You won't believe it,' she'd rung to announce one morning, full of excitement, 'but Rabbi Zimmerman has agreed to marry Gav and me round the pool, in the gardens, if we do it at sunset.'

'Sunset?' I'd asked.

'Yes, so that God won't see, of course!' she

confirmed. 'Gavin's a Catholic!' she whispered in shame, as if announcing that he had committed an unspeakable crime.

Throughout the summer, Maureen and I planned every detail.

'I have more ideas!' she'd regularly announce on the phone like an enthusiastic schoolgirl, and within days we'd be sitting poolside, sharing a bottle of chilled Chardonnay that Maureen insisted on ordering, whatever the time of day. Here we'd pore over tear sheets from glossy American magazines, drooling over the seemingly unfeasible flower decorations as she asked, 'Do you know anyone here who can do this?' or 'Do you think this is fabulous, Izzy, or just a bit too OTT?'

As August came to a close, Maureen's tan had deepened to a shade reminiscent of a 1970s Ambre Solaire advert and she had been told by her dermatologist to take it easy, for the sake of her Botox and fillers. Although her sunglasses increased in size with each meeting and factor 50 peeped from the top of the handbags that matched every outfit, I knew it was time to wrap up the arrangements. At our final Chardonnay-fuelled chat before the wedding, I showed her how we could pull together all the elements she had dreamt about. How the flower sculpture would work with the Jewish hoopa by the pool, how we'd dress the gardens with fairy lights and candles for the twilight ceremony and move guests seamlessly into a heated marquee afterwards. I'd had a sample menu printed and delivered, shown her a photo of the tower of fluffy white meringues that would be the wedding cake and booked a hair and make-up artist who was waiting to carry out a pre-wedding trial after our meeting.

'It's everything I dreamt of!' Maureen announced emotionally, hugging me as a heavy train track of Diorshow mascara wound its way down her cheek and dripped on to my simple white tee.

Now, as I returned her call, with less than a week to go, I only hoped that the big day would live up to Maureen's glamorous dream.

'Isabelle!' I could hear her long nails tapping nervously on the receiver as she said my name.

'Maureen, how are you? Is everything OK?'

'To be honest, no. It's a disaster!' she said with a nervous laugh, trying to keep herself together.

'I bet its fixable,' I soothed. 'Most things are.'

'I'm not so sure, I don't know where to start . . . ' Maureen gabbled, with a catch in her voice. 'I've gone brunette for the wedding . . . I was at the salon all day Saturday, having a pre-wedding pedi, mani, the works . . . when it happened.'

'What happened?'

'They offered me a discount if a junior did the colour and offered to throw in a free treatment. It sounded like such a good deal . . . ' She paused. 'She even seemed to understand the chocolatey-cappuccino colour I was after.'

'Right . . . '

'But when she pulled off the foils, I noticed that she was also pulling out great clumps of . . . my hair!'

I let out a gasp, a little louder than I'd intended.

'It was like something out of a horror movie,' Maureen continued. 'I was sat there with just days to go until the wedding, with my crowning glory around my feet.'

I wasn't sure of the most diplomatic way to ask how bad it was.

'Can you get them to make it look thicker with extensions, maybe? You still have a day left before you fly,' I suggested.

'No, Izzy, you don't understand. There really isn't much left. They've cropped it short, it was the only thing they could do!' Maureen started sobbing, her voice breaking up between huge gulps of breath. 'I've not dared to see Gav yet. We agreed to have a few days to ourselves before the wedding so that I could be with the girls.'

'I'm sure he won't mind a bit! I bet it really suits you short . . . it sounds very fashionable,' I said, trying to imagine it and, of course, be positive.

Maureen was still crying.

I was thinking winter wedding, maybe a fur-trimmed hood, a beautiful hat . . . but none of my suggestions seemed to calm Maureen down.

'Do you think we should just postpone the whole thing?' she asked finally, with a serious tone to her voice.

'The wedding? Of course not!' I exclaimed in a panic. 'I can't imagine why you'd think there was a need to!'

'I don't care how much it costs,' Maureen added glumly. 'I just wanted it to be perfect.'

'It will be!' I assured her. 'If you just think of it as a change of hair arrangement . . . Look, Sara is still booked to do your hair and make-up. I'll call her and let her know. She'll have some ideas . . . She really is the best here, you'll be in good hands.'

'Maybe I should go back and go platinum,' Maureen mulled out loud, tapping her nails again. 'That might just, I don't know, give it a lift maybe.'

'Good idea,' I agreed. 'It suited you blond. Now, go book the appointment. Everything's all organised this end, so nothing for you to worry about.'

'OK, thanks, Izzy, I will do . . . but if I see that junior . . . '

I giggled with relief.

'Look, it will be such an amazing day, you won't give your hair a second thought,' I promised her, before hanging up the receiver.

Looking down at my desk, I let out a big sigh.

'Problems, Isabelle?' Celia asked with an enquiring tone.

'Poor Maureen's had a disaster at the hairdresser's. She's very upset, so it's not ideal,' I answered, 'but not as dramatic as I'm sure the conversation sounded.'

Celia gave me a smile.

'And I'm sure it's something Sara can help with on the day,' I assured both of us.

'Sara?' Celia asked. 'But Sara's working for me on Saturday evening.'

'Sorry, Celia, but I definitely have her booked.' I reeled, my face flushing. 'I've got a team tackling fifteen ladies in Bendinat, and Sara's just focusing on Maureen.'

'But it's been in the diary for months,'

Celia exclaimed, her kitten heels clicking on the tiled floor as she paced over to show me her delicate lilac leather diary. With a perfectly manicured hand, she opened the book at a page marked with a gold silk ribbon. The date was circled and the words 'PM — Charity Golf Event' were penned in her impeccable hand. 'Sara — make-up for Anna' was an entry amidst several beautifully looped notes.

I gulped hard. Just about every good make-up artist on the island was booked to tackle Maureen's wedding guests. Finding another would be almost impossible. And besides, not just any make-up artist would do for Maureen.

'Sara?' I heard Celia pipe in her best phone voice before I could get my head together. 'It's Celia calling. Do you have a moment? I think we have a little mixup . . . '

6

Well groomed

I had always imagined Maureen's Gav to be a sweet, quiet businessman in awe of his older, glamorous and vivacious fiancée. After all, Maureen seemed to be such a big character that I presumed she would be the driving force of any relationship, with a strong, silent type backing her up all the way. But it seemed that I was wrong.

I was up early on the morning of the wedding, before the rest of the house had stirred. The details of Maureen's big day had buzzed like low-level interference at the back of my mind all night and had finally woken me before sunrise. Soon after, I found myself in the office, leisurely printing off schedules and checking last-minute details, sipping a cup of thick Spanish hot chocolate and wearing a big slouchy sweatshirt that I'd pulled over plaid pyjamas and cosy woollen socks. Despite my usual wedding-day nerves, I was enjoying the knowledge that Maureen's big day was the last date in the calendar for several months. I was determined to make it special for her, and to enjoy it myself.

'Good morning, can I help?' I chimed in jolly spirits as the phone rang before 9 a.m.

'Can you help? Let's hope so,' a deep voice boomed back. It was angry and laced with a cockney accent. 'Isabelle Mistry?' it asked.

'Yes . . . that's me,' I answered cautiously.

'Miss Mistry, congratulations on an unhappy groom on his wedding morning,' the voice continued sardonically, in gravelly tones. 'What a *dump* of a hotel you've booked me into. I ordered breakfast a good half-hour ago and it's not been delivered to my room, and I was told on check-in yesterday that there is no overnight dry-cleaning service for my suit for today . . . It's JUST NOT GOOD ENOUGH!' The voice was increasing in volume and speed as the list of complaints continued.

'And to top it all off, apparently I'm too late to book six of us in for a round of golf. I'd like to know what you're going to do about it! And I'd also like to know how you think this hell hole is going to deal with a wedding?'

I felt my hand quiver slightly against the receiver and my brow knot as I struggled to reply. I was already building a mental image of an East End gangster, and I didn't want to make him any more furious.

'I'm surprised to hear you have problems, Mr Shaw. The hotel is one of the best on the island — '

'I don't really care what your opinion is of this . . . this youth hostel!' the voice interrupted. 'I've been paying through the nose for your so-called services, not least for Maureen to fly over God knows how many times to make plans . . . and this is the best you can come up with? Just fix it,' the voice snarled.

And before I could reply, the line had gone dead.

I spent the rest of the day conjuring up a mental image of Gavin Shaw as a modern-day Ronnie Kray. All gold chains, mysterious facial scars, slick suits and a dodgy portfolio of businesses. As the hours passed, I became a jitterbug. I double-checked the table plan, called the florist umpteen times and hauled a grumpy DJ out of bed to check he'd organised his set. I also visited the hotel Gavin was staying in to make sure that the manager and his team were doing all they could to accommodate him. Gavin, I'd decided, was my first ever Groom-zilla, and I was petrified.

To avoid the possibility of confrontation with the man himself, I trawled the corridors of the seamless palace Gavin had labelled a youth hostel in search of Carlos, the hotel manager, a straw Panama pulled low over my face. When I found him, I discovered that Gavin had made quite an impression on several members of staff as well as on me. I heard myself apologising for my difficult client and at the same time asking that the hotel do all they reasonably could for a guest spending so much on his wedding with them. And we hadn't even met.

By lunchtime I had to switch my focus to Maureen. After all, as they say, it was her day. I'd called her briefly and breezily that morning to assure her that the weather seemed to be holding and everything was under control.

'It's already wonderful, Izzy!' she'd told me excitedly from the portable room phone. She was enjoying the last of the autumn sunshine on the vast terrace of her suite, nibbling on a platter of fruit for breakfast as the waves lapped at the rocks below.

'I'm just so glad I've got the day to myself . . . and that I've given you my mobile,' she said, thanking me for the plan I'd devised to keep her teenage girls at bay.

Paris and Natasha were going to be treated to an afternoon of pampering by a young make-up artist who'd indulge their desire to look like Paris Hilton and deal with any

70

tantrums. Nevertheless, Maureen's phone hadn't stopped ringing, and I spent most of my time fending off her guests.

'Maureen? It's Susan,' the first caller had said, uninterested in hearing a response. 'Can't find our bloody hotel for the life of me. Can't believe you've booked us into somewhere so far from the airport. Can you direct us?'

'Hello, Maureen, Veronica Lakemoor here,' a cut-glass voice chimed not long afterwards. 'That hairdresser you've booked for me at twelve thirty . . . I really would appreciate you making the appointment at three, so that I have a chance to play tennis with Peter.'

'Yah, hi, sweetie,' another drawled. 'Can your makeup girl squeeze me in at four?'

By the fourth call, I was astounded that Maureen's friends showed such little regard for her wedding day and were putting their high-maintenance selves first. By the afternoon, I felt like the PA to half of north London, desperately juggling beauty appointments, handing out tips on where to buy shawls in case there was a chill in the air at the ceremony and booking tables for lunch. I was exhausted and desperate to throw Maureen's phone over the edge of her balcony when I checked in on her.

I found the bride in her suite, languishing

like an off-duty movie star. Every surface of the cool contemporary interior was filled with bouquets of white flowers, the air was heady with expensive perfume and bubble bath and Frank Sinatra played gently on the speakers concealed in every room. Maureen's deeply tanned body was enveloped in a white towelling robe, her head wrapped in a matching turban and her face already fully made up. She lounged on the cream leather chaise longue, a glass of champagne in one hand, whilst Sara buffed the nails of the other and her assistant worked on Maureen's feet.

'Hi, Maureen!' I beamed, on seeing the vision. 'How is the bride?'

I didn't know who to greet first, Maureen or Sara. Sara's assistant had double-booked her diary with Celia's charity event, and she had managed to convince the other lady to be made up early. The assistant, obviously still embarrassed, couldn't look me in the eye, and Maureen, of course, was oblivious to the entire scenario.

'Fabulous!' she replied serenely. 'The girls are *really* looking after me!'

'Brilliant,' I cooed, pleased to see her looking so relaxed and happy. 'Is there anything I can get for you? Have you eaten lunch?'

'You're kidding!' Maureen laughed. 'I can't

eat lunch, I'll never get into the frock!'

The assistant let out a giggle and slipped Maureen's feet into her pink marabou mules, now that her nails were dry.

'Champagne, Izzy?' Maureen asked. I accepted gracefully.

'Have you heard from Gavin?' she enquired as I topped up her glass.

'No, not a murmur,' I lied instinctively, knowing that Maureen, being superstitious, didn't want any contact with her groom for at least twenty-four hours before the event, let alone to hear about his complaints.

'So, speaking of the dress, do I get a pre-view?' I asked quickly, in a shameless attempt to change the subject. After all, the infamous frock had been the topic of conversation for many months. We'd debated so many different colours after Maureen had told me that she didn't dare wear white. Red, if accessorised with cream, might make her look as if she was about to burst into a rendition of 'Santa Baby', and silver, she felt, would clash with her jewellery and her skin tone, so she had settled on a pale gold raw silk dress that was backless and cut on the bias, with a cream fur stole draped around her shoulders and feathered Jimmy Choo mules. The guests, she'd spelt out with a dress code on the invite, were all to wear black.

'Of course!' she giggled as I headed off to find the dress in the bedroom, the glass of champagne still in my hand. The room was beautifully minimal; a vast four-poster bed stood in the centre of the marble floor and sheer white drapes billowed at the French doors that opened out on to the terrace.

'Wow, Maureen, more flowers!' I shouted out to her, on seeing several more vases packed with beautiful white roses.

'Yes, my Gavin's so romantic!' she yelled back.

At that moment I felt a buzz in my pocket and realised that it was Maureen's mobile, which I'd put on silent. I placed the glass of bubbly on the white chest of drawers in front of a bank of just-visible wardrobes and pulled the phone out of my cigarette pants to look at the screen. I saw the word 'Gav' and pressed the red button to get rid of him. What could be so important that he'd ignore Maureen's wish that they didn't communicate before the wedding? Nervously I fished inside my handbag for my own phone, leaning back a little on the wardrobe for support, rummaging and cussing the messy contents as I tried desperately to locate it before he had the chance to give me another irate call. Lip balm, used tissue, gum wrapper, sunglasses case . . . I churned through the endless items, identifying them by touch. Leaning back a little further, I heard the mechanism of the wardrobe door click open. I ignored it and delved some more. Then, as the mobile predictably rang, I jumped, my elbow lurching as my hand still tried to feel for the ringing phone and my eyes wide as it knocked the enormous vase of flowers so that it wobbled precariously on the chest of drawers. I swung my body around to steady the bouquet and let out a shriek as I felt something brush against the back of my neck and head — something warm, hairy and itchy.

'Izzy?' I heard Sara's concerned voice at the doorway and turned round to face her. I was trying to brush the invisible beast off my head as she burst into laughter.

I knew by her face that it wasn't the giant wild cat I'd envisaged, and turned to look in the full-length mirror. At first I didn't quite recognise my own reflection, then I saw what Sara, bent double clutching her belly and wiping tears from her eyes, was in hysterics about. A very long chestnut-brown wig was clinging to the back of my head, its tendrils splayed across my back and shoulders, a long fringe hanging over the side of my cheek. I carefully peeled it off, red-faced, and giggled too. Sara managed to compose herself long enough to help me, and in hushed voices we raced to smooth down the tresses and return them to the stand that had been hidden in the wardrobe.

When we both turned around, Maureen was standing at the open doorway, smiling.

'Found the wig, then?' she laughed, in good spirits, having rumbled us.

'God, I'm so so sorry, Maureen,' I started, mortified, before trying to launch into a lengthy explanation.

'Don't worry about it!' she giggled.

There was a silence as she started to unwrap the turban from her head.

'As we're all girls together, you might as well see, Izzy,' she said. 'I went back to the salon and they told me I shouldn't go platinum. But, well, you know me, when I've got something set in my mind . . . ' she started to explain.

She pulled the towel away from her head to reveal a brilliant white shock of shorn hair. It was cropped so short that you could see parts of her scalp, and what was there looked almost silver against the deep colour of her skin. The cut made her face look long, sallow and older than her years. It was a disaster. And one that I imagined would traumatise any bride.

'Sara saved the day with the wig,' she said,

grinning, heedless of her appearance. 'She bought me three to choose from — '

'Here,' Sara interrupted, rushing to the cupboard. She smoothed down the chestnut tresses some more before carefully tugging them on to Maureen's head. I knew her well enough to know that she anticipated tears if Maureen caught her own turban-free reflection on her wedding day. 'Perfect,' she said as she finished straightening it.

'Almost better than the real thing!' Maureen exclaimed as we nodded and smiled. 'To think I felt so bad about them earlier that I wanted them stored from view . . . '

'It really does suit you,' Sara confirmed sweetly. 'Why don't you hang on to it for the honeymoon, until yours grows a little. You can post it back to me from London?' she offered kindly. And despite our best efforts, Maureen let the waterworks flow.

★ ★ ★

That afternoon, with Maureen's make-up touched up and all of the other contractors on schedule, I headed down to the wedding hotel.

I had taken my trusty blue Vespino for nipping around that day. It was the first time

77

that year that I felt a coolness in the breeze prickle my bare forearms and ankles, as I set off along the coastline. Autumn had definitely arrived. The afternoon sun was a pale low orb, set into a pastel blue sky that seamlessly met the horizon and cast soft rays that shimmered on the ocean. It held almost no heat, and yet I could still make out the tiny figures clad in bikinis and shorts on the beach that stretched out before me.

At the hotel I parked the Vespino amidst a fleet of expensive sports cars and executive saloons in the underground car park, shook out my helmet hair and smoothed it into a ponytail before taking a deep breath and stepping outside.

I took the walk through the sprawling hotel grounds that led down to a small private cove, over the velvety green lawn broken only by a seemingly bottomless jetblack sky-pool. Five four-poster sunloungers swathed in crisp white cotton were dotted around the pool. One, I noticed, was occupied by a twenty-something couple, their slim brown limbs delicately entwined whilst a bottle of bubbly sat unopened in a silver ice bucket on a table beside them.

I took the stone steps down to the lower tier of the garden, which stretched out to a vast infinity pool, the edge of which seemed to disappear into the sparkling sea beyond. It was here that the majority of the wedding would take place.

The pool area had been cleared of furniture and was spotlessly clean and ready for the torches and endless numbers of candles that would illuminate the area by sunset. The florist and his team had finished decorating the Jewish hoopa arch beneath which the couple would stand for the ceremony as they looked out to sea. It stood to the right-hand side of the pool, framing the ocean beyond with a thick arc of pure white orchids, their leaves climbing the concealed structure, the head of each fragile butterfly-shaped flower perfectly open and fluttering delicately in the faint sea breeze. A trail of white and blush-coloured rose petals had been scattered on the limestone tiles beneath the arch and covered the aisle like a thick silk sheet, between two rows of perfectly posi-tioned wedding chairs. It was almost impossible, at this moment, with no one around, not to imagine myself standing beneath the beautiful arch as my guests looked on. But I didn't pause to indulge the notion. Instead I turned around to see the floristry team now focused on wrapping the two stone pillars that led to the reception terrace in matching white flowers. Beyond the pillars a team of waiters, smart in their black and whites, stocked the circular bar in the middle of the terrace for the canapé reception. Two guys lugged tall outdoor heaters into strategically chosen positions, a third swept the already spotless floor, whilst waitresses polished the high, elegant cocktail tables and tied blush-coloured bows to the backs of the matching bar stools. So far, so good, I thought, ticking off a mental checklist.

Next I went in search of the florist to check that the bouquets had been delivered to Maureen and the bridesmaids. I took the path that wound behind the reception terrace, lined with rose bushes and laid with an endless red carpet that Maureen had requested lead to the upper area of lawn dominated by the vast marquee. Inside, I instantly spotted Frederik the florist, working swiftly to erect the towering sculptural arrangements of blush-coloured roses designed to give the marquee some magic. He waved from the top of an impossibly high ladder on one side of the room, and in return I gave him a big grin and a very British thumbs up, which made him giggle and almost lose his balance. He always teased me for being a less than ladylike Englishwoman up against the only other Brit he knew on the island — my boss,

Celia. My clumsy mime of holding a wedding posy didn't help to convince him that I could be elegant, but instead made him smile again as he nodded in confirmation that the wedding and bridesmaids' bouquets had been sent.

Happy that all was going to plan, I glanced around the room. Even though I knew the exact dimensions of the marquee to the millimetre, the structure in reality was overwhelming. Still undergoing its process of transformation, it was a hubbub of activity. Lighting technicians weaved strings of fairy lights beneath sheer white drapes and a vast vault of silk that ran across the ceiling, into a gathered central rose, from which they carefully hung a Majorcan glass chandelier. The result was even more spectacular than Maureen and I had imagined. A team of light-footed waiters moved the French-style antique chairs with gold backs to circle the tables, which I now counted. To the left there was a separate raised area with a twenty-foot-square dance floor, a chic bar and a stage. Here, the jazz band were busily setting up their kit. Veronique, the stunning sixfoot African-American singer, gave me a wink as she positioned her mic stand in the centre of the stage, directly in front of a gold fabric banner with Maureen and Gavin's initials emblazoned in white scrolled writing. I waved a hello and left her to her sound check. *My* final check now was catering.

There was a concealed section of the marquee to the rear of the dining area that was thirty feet long and a temporary home to a fully operational kitchen. The generators whirred loudly as a bustling team of workers sporting immaculate chef's whites scurried between workstations, prepping two hundred shot glasses for the amuse bouche, and two hundred plates for the starter. I singled out Pablo leading the team, recognising him from the tasting Maureen had insisted I accompany her to, in Gavin's absence. He was the chef who had been so patient with her and so understanding of the Jewish restrictions she had to impose on his Spanish menu options, which he adapted for her 'with a twist'.

'Isabelle! *Ciao!*' Pablo greeted me warmly, kissing me on each cheek. He was tall, ruggedly good-looking and spoke about food with a passion that was irresistibly Latin.

'How is everything?' I asked, my eyes wandering round the room observing his carefully conducted team.

'*Perfecto!*' he exclaimed, his warm eyes dancing. '*Todo bien!* Oh, and Isabelle. The dining room, I am very pleased. It looks beau-ti-ful. Your people, they have done a wonderful job,' he drawled in his deep, sexy accent.

'*Gracias*, Pablo.' I blushed a little. It was a feeling similar to the one I'd had when Maureen had topped up my glass a few too many times at the tasting and Pablo had joined our table, rolling up the sleeves on his whites to expose muscular tanned forearms and speaking in the most attentive and calm way, not just to us, but to his staff.

'So you have everything you need?' I asked, bringing myself back to the job.

'*Claro!*' he replied. 'It is going to be a great service.'

A member of Pablo's team stood impatiently by us, and unable to ignore her presence any longer, Pablo placed his large, warm hand on my arm to excuse himself whilst he turned to speak to her in Spanish.

'Isabelle . . . now I must work,' he said, turning back to me some time later. 'But please,' he begged, his eyes suddenly large and fixed on mine, 'come later, for something to eat. I will save you something, for when you finish.'

I nodded apprehensively and turned to leave. Was he flirting with me? I thought of Harrisson and of my less than perfect appearance and shrugged it off. There was no denying that there was a certain something about Spanish guys, some kind of charm that always made you feel like the only woman in the world. And I guessed there was nothing wrong with enjoying that feeling, that flirtation. I floated out of the marquee and back down the red carpet, past the scented roses, to the reception area. Here lines of perfectly spaced candles led down to the pool. The scene was spectacular. I thought of Maureen and patted my hands together in excitement. Yet I had forgotten, momentarily, about one not so small detail. Gavin. I checked at reception to make sure that he had everything he needed in his room. Then I put in a call to the best man, Sean, who confirmed that he had seen the man himself just ten minutes ago. He was going to shower and change, then bring Gavin to the ceremony area ten minutes before the big event to collect their buttonholes. That would be my chance to smooth things over and make sure Gavin was happy before Maureen arrived.

The next hour passed by in a haze. Wedding guests gathered for a pre-ceremony glass of champagne. I eyed the ladies in barely-there designer dresses and impossibly high heels and wondered which of them I'd had to run errands for. I marvelled at the size of the rocks in their rings, the baubles that dangled from their ear lobes and the jewel-coloured handbags that most had teamed their uniform black dresses with. There was no doubt that many had overcompensated for Maureen's all-black code with flamboyant accessories. The old guard had donned elaborate hats and sedate suits, whilst Maureen's friends looked like overgrown WAGS — all big hair, unnatural make-up, fake tan and flashy jewellery.

The bridesmaids arrived next, looking like teen-movie heroines, all pink shimmery mini dresses, gooey glossed lips, perfectly straightened hair and clear perspex Dior platforms that they could hardly walk in. The elder daughter was accompanied by a sheepish-looking Spanish boy, obviously uninvited.

I took a quick head count, made sure that a waiter placed an extra chair for the impromptu guest and made my way to where I had arranged to meet the best man, texting Sara, the make-up artist, a ten-minute signal for Maureen to leave in her wedding car. As I was signing off, I felt a tap on my shoulder.

'You Izzy?'

'Yes!' I spun round, adopting my winning wedding day smile and clutching a box containing the white orchid buttonholes.

The man standing in front of me was just a little taller than me, about five foot six. From the back, he would have looked like a skinny teenager, or an usher, in a sharp pale grey suit, but his face, topped with a crop of auburn hair, was lined and ruddy and showed its years. His voice was powerful and low, but his stature was slight.

'Buttonhole?' I offered, waiting for him to introduce himself.

'Which one's mine, then?' he asked.

And then something clicked. He was the only man at the wedding wearing a shocking pink tie. A tie that matched the lining of Maureen's pale gold dress.

'Think I owe you an apology,' he sniffed, as I sought out the only pin with a pearl and offered it to him. 'I was a bit hasty earlier . . . and what with the nerves . . . Anyway, it's looking beautiful,' he offered, looking at the ceremony area before him. 'Maureen's going to love it.' I smiled sweetly, but before I could speak, another man had slipped an arm round Gavin's shoulder.

'Blimey!' the bloke exclaimed. 'Don't set him off again, love. 'E's the only bloke I've ever caught cryin' at his own weddin' . . . although,' he added, 'many of us have blubbed for years after!' I didn't know which was worse, the sexist joke circa 1970, or the ridiculous vision of Gavin that I'd built up in my head.

I spotted the rabbi over Gavin's shoulder and heard the wheels of Maureen's car on the gravelled drive. 'The bride's here!' I told the men, shooing them into place.

Maureen's face glowed in the candlelight. She looked perfect. Perfectly happy and perfectly beautiful, and I glowed back at her with pride. As we had planned, she made her entrance whilst the sun set over the sea and the strings played. Gavin stood by the rabbi, tears rolling down his face, as his bride made her way down the aisle. The congregation, having initially fallen silent, met her with a standing ovation.

'You haven't noticed,' said a voice next to me that I realised was Sara's.

I turned to answer her with a 'What?'

'Maureen . . . look. She's dumped the wig.'

7

Speaking Spanglish

'Everything went to plan!' I explained
excitedly to Harrisson when I called him the
following morning. I was alone in the office,
save for Pepillo, who had snuck up to sit at
my feet whilst Celia was out at a meeting, and
I was thankful to have some time to ease
myself into the day. My head was a little
fuzzy, as Maureen had sweetly insisted that I
stay to have a drink with her, which turned
into several as the jazz band played their final
set. I was keen to share with Harrisson my
relief at surviving the wedding, and my
feeling of anticipation at being able to focus
on house-hunting for us.

'Honestly, just as I get to the last wedding
of the year, it all goes without a hitch!' I
giggled, proud of myself.

'Good for you . . . I bet they loved you,' he
answered.

It was one of his stock phrases, and his
autopilot tone let me know that I was
disturbing him at work. It was difficult to
imagine him in an office in the East End of

London, where I knew he was based for the next few days, art-directing a campaign for an edgy young ad agency. I could hear loud retro hip-hop playing in the background as we spoke, and imagined him surrounded by ironic contemporary art and twenty-something girls wearing similar pieces as anti-fashion statements.

'Well, everything looked beautiful and even the dreaded groom turned out to be fine after some nervous barking. Maureen was ecstatic!' I responded honestly, knowing to keep things short. 'But I'll tell you more another time . . . I'll leave you to it!' I added hastily.

'Thanks, babe . . . I'll have more time later,' he soothed. 'Glad they loved it . . . as long as no one loved you too much,' he added, before starting to sign off.

It was a little corny, but it made me smile. A touch of jealousy was a good thing, to keep him on his toes.

'Well . . . I'm off to organise seeing some more properties for us tomorrow,' I couldn't help reminding him before saying my goodbyes. 'Wish me luck.'

'That I will do,' he quipped back. 'If your experience is anything like our last, you'll need it!'

That morning, I failed to see a flurry of emails hit my inbox. I was too busy surfing estate agents' websites, dreaming of houses and apartments for our new life, imagining how tumbling stone wrecks could be transformed with a renovation, and trying not to waste time marvelling at the mansion apartments in the ancient Arab quarter of Palma, with their intricate patterned tiled floors, grand proportions and price tags to match. My only other distraction was Pepillo, who sporadically scratched at my bare ankle with his paw, in hope of a pat on the head. By midday, I'd come to the conclusion that Palma was unrealistic unless we wanted to live in a shoebox without any outside space, air-conditioning or heating. And so were the more glamorous resorts that I figured Harrisson would like, as well as the pretty Spanish towns that I preferred. My eyes were starting to feel the fatigue of a flickering screen coupled with a hangover. The sun, now level with the office, streamed in, its glare magnified by the glass at the window, and swamped me with a sleepy feeling. Pepillo barked at me to be fed.

I succumbed to his impatience and decided that a five-minute break away from the computer would be a good idea. Downstairs, I scrabbled on the floor in search of his dishes, which he'd pushed beneath Celia's kitchen units in an attempt, I presumed, to catch every last morsel of the previous meal with the tip of his tongue. The two ceramic bowls lay out of reach, pushed up against the wall at the back of the cupboards, so I went in search of a broom to help fish them out. Pepillo looked at me in bemusement with his one good eye before flattening out his body and wriggling as far into the gap beneath the cupboards as he could. As far as he was concerned, I'd started a race. When Celia walked into the kitchen, she was greeted by the sight of his tail wagging in the air and the lower half of my legs sticking out awkwardly from beneath her units. I was trying to reach the dishes with the broom handle and fight Pepillo for them at the same time.

Predictably I banged my head whilst squeezing my way out, and Pepillo emerged with his covered in cobwebs.

'Just look at you both!' Celia laughed.

'Don't!' I exclaimed, rubbing my head and walking over to the fridge to find the chicken she'd left in a terracotta dish for the hungry dog.

'I take it that it all went well last night?' Celia asked, eyeing my dishevelled appearance.

'Yes, Maureen was really happy . . . it was a lovely wedding.'

Celia was immaculate in beige Capri pants,

91

quilted ballet pumps and a crisp white cotton shirt, clutching a ruby-red Hermès Kelly bag.

'How did this morning's meeting go?' I asked.

'Yes, very well indeed.' She smiled. 'I was thinking, why don't I rustle up something for lunch for both of us?' she offered, placing the bag and a pair of classic Chanel sunglasses on the kitchen table. 'And we can talk all about it.'

Celia and I hadn't eaten a meal together for weeks, and the idea of someone cooking something hearty for me was more than just a little appealing.

Whilst I embarked on setting the table outside just the way that Celia liked it — two Spanish lace tablecloths, layered, her heavy silver cutlery, linen napkins — I could smell the sweet sticky scent of onions and garlic sizzling in Celia's heavy Spanish pan. By the time I'd leisurely plucked some wild flowers from the end of the garden to place in one of her antique glass vases, the welcome sound of clattering crockery came from the kitchen, interrupting the silence outside. Celia emerged clutching a large ornate platter topped with a hot, fresh tortilla and a delicate porcelain bowl brimming with bright green leaves, before heading back to the kitchen for bread, olives and a bottle of white Rioja from one of the cases she regularly had delivered from the local vineyard.

Lunch, in the fading sun of Celia's terrace, was perfect. The well-kept garden was bathed in a golden glow of low autumnal light, and save for the occasional bleat of a donkey in the distance, it was wonderfully quiet, the air soft and scented. At first, and as usual, Celia was formal, telling me about her meeting with potential new clients and asking me all sorts of professional details about Maureen's wedding, her blond chignon nodding against a vibrant background of purple bougainvillea as she listened. Yet over the course of a leisurely afternoon, as we nibbled at the oily olives, helped ourselves to seconds of the delicious tortilla and refilled our glasses, she seemed to relax and eventually drop the formality of our working relationship, for the first time that I could remember.

We gossiped about a recent event that Celia had organised at Marta's family's vineyard, and shared wedding stories from the past year. And it wasn't until 4 p.m. that I was back inside, clearing the plates and rustling up a pot of coffee on the stove, whilst Celia pulled a shawl around her shoulders at the table and Pepillo gnawed at an old tennis ball. When I re-emerged on the terrace, Celia looked thoughtful. She smiled gently as I placed the coffee pot on a slab of marble on the table and passed her the silver sugar dish.

'You know . . . ' she started, her focus now back to me, 'it's such a shame that things didn't work out between you and Tomas. I had secretly hoped they might,' she added quietly, without catching my eye.

I was surprised both at her choice of subject matter and at her admission. It was the first time she'd acknowledged that something had happened between us, and I had doubted that she'd found me suitable for her intellectual son.

I smiled and tried to keep a steady hand pouring the coffee.

'At least you both seem closer now,' I offered. 'You've spent some time together this year.' I'd never heard the full story, but I knew that Tomas and Celia had drifted apart since Tomas's father had died and had only just started to become close again.

'Yes, quite.'

'Milk?' I asked. She nodded.

'I can imagine having far more frightful daughters-in-law!' she said, and we both laughed. 'Really, I don't think I've had a chance to tell you, Isabelle, quite how much fun it has been to have you here,' she added, her eyes now meeting mine, a little glassy from the wine.

'I really appreciate that, Celia,' I said, holding her gaze. 'It has been for me too. But why are we talking in the past tense? You're not about to tell me I'm fired, are you?' I giggled, trying to lift the moment.

'Gracious, of course not!' she chuckled. 'I couldn't have imagined that things would work out quite so well in the business . . . ' She trailed off at the end of the sentence and I guessed that her thoughts had returned to her son.

'Look, I really am very fond of Tomas,' I told her, seriously, 'but something didn't quite work or gel for us, I guess.'

'Well, that is something that can't be helped,' she agreed. 'Although it is completely evident that you light up when you're with Harrisson,' she added.

'I guess I do,' I agreed, feeling content.

'I'm happy for you, just as long as you're sure he's the one.'

I sat back down in my chair and pulled my knees up to my chest, hugging them for extra warmth in the coolness of the afternoon.

'It just feels right,' I told her. 'I didn't ever think he'd commit. But he has. I didn't ever think that I'd settle anywhere, let alone here, but I adore it and I can't imagine anywhere I'd rather be. And I feel so lucky that he's happy to make a go of it here, because he knows that . . . what's not to love?' I beamed.

'It is all wonderfully romantic.' Celia smiled, with a twinkle in her pale blue eyes, as she leaned in a little closer. 'Just don't rush into things,' she added before lifting the porcelain cup to her lips, leaving a camelia-coloured Chanel lipstick stain on the chalky white china.

'You sound like you're speaking from experience,' I offered.

'Well . . . ' She laughed. 'So many stories.'

'Great, I'm all ears,' I teased her in eager anticipation.

'Now that would take another bottle!' she smiled, finishing her coffee. 'And I suppose, dear Isabelle, that I had better check my emails and make some calls before the day is completely through.'

'Yes, me too,' I said, disappointed, yet remembering that she was paying for my time. 'After all, my day off is supposed to be tomorrow.'

'So tell me, what does the day hold?'

'I thought I'd view some more houses,' I told her. 'But, well, to be honest, I've been finding it hard to spot anything vaguely inhabitable that's within our budget.'

'Are you looking at the international websites or the local ones?' Celia asked, standing up from the table.

'Oh, the international ones, of course, for the English!' I laughed, grabbing the coffee cups to take inside.

'For what it's worth, try the local *inmobiliaria* sites. You'll find that the property as well as the prices is geared more towards the locals,' she advised sensibly.

That evening, as the sun finally set over the mountains and we cooped ourselves up in the office, I started to investigate the Spanish estate agents' websites as Celia made her calls. I skimmed over endless property details, being mindful of exaggeration and focusing on pictures and prices. There were a few properties in the east of the island, by the salt flats or the potato-growing region, that sounded remote and maybe one culture shock too many for Harrisson. There were strips of farming land and olive groves in desirable locations boasting *cassitas* ripe for development, but without water, electricity or more than one room. Turning what presumably would have been home to livestock into a fully functioning home seemed too great a feat of planning permission and serious building work. I even failed to find a replica of Harrisson's 1960s retro dream flat. Yet what I did find was an estate agent advertising the historic townhouses I had always loved in Sóller.

It was a part of the island that I couldn't help but fall in love with when I had visited with Tomas earlier in the summer, but I knew that its port, food market and genteel Parisian influence would also appeal to Harrisson. Memories of the beautiful town square, the tree-lined avenues, the old-fashioned bakeries and the charming wooden tram spurred on some eager scrolling of web pages. I even convinced myself that a long drive to work at Celia's from the beautiful haven of the mountain town would all be worth it.

Of course, I found that the fine examples of houses, with beautiful cobbled entrance halls, art nouveau façades and plenty of space, were at a premium, but smaller, more rustic versions on the edge of town, with less outside space and needing a little work, didn't seem to be completely out of the question. Nor did apartments in the town, unlike those with sea views in the port. As the office clock ticked towards the agents' closing time, I decided to embrace my jittery Spanish and call, having seen one house that might, just might, work. I jotted down a few sentences on my notepad and agonised over them for a few moments before picking up the receiver.

'*Buenas tardes*,' I pronounced carefully. '*Quisiera hablar con* — '

'English?' the voice at the other end interrupted me.

'Yes, I mean, *si*.' I sighed.

The agent's English was polite and basic, but certainly better than my Spanish and without any risk of misunderstandings. I was thankful to be able to book appointments for the following afternoon. Unlike an English estate agent, I found that Francisca, the friendly Mallorquina, was insistent that she'd not only show me the property I'd asked about, but everything she had on her books in a similar price range. Slightly baffled, I agreed and made a time to meet her in the town square the next day.

Later on that evening, I put in an excited call to Marta. I wanted to tell her all about Maureen's wedding and how I was finally taking on some serious house-hunting, to set up home on the island with Harrisson. I knew she'd love the news and I was secretly hoping that she might have time to accompany me on my viewings in Sóller. I was sure that her Spanish and her general level-headed know-how would come in handy.

I was disappointed to find that there was no answer at the vineyard. I'd made the call from a small snug that Celia grandly called 'the library'. It was a square room with an elaborate crystal chandelier that hovered over the original patterned tiled floor. There was a wall of books that ranged from old encyclopedias and textbooks on botany (which I presumed belonged to Tomas) to hardback classics and well-thumbed paperbacks on the wooden shelves that bowed slightly under the weight of them all. It was a quiet, dark room that felt like an escape from the rest of the house, and although Celia hadn't ever suggested that it was private, the few times I'd found myself there, I had a feeling that maybe I shouldn't be.

I placed down the receiver and heard the bell of the old-fashioned phone 'ting'. I stayed perched awkwardly on the edge of the high-backed chair at Celia's writing desk and let out a sigh. I'd never quite got used to spending so much time alone, rolling around someone else's home. But after an afternoon of chatting with Celia, I prepared myself for spending a night on my own in my room. I looked over to the bookshelves. I was sure that Celia wouldn't mind me borrowing a novel, but I wasn't in a rush and I let my eyes wander lazily around the room. The fireplace on the opposite wall was handsome, its grate filled with dusty logs. A beautiful Venetian mirror, its glass softly mottled with age, hung above it. There were black and white photos on the mantelpiece of Celia, her late husband

and Tomas. Tomas as a boy, proudly holding up a huge catch, a fish almost as big as the child himself. Tomas as a graduate, collecting his degree in an outmoded gown and mortarboard hat that aged him thirty years. And a black and white photo of Celia in her twenties, modelling in a Mary Quant-style minidress and knee-high boots, her long blond hair cut into a blunt fringe, her profile elegant and sharp. I smoothed my hands over the mahogany desk, noting its tiny drawers, the well that Celia had filled with a glass jar of jet-black ink and the beautiful gold fountain pen that lay beside it. I resisted the temptation to open a drawer, to turn the tiny silver keys that kept each one tightly locked, and walked over to the bookshelves.

Celia's taste was eclectic and romantic. Jane Austen novels nestled alongside Dickens classics, Albert Camus rubbed shoulders with Arthur Miller, and P. G. Wodehouse hardbacks were neighbours with Evelyn Waugh. It was a very English collection, broken only by a scattering of Marques and Isabel Allende, a nod, I supposed, to Spanish culture. I pulled out a few of the latter, reading the back-sleeve blurbs, crouching down to do so. I was looking for something fun. *One Hundred Years of Solitude* wasn't really cutting it, and just felt like a comment on my current situation. I was just about to give up when something caught my eye on the very last bookshelf to the right. A row of brightly coloured hardbacks, which revealed themselves to be trashier and far more exciting reads, including salacious biographies of starlets and political figures, and a racy Jilly Cooper novel. I slid the latter carefully from the shelf and headed upstairs.

8

Good 'ouzees

There is something very British about our strict sense of punctuality that doesn't seem to translate into Spanish culture. I was determined not to be late on the day that I'd organised to meet Francisca. I'd skipped the brunch I'd planned for myself, having got wrapped up in answering emails and waiting for a delivery of water to fill Celia's well, so that I could take a shower. Afterwards I'd raced down to the car without a jacket, my hair still wet and sticky with the conditioner I'd forgotten to rinse away and I fought off Pepillo, who assumed he'd be coming along too. As I jumped behind the wheel, I checked the clock on the dashboard and revved the engine. I'd left just enough time, traffic permitting, to drive up to the north-west of the island and make it to our meeting place, as agreed.

With my foot applying as much pressure to the accelerator as I could muster and one hand guiding the wheel as the motorway rose steeply towards the mountains, I tried to tune in the ever-crackly radio. I settled on Radio National España Tres, in a vain attempt to improve my Spanish. The broadcasters spoke at a lightning speed I found impossible to keep up with. I suddenly had a pang for Marta's help. I must be crazy to think I could house-hunt in Spanish.

As the motorway turned into single-file traffic, I passed fields of olive trees that stretched towards the towering mountains lining the valley of Sóller, just as my mobile rang.

I turned down the radio and scrambled in my bottomless bag with my left hand, keeping my eyes fixed on the road.

'Hello!' I beamed happily.

'*Hola, cariño . . . soy Raimundo!*'

It was Ray, my best friend from London, who visited the island as much as possible between TV contracts to stay with his Latin lover Ramon, a classical guitarist. During his trips over, he'd learned just enough Spanish to charm and cuss, two activities that were vital in Ray's world.

'Hey, are you here?' I asked, excited at hearing his voice.

'Sure am. Cooped up in Ramon's arms as we speak!' he cooed. I could hear the sound of husky breathing and what I assumed was Ramon nibbling at Ray's neck.

'Purrlease,' I scolded. 'Too much information . . . Listen, I'm on the road. Can I call you to chat later, *amigo*?'

'Where you heading? I'm actually looking for some fun today whilst Ramon is busking in the city. You know I'm just not the kind of guy to hang out on street corners with those people being human sculptures and holding a hat for someone else's coins.'

I chuckled at the thought.

'Sorry, hon, but I'm house-hunting. I'm not sure it's your thing.'

'Not my thing? Izzy, you need me there.'

I remembered how he always slated what he called my 'slag pit' in Notting Hill.

'So where are we going?' he added.

'Sóller,' I answered.

'Where?'

'Ask Ramon and he'll tell you where it is.'

I could hear Ramon cursing in the background.

'To put it politely, he says it's hours away!' Ray replied.

'Rubbish!' I laughed.

Despite the new fast road and the tunnel that carved through the mountains, making Sóller easily accessible from Palma in around half an hour, the Majorcans from the south couldn't seem to forget the days when it took several hours winding around the mountain roads to reach the town, and it had often been quicker to go by boat.

'Did you hire a car? If not, there's a train you can catch from Palma. It's wooden and brass, really pretty, and it comes through the mountains,' I added, trying to tempt him.

'Ramon is waving his arms at me like a madman and yelling *'touristas'*. I'll drive. I hired a divine open-topped Porsche.'

'Of course you did,' I giggled. 'I'm meeting the estate agent in the town square really soon, though, so why don't I meet you for lunch and then you can come to the afternoon viewings?' I compromised.

'OK, when and where, Izz?'

'Let's say two p.m. in the main town square, to keep things simple. We'll find somewhere to eat from there.'

'*Hasta luego, cariño!*' Ray chimed.

I said my *adios* just before paying the toll at the beginning of the long dark tunnel that burrowed through the mountain. I hadn't driven to the town before. My one and only visit had been chaperoned by Tomas, and we'd parked by the botanical gardens on the outskirts and walked through to the square. I tried to see if I could spot any familiar landmarks as I flew out of the tunnel and down the winding road with the mountains towering either side of me. My ears popped and I noticed how close I felt to the clouds.

I remembered passing the stone houses dotted into the mountains when I'd visited before, the place where families came to slaughter a pig for supper, and the sign I thought had looked quite chic, quite Scandinavian — a white cross on a red background and the name of the town — which Tomas informed me, to my embarrassment, simply meant that there was a pharmacy in the area. I smiled, thinking of Tomas and our disastrous date. Checking my mirrors, my window now wound all the way down and the radio still blasting, I took a last-minute right-hand exit off the round-about, having spotted a parking sign. I'd forgotten to signal, and someone quite rightly honked their horn.

The road narrowed as it wound its way towards the town square, with rows of historic stone townhouses standing proudly on each side. I had a minor panic at spotting the first give-way sign. Give way! The road seemed just wide enough for one small car not to scrape both its sides as it squeezed through, let alone allowing space for two. Then I realised that it was a back up, wait, and then when the coast was clear bomb down to avoid repeating the whole thing again type situation. Just as I had got the knack, the road widened again and the streets were studded with shops. There was a knitting shop that looked like it had been there for a hundred years, a Moroccan tiled restaurant and a wonderful bakery on the corner. People walked in the streets and silver tramlines crossed the road that swept around the square to another maze of back streets. Finally I could see a car park up ahead in a pretty residential square shaded by tall green leafy trees — perfect, but with no spaces to be seen, totally useless. I carried on and followed a narrow *calle*, waiting my turn at the one-way sign and breathing in as if that would allow the car to fit. I found myself in quieter roads away from the square, lined with tall trees and handsome houses built in the Parisian art nouveau style that seemed unique to Sóller. With all of my concentration on the road, I had slightly lost my bearings, but focused on squeezing bumper to bumper into a tiny parking space. Looking at the time once more, I grabbed my handbag, put a hand through my now dry hair and walked as briskly as I could, taking in the slightly cooler mountain air as I made my way back to the square.

* * *

Of course, Francisca was late. Not just five minutes, even ten minutes, but spectacularly late. It bugged me. We'd agreed a time. As twenty minutes passed, and then thirty, I thumbed the pages of the local newspaper, looking at the pictures. After a while I discarded the paper and studied my surroundings instead; after all, I barely understood a word of the Catalan it was written in. Children played by the fountain whilst their families chatted. Each café was filled with both locals and tourists. There was a group of cyclists gathered around one table, old Spanish men in their flat caps at another drinking brandy and all kinds of people and nationalities in between. The church beyond the fountain was majestic and forbidding, the grand town hall next to it awash with activity, with children sitting chatting on its steps. Then a whistle sounded and the tram came belting through the square, its brass carriages rattling into the centre of the town.

'Issabelle?' a voice questioned as the body it belonged to cast a shadow in front of me.

'*Si, hola!*' I beamed. 'Francisca?' I looked up at the smiling face the voice belonged to and couldn't stay angry. Francisca looked warm, friendly and not in the least bit apologetic for being so late.

'*Si! Encantada!* It is wonderful day for being in Sóller, *verdad?*' she said sincerely, and I couldn't disagree.

Francisca pulled up a chair and ordered a *cortado* coffee with a single gesture to a waiter, eyeing the empty coffee cups I had already lined up.

'You arrive early to take in the atmosphere of Sóller? Clever!' she announced, and I realised it was time to fit in with the Latin time zone, or at least relax about it.

'OK, today we look at very good 'ouzees,' she continued, telling me that she had eight properties she thought I should see. I gulped at the thought of eight and suggested we look through the details together first.

The sun shone on Francisca's chestnut hair as she lit a cigarette, holding it firmly down by her side, in case, I presumed, the smoke bothered me. As she sipped her coffee very slowly, she took her time describing each of the properties. The first, a second-floor apartment overlooking the square I apologetically discounted as being too noisy. The second I discarded on location, as it was situated way before the tunnel and practically overlooking the main road. Finally we narrowed the properties down to four that sounded like they had real potential. Three we'd view before lunch, we decided, planning a route by foot; the fourth, which sounded the most promising, we'd see later that afternoon, after siesta, Francisca confirmed.

'*Vamos!*' she suddenly announced, picking up the tab and protesting at my attempt to add some coins, and we strolled off at her leisurely pace. She smiled a hearty '*hola*' at every other person passing through the square, and I felt before we'd even seen a single property that I was getting a lesson in laid-back living.

'You know everyone!' I laughed.

Francisca shrugged. 'I have always lived in Sóller,' she said matter-of-factly.

At the edge of the square we turned the corner into the Calle de sa Luna. The first house, Francisca told me, was on this very street. I couldn't see how, as it was a busy shopping centre with narrow roads, which, she told me, became part of the market on Saturday mornings. It was home to a beautiful old bakery, a traditional butcher's, two bookshops, restaurants, galleries and shops filled with artisans' products, old and new. Being a working town, there were pharmacies and no-nonsense hardware shops nestled between the gift shops, delis and boutiques that attracted the tourists. Halfway along the *calle*, rows of townhouses started to be dotted between the shops, their handsome façades shut to the busy road, their shutters closed tightly, their large wooden doors bolted.

'These houses are *muy antiguo*,' Francisca told me. 'And at the back, some have good garden.'

Three and four storeys high, some of the houses had intricate tilework, Juliet balconies or art nouveau flourishes. I imagined myself in the centre of town in one of these elegant homes that opened up to a quiet oasis away from the street. Yet before I could get too carried away, Francisca announced 'ya estamos aquí' at an alleyway that led off the main thoroughfare. Unlike some of the pretty cobbled side roads that cut across the main *Luna*, this was a dusty track. There were some carpentry workshops, a car repair shop and an ugly block of flats next to a larger building with a shuttered front that seemed to be undergoing some construction.

'This is . . . unique house,' Francisca offered sweetly, smiling when she found the right word. Before I could comment, she was leading me up a few steps past the shuttered window and knocking loudly on the door before using her key. She turned to me to explain.

'I am loud because the owner does not hear so good.'

As she was about to turn the lock, an old man with a stooped back and a heavy woollen cardigan over a rumpled shirt and trousers greeted us.

'*Come va?*' he asked Francisca, kissing her on both cheeks and putting out a hand to shake mine. A smile stretched across a face that despite being creviced with lines still looked as mischievous as a boy's.

We walked into a long, dark hallway, which at one end opened into an open-plan living room, and traversed into an L-shaped maze that was confusing and dark. Bedrooms seemed to spring up everywhere. A kitchen lay between two small doubles, a kitchen with no units, just a camping stove and a brand-new fridge in the corner.

'He says that the kitchen is left, so that the new owners can create whatever they want,' Francisca translated.

When I peered into a bedroom with no window and space for just a single bed, Francisca asked the man a question in an amused tone.

'This room he says is flexible. For baby or for office.' She smiled. 'And this one, it has a bed, but next to the kitchen, maybe dining room?' she added, translating yet again.

As I tried to make sense of the layout, the owner shuffled behind us, smiling whilst giving a spin to rival any cut-throat London estate agent on the empty rooms walled with concrete and breeze blocks and the airless walkways without any natural light.

Francisca looked equally perplexed.

'This is my first time in this house too,' she told me, as we negotiated a narrow staircase to the second floor, where a single bare light bulb swung above us on the landing. Here we found further bedrooms, and a large room with bare plastered walls, where some plumbing was in progress.

'The bathroom . . . ' she said.

'So that the owner can have it how they like?' I offered.

'*Si*,' the man beamed, pleased that I was getting the hang of things.

At the end of the tour, he proudly took the lead and signalled for us to follow him to the back of the second floor. Here we were suddenly out in the open air as the cheap terracotta tiles that had been laid on the floor stretched out beyond the walls of the final room and straight on to the industrial street we had entered the house from. It was a far cry from the lush green garden I'd been daydreaming about. As I tried to make sense of the confusing house and see if there was any beauty beyond the concrete, I could hear Francisca chatting frantically to the man in

Catalan. At the end of the conversation she let out a big sigh.

'OK, with the house alone it is one price. And for the terrace . . . there is an extra price.'

'But the terrace is only accessed through the house, isn't it?' I asked her.

Francisca turned to him again with more questions.

'Yes, exactly,' she confirmed. 'And I have to tell you, Isabelle. For the terrace there are no papers, it is not legal.'

I looked at the little old man and then up at the house. It was a mess. 'I think it's time we saw the next one!' I said diplomatically and we made an exit.

Back on Calle de sa Luna, Francisca flipped through her folder of property details and planned our route to the next house, seemingly unfazed. I kept an eye on the cobbled pavements that wound unevenly before us. As we reached the end of the street, the tall buildings gave way to a bigger vista.

En route, we discovered through our muddled mix of Spanglish that we understood enough to learn the basic things about each other's lives. Francisca, I discovered, was warm, jolly and older than she looked, with three kids at the local school and a husband in construction. We spent a long sunny morning looking at pretty stone houses that all had their charm, but not one of which quite worked for Harrisson and I. Finally, the clock in the market square chimed twice, signalling that it was time to take a break for lunch.

'I hope you don't think I'm fussy!' I apologised to Francisca as she dropped me back at the square.

'No! Of course, this is *muy importante*, you take the time,' she replied kindly. We agreed to meet in two hours' time and she scuttled off home to make lunch for her family.

Ray, of course, was nowhere to be seen. True to our plan, I waited in the square, pouncing upon one of the last unoccupied tables outside a café and ordering a glass of white wine along with some bread and aioli to fight off my hunger pangs. The late-autumn sun was low in the clear sky, peeping through the gaps in the grand buildings that seemed to guard the plaza. From my tiny table there was plenty of people-watching to indulge in. The square buzzed with the sound of tourists and locals eating with their families, and hikers and cyclists taking a break and advantage of a *menu del dia*. I heard voices in French, German and Spanish, watched local ladies carrying straw bags brimming with

116

groceries taking a *café con leche* in the sun. Half a glass of chilled white Rioja later, I craned back my head, letting the bustle wash over me, feeling the warm rays against my face.

Dozing and feeling mellow from the effects of the wine, my brain vaguely registered a screeching of brakes. I knew before I opened my eyes that it would be Ray. I'd never known him make a quiet entrance anywhere. Sure enough, as I looked to my left, a bright orange Porsche was blocking the road and blaring house music. I sank into my seat a little, as Ray waved at me frantically from the convertible. I called him from my mobile.

'Hi, Ray!' I greeted him, turning to look at him as I spoke. 'Glad you made it! I'm staying glued here because if I move, we'll lose the table!' I told him, excusing myself for not going over.

'But have you tried to park in this bloody place? It's impossible!' Ray moaned. 'Do you think I can just leave it here?'

'Of course not!' I laughed

While Ray went to find a place to park, a smiling waiter, his gleaming metal tray held at shoulder height, delivered more bread and wine. Soon afterwards, before the beads of condensation could trickle down to the stem of my glass, Ray was back, walking towards me in baggy khaki shorts that only just stayed belted low on his hips, the tightest distressed tee and flip-flops. His razor-sharp haircut looked edgy and salon fresh, and amidst the more classically dressed Spanish he stood out a mile. I couldn't help but think of London as he waved frantically at me, smiling from behind huge sci-fi shades.

'Ramon was right, back end of nowhere!' he announced, pulling up a chair to join me.

'Don't you think it's beautiful?' I asked, but Ray was more interested in signalling to the waiter to bring a menu, as I rambled on about the delights of the historic town.

Through a simple lunch of garlicky prawns and a generous salad, Ray told me all about his fling with Ramon whilst I enthused about my romance with Sóller.

'Latinos make the best lovers,' said Ray. 'Ramon has such passion. Although you don't want to upset him; when that fire in his belly turns to anger . . . bang!' he announced, dunking a peeled prawn into aioli and devouring it whole. He took a sip of wine and studied the square for a moment, having devoted half an ear to my monologue about Sóller.

'OK, so I get why you like it here. It *is* pretty, I'll give you that. *Loving* the architecture. But you sure you want to be tucked away in the mountains? What will you do at night?'

'There are bars and restaurants,' I laughed.

'But no clubs till Palma.' Ray smiled. 'And don't try to tell me you're not the same girl I knew in Notting Hill.'

'But that's just it,' I told him. 'I don't think I am any more. I just want a quiet life here, with Harrisson.'

Ray eyed me suspiciously, as if my body had been abducted by an alien life form pretending to be me.

I peeled the head off another prawn and dunked my bread in the plate of juices.

Ray signalled to the waiter for a third glass of wine.

Over the next hour we gossiped, laughed and, when we got a little too giggly, ordered *café solos*. Before we knew it, Francisca was standing in front of our table.

'Come join us!' I beamed up at her.

'Eeeesabelle,' she smiled, eyeing Ray.

'Oh sorry, Francisca, this is Ray, Ray, Francisca.'

Ray wiggled his fingers in the finger bowl, wiped his hands on the linen napkin and held one out to shake Francisca's. She laughed and moved forward to kiss him on both cheeks in the more traditional and less formal Majorcan way.

That afternoon Francisca led us through an area of the town I'd yet to discover — L'Horta in the local Catalan, or La Huerta in Spanish, meaning the garden, she explained. It was easy to see why. Perched between the town and the port, it was a lush and vibrant area where houses had a little more land, and plots were divided up into well-kept vegetable gardens and fields brimming with orange trees, all surrounded by the Sera Tramuntana mountain range, of course. In the fading sun of the afternoon, it looked beautiful.

'God, this is remote,' Ray commented as I shot him daggers.

'And here there is a small shop . . . and here is where the tram comes.' Francisca continued with her tour, seemingly oblivious. On cue, the tram rattled by.

'Lovely!' I commented, elbowing Ray in the side, as if we were misbehaving schoolgirls.

Francisca stopped at the local church. It was small and pretty, with a wooden bench outside that seemed to have been adopted by cats seeking out the last of the sun, I presumed Francisca was about to point it out as a landmark, but she didn't.

'*Estamos aqui*,' she announced. 'We are here,' she confirmed in English as she turned and pointed to a three-storey building opposite. 'This is house for sale.' She smiled.

'Good orientation, no?'

She was right. It was a good spot. Overlooking the church and a small orange grove that lay opposite, the old stone townhouse, with its emerald-painted shutters, had an undeniably lovely view.

'But!' Francisca exclaimed, holding up a finger. 'Of course, for this price it needs a little work.'

Ray moaned audibly.

'Of course.' I nodded in agreement, following Francisca across the road, with Ray in tow. On reaching the vast wooden doors, which must have been twenty feet high, Francisca fumbled with a huge, rusty antique key that looked almost half a foot long to open them.

'Fabulous,' Ray cooed, touching the oversized mahogany.

We craned our necks to see inside as Francisca finally pushed open one of the enormous doors. Following closely behind her, we stepped into a large, dusty hallway that was almost pitch black. Francisca ran a hand down one wall to feel for a light switch and lit up the hallway with a single dangling bulb. Huge spider's webs hung like sheets of Spanish lace from the high ceiling. The large space appeared to be empty except for a second set of huge glass and wooden doors, set into an arch.

121

'*Son muy antiguo.*' Francisca nodded, opening the doors and pointing up to the heavy beamed ceiling. Her footsteps echoed across the terracotta-tiled floor, our eyes following her.

'It's a bit 'Most Haunted',' Ray muttered, and as if on cue, Francisca, at the very back of the hallway, opened the heavy wooden door that led out on to a small terrace, letting light flood in.

The stream of daylight highlighted both the good and the bad things about the house, as our eyes adjusted. The terracotta floor, although coated in years of grime, appeared to be in good condition, but the arch that surrounded the door was painted in a faux marble effect, and neither side of the empty space separated by the big doors looked large enough to serve any other purpose than a hall.

'This is good house,' Francisca commented as I walked towards the doorways to take a look at the other rooms that led off the main hall.

There was a tiny kitchen, a shallow room with just one wall of units, which looked like they'd been fitted in the seventies, and an upright cooker from the same period.

'All mod cons then,' Ray giggled as I flicked up an old-fashioned light switch, which caused a buzzing sound and a fleeting flicker of the bare bulb that dangled from the beamed ceiling. I leant over the sink to push open the shutters in compensation.

'Well, you can put in a fridge and a washing machine, but buying that view's not so easy,' I said, looking out to the back of the church.

'*Si*,' Francisca agreed from the doorway. 'To put in plumbing is OK, I think.'

Ray giggled as I turned to face them both, and I looked down to find my favourite silk knit smeared with a line of grey grime from the sink.

'Here we have bathroom,' Francisca said, leading me to the tiny room next to the kitchen. It was equally basic and appeared, at best, to be semi-functional. There was a rust-stained hip bath that looked just big enough to accommodate a child, a tiny sink that was loose against the whitewashed wall and an old-fashioned toilet with no seat and a chain dangling from a large black cistern. As I mulled whether the uneven and cracked red floor tiles were 'good' old, in a retro way, or just bad, I heard Ray gasp, and I rushed to see what he'd discovered at the other end of the ground floor.

I found him with Francisca in a small, square room featuring nothing but an unmade bed and a musty, sweaty smell.

'The tiles, Izzy. Deee-vine,' he cooed, gazing at the patterned Moorish floor that graced the otherwise nondescript space. I let out a sigh of relief.

'*Antiguo tambien.*' Francisca smiled, tapping the ceramics with one foot before opening up the shutters to reveal the view of the church opposite.

'Look up,' I said to Ray, pointing at the pretty cornicing that ran around the ceiling and the rose that decorated its centre.

Ray looked thoughtful.

'*Mira*,' Francisca said, breaking the silence. She beckoned. 'Come.'

We followed her out to the terrace. It was a small space, but the view of the mountain that led up to Deià was stunning.

'That's not part of it?' Ray asked, pointing to a swimming pool that lay a few metres beyond the steps leading down from the empty terrace.

'Of course not!' I tsked, as Francsica shook her head. 'You'd probably need to add another hundred thousand to get that!' I giggled. 'Isn't the view enough?'

'But how could you live,' Ray whined, 'being able to see the pool from this low wall and not being able to dive into it?'

Francisca laughed and opened up a small,

shed-like room that led off the terrace. It smelt old and musty and was stuffed with furniture and boxes that still couldn't conceal the cracked plaster walls.

'You could open this to make larger *terraza*,' she offered. 'Or keep as room. Of course, you can put flowers, furniture — ' she continued.

'This, Izzy, is a big job,' said Ray, interrupting.

He was probably right. I didn't have a clue about how to use a paintbrush, let alone think about the logistics of a new kitchen and bathroom, but nevertheless, I wasn't about to dismiss the house altogether. I looked up at its handsome façade, the old stonework, the pretty shutters. There was something that felt good and solid about it. Something elegant about its proportions and high ceilings.

'No, ees normal, ees OK,' Francisca assured me, interrupting my thoughts. 'The reformation . . . I can help with this.'

'Well,' I sighed, looking at Ray, 'we haven't even been upstairs yet.'

'You go.' Francisca smiled. 'You go with your husband to see upstairs.'

Ray and I were laughing so much at the thought of us being married, that we had to disappear to hide our giggles.

We explored the first and second floors,

racing into each room to open shutters, and with each fling, which Ray performed dramatically, as if bursting on to an invisible stage, the views just got better and better.

The whitewashed bedrooms were a good size, some with the original tiled floors, all with high ceilings, but there were no further bathrooms. On the top floor, there was a room that looked familiar — a cold stone space with a bare concrete floor and a cupboard with hooks on its walls. 'This is the room they would have used to prepare and hang meat,' I told Ray, who winced.

'I'm not going to even ask how you know that,' he said before turning to go into the final room.

'Now this is a view,' he shouted as I heard the shutters creak open. At the highest point of the house, the room was almost level with the bell tower of the church and looked across to the houses, orange trees and mountains beyond. We both leant out of the window to take it all in. The air outside was soft and silent.

We both jumped a little as the church bells began to strike five, and laughed again. Then, from the street below, the noise of workers' vans and loud Spanish male voices began to emerge, followed by the rap of the heavy brass knocker at the door.

From inside the house we heard the sound of workmen's boots on the floor below and loud, animated voices. Back downstairs, Ray and I were politely greeted by a team of electricians, who sighed at the contents of the black box in the hallway and the cabling that ran on the outside of some of the walls. Next, a team of plumbers arrived, their boss's name emblazoned on their T-shirts, taking notes as they nodded their heads at the state of the bathroom and kitchen. Three builders followed, wearing paint-splattered clothes, as if they'd been pulled from another job. They surveyed the rooms and scratched their chins thoughtfully, chattering in Spanish. Before long the house was a hubbub of activity and Ray and I looked on, bemused and bombarded.

'Eesabelle, see, ees easy,' Francisca assured me. 'You look worried at how much work, so I organise these, to show you ees OK.'

'Gosh, I'm not even sure if I'm interested — '

'No, ees no problem,' she interrupted, putting a hand on my shoulder. 'How you know if you want the house, unless you know *todo possibilidad*, no?' she offered. 'My husband, he come now,' she told us. 'To give you *un presupuesto* — a quotation.'

'Quotation?' I asked, unbelieving.

'*Si*, quotation, thees right word, no? He will talk to your husband . . . Ray?'

'Oh, he's not my husband.' I blushed. I wasn't sure what to try and explain first, but there was little time to contemplate. A serious-looking man, whose van screeched up so close to the front door that it looked as though he might try to drive inside, was soon standing in the doorway. He spoke in fast Catalan, which Francisca translated, licking his pencil to make notes in a small leather book as he walked around the house, contemplating every detail.

'Come,' Francisca cooed calmly, starting a tour that would lead to every room and a million questions on what I wanted here and there, whilst the other trades seemed to amass in even greater numbers. As I hesitated and stumbled over answers and found there was little alternative but to go along with the process, Francisca's husband called upon the various men to give this advice or that. All the while, I could see numbers and sketches mounting up on his thinly lined pad.

Some time later, Ray caught my eye from the kitchen doorway. I shrugged apologetically and tried to mouth 'sorry'. He signalled 'square' and 'drink' in return, along with a dramatic motion that looked like he might die of thirst otherwise. He excused himself as he

128

passed each electrician, plumber and builder, who were insistent on politely and individually saying their goodbyes to Señor Ray, the man of the house, with an English handshake. Ray turned to give me a final 'what the?' motion with his shoulders before he vanished.

As he did so, a man and a woman appeared at the door, peering in keenly to see what all the hubbub was about.

'*Venga*.' Francisca signalled to the couple and to my amazement they came inside.

'This,' Francisca announced, 'are good neighbours. Paco y Ana.' Then, to my alarm, 'This lady is interested in your house,' she told them in Spanish.

'*Encantada*,' Ana answered cheerily, coming forward without hesitation to give me a kiss on both cheeks. She had a warm, round face and clasped my arms at the shoulders in a tight grip as she eyed me up, a wide smile beaming back at me.

'Your house,' I repeated. 'I see. It's lovely, but I'm seeing *many, many* houses,' I stressed, embarrassed.

'Paco y Ana own this house and live in the next one,' Francisca explained. I smiled at Paco and nodded with a friendly smile.

'Yes, good place to live,' I found myself saying, despite not wanting to give them any further misleading encouragement.

Ana and Francisca spoke for a moment in Catalan as the workmen left.

'It's been good to meet you.' I started to excuse myself in my best Spanish. 'I must go and find my friend.' But Ana wasn't having any of my excuses.

Although I didn't understand her dialect, she led me outside to proudly present her own well tended garden, including a vast outdoor kitchen that looked as though it could cater for the whole town, and, of course, her prized swimming pool. Next, through Francisca, she ran through all the good points about the house for sale. She explained that the house was very large and until recently had had three families living in it, one on each floor. As the ladies spoke, Paco looked on silently. A sweet man in his seventies, I presumed, he was half Ana's size in both stature and presence. Half an hour later, as his smiles diluted into a more apologetic look, he finally encouraged his wife to leave.

It was late by the time I said goodbye to Francisca and started to make my way back to the square. Seeking out some quiet, I took the winding country lane as the dusky light set in. The stone houses that peppered the way started to light up and the trill of birdsong filled the otherwise quiet and fragrant evening air. Although I was in a town I barely knew and retracing steps I only vaguely remembered, I felt safe. As I crossed the bridge over the river, the rabble of ducks quacked animatedly, the natural spring water rushing beneath them. I crossed the tram tracks. A scooter whizzed by with two kids chatting excitedly, a girl jogging with her dog nodded me a 'buenas' and I started to recognise the streets that led into town. The walk descended towards the square via cobbled streets that had worn slippy-smooth and cool, narrow alleys. Outside the handsome stone houses, plants in large terracotta pots lined the pedestrian streets.

Back in the square, I looked for Ray in several of the bars. With no sign of him, I finally took a seat at the fountain and checked my phone. I had a missed call and a text. Ray had waited another hour for me, then gone home to Ramon. I couldn't blame him. My head still fuzzy with all the excitement of the day, and the confusion of the final house, I took my now weary legs to find my car and start the long drive back to Celia's.

9

It's not a house, it's a home

'You *are* kidding me, right?' was Ray's initial reaction when I told him the next morning that I might have fallen for the house in Sóller. The truth was that I'd been thinking about it all night, planning the rooms and furnishing it in my head, and first thing, before I had got it together to call Harrisson, I knew that I needed to try out the idea of the house on Ray. Besides, it also gave me the opportunity to apologise to him for the chaos of the previous afternoon.

'But it's *so* not you . . . that spooky, dusty old place that needs a hundred thousand euros spent on it to bring it crashing into the twenty-first century . . . and it is definitely not Harrisson,' he told me bluntly. 'Not one thing about it is Harrisson.'

'But it could be,' I tried to assure him. 'The basics are all there. Think of it as having good bone structure,' I argued, in a language I thought he might understand.

I was lying on my bed, having thrown the shutters open, to greet the early-morning sun as it shimmered across the valley. Ray continued to protest loudly down the mobile phone pressed tightly to my ear.

'You're crazy, Izz!' he told me. 'Why not go for a simple new apartment and compromise on size?'

'So you don't think the house could be great, with a lick of paint and some gorgeous furniture?' I asked hopefully. 'Those views are so beautiful . . . there are so many rooms with so many possibilities, so much space — '

'I think you've lost it, to be honest,' Ray interrupted with a sigh. 'You'd have to sink so much cash into doing that place up to make it vaguely inhabitable, even for an unfussy couple, which you most definitely are not! You'd be better to flatten it and start from scratch. Have you any idea, Izzy, really? You'd better brace yourself for when that quote comes back from Francisca.'

'Ah . . . yes, that.' I laughed with embarrassment. 'It's just so pretty,' I cooed pathetically.

'Well,' Ray said like a man defeated, 'sounds like, despite all reason, you've got your heart set on it.'

'I think that maybe I have,' I confirmed. 'I was going to run it by Harrisson,' I said with uncertainty, imagining Ray with his head in his hands. Instead he laughed out loud.

'*That* is one hard sell to a Londoner,' he

warned, and I had to admit that he was probably right.

★ ★ ★

Celia and I had planned an office day. With the final wedding of the season now firmly out of the way, we were in the leisurely situation of being able to plan ahead. The idea was to go through the enquiries we had received for next year and divide up the new workload. Then, Celia had rather elaborately decided, we'd spend the rest of the afternoon looking at the trends for weddings and brides for the new season.

After a simple breakfast of *pa amb oli* and a strong black coffee at Celia's kitchen table, I headed up to the office. I'd left a carefully drawn-up synopsis on my desk of all of the enquiries I'd had to date from serious brides, noting their budgets, number of guests and all the key details and initial wishes they'd relayed to me, along with as much personal information as I'd managed to glean about each couple. I'd come to know Celia well enough to pre-empt that she would expect my list to be both incredibly organised and meticulously detailed.

Celia, I discovered, had different ideas. That morning, I could barely push open the door to the office. Wedding magazines, swatches of organza, vast lengths of silk ribbon, menus, hotel details and CDs of music teetered in impossibly high piles on every surface. Celia had emptied cupboards, and ordered in lavish books on floristry, samples of wedding cakes, cup-cakes and dresses by Spanish designers. I felt as though I'd stumbled into the grotto of a fairy godmother of wedding planning, and it was a total surprise.

'It's all gorgeous,' I gasped excitedly. 'But . . . '

'I know,' said Celia from the far end of the room. 'You thought we'd do the serious stuff first? The planning? Well, what kind of fun is *that?*' she chimed in a playful voice.

Celia was immersed in unveiling the last of the wedding dresses, unwrapping a box brimming with rose-pink tissue paper to reveal the most delicate wisp of crème-brûlée-coloured lace I'd ever seen. She'd looped a seamstress's tape measure around the shoulders of her neat 1950s-style dress and peered down the bridge of her perfectly powdered nose and beyond her gold-rimmed reading glasses to inspect the gown more closely. She finally slipped it on to a silk hanger and hung it on the edge of a folding screen that was already decorated with a good number of others.

'Besides,' she continued, turning to look at me, 'not only do we want to assess the key trends and our contractors' handiwork for next season . . . but when we've got a bride in our very midst, there really is no time like the present.'

I drew in a deep breath and it all became clear. I gave Celia a huge grin and looked around at the delicious contents of the room, so carefully prepared. If I'd been with anyone other than my boss, I caught myself thinking, I would have squealed.

'Right,' Celia announced, as if getting down to business, 'I would imagine that you are just itching to try on dresses?'

I beamed back a smile. 'For the brides of next year, of course,' I teased, floating over to the screen.

That morning Celia and I had the most fun. I paraded in dresses and encouraged Celia to try at least one vintage number that had arrived in her size, which she topped with a feathered fascinator. We debated the fashion trends of big bows and classic elegance and discussed how to conjure a stylish take on a modern-day fairy tale as well as adapt contemporary Spanish style for our English brides. We toyed with table settings, favours, accessories and French macaroons. And we assessed the make-up artists, florists and decorators all vying for business.

All the while Pepillo cowered beneath Celia's desk, thrown by our uncharacteristic activity and creative chaos.

By the end of the afternoon, having nibbled at wedding cake and sugared almonds instead of stopping for lunch, we had run out of energy to tackle our so-called planning. There was just time to carefully file and pack up the office, taking notes of our coveted findings.

High on ideas for my own wedding day, I jotted down my personal favourite finds in a crisp new notebook that I'd been saving for the very purpose. From the office window I could see Celia lazing happily in the garden below, humming to herself as she sipped a G&T and listened to her favourite classical radio station as the sun began to set over the valley. Pepillo sat calmly at her feet, seemingly relieved that order had been restored. It was the perfect time to pick up the phone to Harrisson.

'I think I've found *it* and you'd better come and look,' I sing-songed at hearing Harrisson's laid-back 'yeeelo'.

'Babe?' he answered cheekily. 'Are you being naughty? I'm still in the office.'

I giggled at my own innuendo.

'NO! A HOUSE!' I blurted loudly, unable to contain myself.

I heard Harrisson take a deep breath.

'Are you free this weekend? I think you're going to love it,' I continued, not waiting for an answer. 'It needs a little work, OK, so a lot of work, but it's a real find. Beautiful two-hundred-year-old townhouse with tons of rooms, a great little terrace and a fantastic view,' I reeled off at super-speed, almost without pause for breath. 'There are some things about it I think you'll love — some amazing antique tiles, beams, all that kind of stuff,' I continued without hesitation. 'And the price, well, we can *actually* afford it!' I announced proudly. 'And have cash spare to do it up, although I have to prepare you, it does need *quite a bit* of money spent on it, but I've already been looking into that . . . '

'Izzy, Izzy, slow down,' Harrisson pleaded with the catch of a laugh in his voice. 'Why don't you send the details over to me, like you have with the other cooky places you've seen?'

He wasn't taking me seriously.

'This one's different,' I pleaded. 'The details aren't great, because they're from a Spanish agent, so you might miss something in translation,' I added, pleased with my creative thinking on the spot. 'And anyway, you can't get a sense of its position, the views, the surrounding area — all a real bonus. It's in my favourite part of the island, you know that place I told you about . . . Sóller.'

'Yeah, I remember,' Harrisson recalled, sounding more interested now. 'Isn't that where Posh and Becks stayed, at that hotel in the port up there?' he said, perking up.

'The Esplendido?'

'That's it!' he confirmed. 'It looked kinda cool.'

'Well it is,' I said, 'but obviously the house is nothing like that . . . although it's only five minutes away from there in the car,' I tried invitingly. 'So, you're not shooting this weekend, are you?' I asked, trying to lead him.

'Izzy, Izzy, Izzy . . . I can tell that you're not going to give this one a rest until I see it,' he said, and I felt my heart leap in anticipation. 'I'll book flights.'

★ ★ ★

'Jesus, Izz, I'm just not sure if this sort of project is the right thing for us,' Harrisson said finally, after some of the initial shock at the state of the house in Sóller had sunk in. 'I mean, this is the kind of thing property developers take on, proper professionals who

139

do it full time,' he added, peeling away a chunk of mottled plaster from the living room wall. 'This isn't just decorating, this is major . . . I mean, there really isn't a proper kitchen or a bathroom even.'

We'd been in the house with Francisca for an hour, and until now Harrisson had just walked around silently. I couldn't even tell if he liked what he saw. All I did know, returning to the house, was that I had set my heart on this being home.

I'd tried to stay calm and let Francisca lead the viewing, but I couldn't help pointing out the things I loved in each room, just in case, having come all this way, Harrisson missed some of them.

'So do you like it?' I turned to ask him finally, when I thought we were alone in one of the bedrooms and I could bear the silence no longer.

Harrisson put his arms around me, in a way that signalled he was about to give me bad news.

'Sure, it's a great little house. But it needs a lot of love and hard work, babe, you can see that.'

'I know,' I said, deflated, looking down at the beautiful tiled floor.

'But thees no problem,' Francisca inter- rupted happily, making an entrance from the hallway. 'Here in Sóller I have all of the contacts to start right away on the reform. They do work. You do nothing.'

I looked up at Harrisson and smiled a smile that I hadn't used since begging my dad for a completely inappropriate pair of school shoes as a teenager. Harrisson shook his head at me and raised a brow in a way that told me that my tactic just wasn't going to work.

'Theees is for everything, but of course, you can adapt,' Francisca said, handing over the typed-out quotation she'd prepared after my last visit.

Harrisson baulked at the figure.

'I can imagine,' I admitted, blushing slightly, 'that I might have got just a bit carried away talking to the builders.' I giggled nervously and thought for a second. 'But you've got such a great eye, it seems kind of mad not to take something and make our own mark on it. You do it every day with art directing; you could project-manage the house here. It would be just the same. And cut the price right down. And we can prioritise what needs doing and not spend *all* of this, obviously,' I argued, surprising myself with my off-the-cuff thinking.

That afternoon I gave Harrisson my own tour of the town. The chef in him loved the vast indoor market, seeing the traders selling their locally grown produce, fresh fish and deli treats. The aesthete in him loved the architecture, and the laid-back side loved the lazy pace and the relaxed vibe. But it was the port that really sold Sóller to Harrisson. He couldn't quite get over the fact that just a few minutes from the historic town, surrounded by mountains, you could find yourself at the beach. A small beach, but a beach with golden sand, surrounded by a few great little bars and restaurants that he undoubtedly could see himself regularly escaping to. We walked the length of the bay hand in hand, stopping for an afternoon drink on a terrace overlooking the water and again at a traditional tapas bar on the farthest side, where the view of the fishing boats bobbing beneath the towering mountains was breath-taking. As the afternoon was closing in, we watched the fishermen arrive back in port and reel in their nets.

'You hungry?' I asked, taking my eyes away from the view and back to study Harrisson. He'd been quiet and seemingly lost in thought for what had felt like hours. Behind his Ray Ban Aviators, his eyes were fixed on the table.

He swirled the last of his white wine around the bottom of a short Pyrex tumbler, finished the contents and eventually looked up at me.

'No. I'm cool. But I think,' he said, with a smile, 'that I like these tumblers. We should get some . . . for the new house.'

10

Black money

Deciding that you're going to buy a house in Majorca is one thing. Doing it is very different altogether. After Harrisson had gone back to London, I was left to find out all of the details, make the contacts and draw up the plans. And nothing was as I thought it might be.

The systems, paperwork, people and processes were all alien to me, and it wasn't just a question of language. Yet I figured that if I could get my head around the intricacies of buying a house on the island, maybe I'd be a step closer to understanding how everything worked for when we finally lived in Sóller.

I tried to keep Harrisson up to speed, telling him how I'd had to get this certificate or that document. About valuations, meetings and trips to the town hall, and all of the complications. The fact, for example, that the house wasn't listed under the number the owners had given it, but as part of the original building, which all had to be changed by a very serious-looking man with a pencil at the town hall. Harrisson listened half-heartedly to my stories whilst drinking in a bar, walking down Oxford Street or sending emails from work.

'You won't actually believe me,' I told him one evening, when he asked how it had gone that day at the bank. 'The bank manager asked me how much we had agreed to pay in black money!'

'What do you mean, black money? Have you been watching too much American TV?' he quipped.

'Cash. The bank manager asked me. She came straight out with it.'

'What are you talking about, Izz? We're getting a mortgage.'

'Of course we are, but apparently we're expected to give the sellers some cash too. I asked her how it works and she said that it's standard to agree the price that goes on all of the official documents, then extra in a cash bundle, so that the sellers have a chunk they don't need to declare.'

'That's crazy!' he laughed.

'I know! Then, when you're at the *gestoria* . . . the equivalent of the solicitor,' I explained, 'the suits all leave the room so that you can hand over the envelope to the seller.'

'Of cash?'

'Yeah! Only, although they all leave the

room, everyone knows exactly what's happening. Everyone does it apparently.'

'Bizarre,' Harrisson said. 'How much do they want, then?'

'Twenty thousand euros,' I told him

'Can we do it?'

'Yes, the bank have budgeted it into our figures for us.'

'Really? Well, I guess it will make things more interesting.'

'For you maybe!' I told him. 'That's one big envelope to carry around in a handbag.'

Throughout what seemed to be the endless preparing, chasing and signing of papers for the house, I started organising next season's weddings with Celia and embarked on a strict diet regime in preparation for my own. Having got very comfortable with Spanish food, Spanish wine and a slower pace, the regime had to be as big as the bulge I was now fighting to tackle.

At first I assumed there would only be one solution in the absence of Remi — my fashionista friend and the ultimate body fascist — and that came in the shape of Ray, my self-appointed boot-camp trainer. For session one, he'd lured me out of bed at some ungodly hour with the promise of a gentle jog along the beach front at Portixol, followed by breakfast. He even told me we'd burn so many calories that it would be OK to indulge in 'really good eats' afterwards, so as I prepared myself in inappropriate yoga togs in the absence of proper running clothes and donned my Converses in lieu of sensible trainers, I told myself that there was a big breakfast of *huevos rancheros* at the end of what might be a long, dark tunnel.

Ray, I discovered on that deceptively sunny and cheery bright morning, had lied. Outrageously. He arrived with Ramon and a fleet of gorgeous, toned twenty-something girls in tow, all sporting the latest looks in Lycra, perfect skin, sunglasses and sleek ponytails. Ray, it transpired, had conveniently forgotten to mention that he was part of a German running club that had been set up by an ex-model who had come to live on the island with her Majorcan husband, who played for the island's professional football team. Ray and boyfriend Ramon were the honorary male members, I noted, sizing them up, on account of Ray's colourful line in Lycra cycling-style running shorts that left not a stitch to modesty and Ramon's vest top, strategically ripped to reveal bulging muscles. I looked down at my own wobbly waistline, chunky thighs and unsuitable attire and groaned, mouthing 'I hate you' at Ray as he pointed to the statuesque blonde who was going to lead the run and was gathering everyone together.

Minutes later, after a welcome greeting in which the running club embraced me with looks of pity, I watched baffled as everyone removed their shoes. 'Come on, Izz.' Ray ushered me along as he sidled up to me. 'We're going barefoot, on the sand.'

'We are?' I asked in disbelief.

'Yes, it's great for the calves,' he said, 'keeps things interesting. To be honest, Izz, it could be a kind manoeuvre by Uli, on account of your battered Converse.'

My blushes soon turned into scarlet-faced gasps as the pack set off, at speed. Running on sand, I discovered for the first time, was more accurately hell on the calves, and after five minutes of struggling to keep up, I was bent double as the ponytails all swished by. I took a minute to catch a breath. Gorgeous girls on rollerblades whizzed past on the promenade above us. Joggers ran with their dogs. A white-haired sun-worshipper was swimming in the late-autumn sea. Even he put me to shame. I jumped a little when I felt a hand on my shoulder.

'Isabelle,' a deep voice soothed, a little husky and out of breath. 'Don't worry about it. The Spanish would say you look beautiful as you are. You don't need this running.' It was Ramon, Ray's boyfriend, who'd sweetly dropped behind. 'I told Ray that I'd stay with you,' he explained. 'That he should go ahead.'

I could see Ray's tiny butt in his crazy shorts disappearing into the distance as he ran effortlessly alongside the girls.

'Look at him!' Ramon laughed. 'He loves it! Me, I prefer to take things slower . . . you know, *tranquillo*. Coffee and a cigarette?' he finally offered.

'You sure I'm not keeping you from — '

'No, you are doing me a favour,' Ramon interrupted. 'I am killing for a cigarette,' he drawled in his almost perfect English. As I got my breath back and we walked chatting towards the nearest café, I realised that despite the beautiful scenery, there had to be better ways to get your body into some kind of shape for a wedding.

11

The big handbag

I missed Harrisson, and as I was telling Marta, I desperately wanted him to be part of the whole process of setting up our life together from the outset. It was a warm autumn afternoon at the vineyard, the kind that lulls you into a false sense that summer might just creep on for ever. Half an hour after Marta's extended family had left the lunch table, we were still chatting over strong black coffee in the vine-covered courtyard, surrounded by the flat earthenware dishes that had held large portions of her grandma's home-made almond cake and ice cream. The low sun cast dappled shadows through the vine leaves and on to the old stone floor as we spoke; the air felt warm and the only sound for miles was the distant tapping of canes as the local farmers encouraged their crop of almonds to fall from their trees into nets.

'But everything is good now, no? The house, Harrisson coming to live . . . ' Marta soothed my concern. 'I know, but I just worry that if he's not involved now, it will be like stepping into someone else's life when he arrives . . . do you know what I mean?'

'*Claro*,' Marta agreed. 'But I am sure he has his reasons, no? He has many things to take care of in England,' she said sensibly.

I nodded in agreement, stirring my *café solo* with a spoon out of habit, having resisted the urge to add sugar to it.

'So you have to let him do what he has to. But I would say also,' she added with a twinkle in her eye, 'it is better you make the decisions now, whilst the man isn't here to . . . what is this word . . . interfere!'

'True.' I nodded, laughing.

Marta took a sip of her coffee, bringing both hands to the cup and her clear brown eyes to meet mine.

'Isabelle, you worry too much,' she said, placing the cup back down.

'I guess you're right,' I agreed. 'When things are going well, I should just be getting on with making them happen.'

'*Exactamente*. You English, you want everything so fast,' she said accurately. 'Let life be . . . a little more straightforward.' She gestured. 'At its own pace.'

'Straightforward,' I sighed. 'If only! Celia told me this morning that Tomas is coming to visit this week.' I gave Marta the news partly because I knew she'd want to see her old friend, and also because I wasn't sure how long he'd stay and how things would be when Harrisson turned up too. And of course, not least because since Celia had told me that Tomas was due to arrive, I'd been into a panic.

Marta looked at me with wide eyes. 'But that is OK,' she insisted. 'You are all . . . how you say, grown up, and Tomas, you know, he is always a gentleman.'

She was right. It was going to be difficult, but if I was going to stay on the island and work with Celia, I needed to get used to the idea of both Tomas and Harrisson being around.

I smiled and told myself that I was probably looking for problems where there weren't any.

Marta, on the other hand, had plenty of problems with the men in her life. So as I dismissed my own worries, I told myself to count my blessings and asked her how things were going with the businessman she'd been dating in the city. It was just the beginning of a conversation that dominated the next couple of hours and another large pot of coffee.

★　★　★

Two weeks later I found myself in the notary office in Palma with a pile of paperwork on my lap and Harrisson by my side, waiting to go into the boardroom to sign the deeds to the house.

Harrisson squeezed my hand as I looked up at the clock on the wall. We were early. The office smelt of cleaning fluid and its shiny white tiled floor glimmered under the glare of the fluorescent ceiling lights. Perched on the edge of a boxy sofa that looked as though it had been there since the 1970s, with huge cheese plants towering over us at either side, I suddenly felt nervous. I had a bag full of euros and a head full of the kind of horror stories that dominate those TV programmes where English people buy a house abroad only to find that there's a motorway planned that will run straight through it. I looked out of the window at the scene of backed-up traffic on the rainy street below.

'It's almost nine,' I mumbled to Harrisson.

'Chill out, Izz, they'll be here,' he assured me, flicking through a magazine, his eyes fixed on the pages. The quiet waiting room wasn't conducive to pursuing conversation.

I sighed with anticipation and let my mind wander back over the events of the previous weekend, just after I'd seen Marta at the

153

vineyard. I had stumbled out of bed and downstairs early on Saturday morning in an oversized Blondie T-shirt, big thick socks and bird's nest hair, in desperate search of coffee. I had a morning at home whilst Celia was in the city and before Harrisson arrived that afternoon. It was one of those rare moments when I was in the house alone and could feel completely relaxed and off duty. I scratched my sleepy head as I put together the metal mocha pot and grunted a hello to Pepillo, who opened his one good eye in recognition from his rug. I scoured the room for a newspaper, wandering over to the kitchen table to read the headlines on a discarded local paper whilst the pot bubbled on the stove.

'Hello,' said a voice cutting through the silence from the doorway. I jumped, turning around, my heart pounding furiously.

It was Tomas.

'Jesus!' I shrieked with a mixture of shock and disbelief. 'You almost scared me to death!'

I looked down at my bare legs and pulled my T-shirt down instinctively.

'Sorry . . . ' he apologised, looking sheepish.

I blushed. I wasn't sure if I was more embarrassed to be caught by the man who'd proposed marriage to me because I thought I was at home alone, or because I looked such a state.

'Bad timing,' he offered awkwardly.

'I didn't know anyone was here,' I explained. 'Obviously,' I added, referring to my appearance.

'I, er . . . skipped eighties music, being here,' Tomas replied, eyeing my T-shirt with embarrassment. 'We didn't get English TV then . . . I'd never heard of *Top of the Pops* . . . ' He looked good, I couldn't help but notice as his voice trailed off. Good in a classic English grown-up public schoolboy kind of way. His forearms, beneath roughly rolled-up white shirt sleeves, were muscular and tanned from gardening, his blue eyes bright and enquiring behind his glasses. His skin had that familiar clean, fresh smell he always had.

'I wasn't due to arrive until tomorrow, but I caught an early flight,' he explained, seeming to feel the need to fill the silence. 'Didn't seem much point hanging around for another day, just waiting to fly over . . . '

And just at that moment, Celia returned early too. Before we had a chance to drop the awkward façade, or to face the inevitable conversation about the proposal. Of course at that precise moment I was relieved to be able to excuse myself and run upstairs to get dressed and ready for Harrisson's arrival. From Tomas's incredibly polite manner that afternoon, when he made sure that he was around to shake Harrisson's hand and pat him on the back in a 'best man won' kind of manner before disappearing to avoid any unnecessary small talk, I presumed that Celia had already filled him in on Harrisson's trip. Tomas, like before, had made it easy for me and kept a low profile around the house. Marta, I realised had been right: he was a gentleman. Harrisson, on the other hand, being cool rather than courteous, pretty much ignored Tomas and didn't once mention his presence. But I'd started to feel that we should at least try to be more hospitable, ask Tomas to come out for a drink and maybe invite Marta too. After all, I mulled, looking around at the notary's office once more, he was Celia's son and therefore would figure pretty long term in our future.

The receptionist smiled at us from a desk in the corner, between answering calls in lightning-speed Spanish. A young guy in jeans, looking uncomfortable, sat on the sofa opposite us.

'Wonder why he's here?' I whispered to Harrisson.

He raised an eyebrow at me. 'You're so

impatient!' he whispered back. 'And nosy!'

I smiled up at him as Francisca and our German bank manager arrived at reception. They were followed moments later by our neighbours and sellers Paco and Ana, who had dressed so smartly for the occasion they were almost unrecognisable. There were smiles and nods of recognition all round, and then the receptionist announced to the mystery young guy that he was not required at the meeting. Francisca leaned in to translate.

'He is the relation of Paco y Ana,' she told me, 'and also your neighbour, but he does not need to sign.'

Finally, as the clock above us showed that it was almost 9.30, the receptionist signalled for us to make our way to the boardroom. Here we were introduced, very formally, to the notary, a frail grey-haired man who sat at the head of the table.

For the next two hours he read through each line of the documentation for the house in Spanish. Our neighbours had a copy in Catalan, whilst Lena, our bank manager, and Francisca kindly leant over to translate for us whenever our brows knotted in confusion, which was frequently. It was a process that seemed to last for ever. We agreed the terms of the mortgage, that the deeds were correct, that we had checked the future building plans at the town hall ourselves, and that as the new owners we were responsible for everything on our property in the context of our small neighbourhood of three houses, including, it was specified, the old water pipes. I was too excited about our purchase to be bored by the formalities and kept grinning over at Harrisson, who almost laughed when, as I had told him would happen, the notary and the bank manager left the room so that we could hand over the cash to the buyers when Francisca asked 'You have the black money?'

'*Si, claro*,' I answered confidently, shuffling an A4 envelope of cash in Paco's direction. He smiled a mischievous schoolboy grin and stretched his hand tentatively across the table to take it. But as he glanced in the direction of his somewhat formidable wife, she swiped the envelope and in one swift motion had concealed it in the depths of her enormous handbag. Within seconds the clasp was tightly shut. Paco gave me a little defeated shrug and Ana kept the bag tightly clenched to her chest for the rest of the meeting.

When everything was signed and sealed, we rushed down on to the street, clutching the paperwork, with its just-dry signatures and the stamp of the notary, that said that we owned the house. Despite it being a damp and drizzly morning, Harrisson literally swept me off my feet. As he spun me around, Palma whizzed by in a blur.

'Now,' he said, waving our set of keys, 'let's go celebrate with a big brunch and a Buck's Fizz, before we make our first visit . . . home.'

★　★　★

That afternoon, a little giddy from too much champagne, we visited our new house in Sóller. As the bells tolled at the church across the road, Harrisson caught me off guard by whisking me off my feet for the second time that day to carry me over the threshold. We collapsed in fits of laughter as we dived head first into cobwebs and stepped across the dusty floors into the empty shell of our uninhabitable house, but we didn't care: It was ours and it was going to be beautiful.

Once inside, I dashed over to the doors that led to the terrace at the back of the vast hallway and pushed them open to let in the soft winter daylight. I wanted to see everything. I whizzed around the downstairs of the house, opening the heavy emerald-green shutters, whose warped wooden frames and rusty fittings creaked and groaned in protest.

'The view *is* amazing, isn't it?' I heard

Harrisson announce proudly from the ter-race.

'Sure is!' I yelled back. I was in the bathroom. Despite the toilet being in a grimy state, I'd dived in there after the long journey. I pulled at the old-fashioned chain and it came away from the cistern. I let out a little yelp of surprise.

'You OK?' I heard from the distance. I giggled and then went to turn on the tap in the sink. No water.

I went back outside and found Harrisson.

'I'm going to go round to Ana and Paco's and ask them where the mains tap for the water is,' I announced.

'OK, best you go, with your Spanish,' he answered. I was already trying to carefully figure out what I needed to say.

I went off mumbling to myself and closed the big wooden door behind me. Outside, the late-afternoon sky was clearing and a mist of clouds hung around the mountains. The air smelt dewy from the earlier rain. I knocked on our new neighbours' door and it opened instantly, as if they already knew I was there.

'*Hola! Como va?*' Ana exclaimed with a big friendly smile. Paco came to join us, and following a mixture of stilted rudimentary Spanish and elaborate hand signals, he seemed to understand that we had no water and ambled outside to turn on the mains. I thanked him overenthusiastically and went back to Harrisson, but as we were exploring the first floor of the house, there was an insistent banging at the door. When we opened it, Paco stood in front of us, rambling in his frantic Spanish punctuated by exaggerated mimes. Harrisson and I looked at each other blankly, unable to understand, until finally Paco stepped inside, exclaiming '*mira!*' and raced up to the first floor, pointing to the window. In the garden beyond, Ana was single-handedly tackling a dramatic flood that in England would have prompted a phone call to the fire brigade. It was instantly clear that our mains water pipe had burst, and a gushing torrent was rushing straight into Paco's beloved crop of tomato plants, flooding their sparkling patio and pool. It didn't look as though it would take long for the whole area to be immersed in several feet of water, mud and rust.

Paco shook his head in disbelief and looked down at the scene. Ana, wearing the tiniest pair of shorts, which she seemed set to burst out of, was attacking the water with a single mop and a bucket. Our old pipes, it seemed, were the reason for the chaos, and my mind flipped back to the notary's office earlier that day and the stress on the pipes being our responsibility. I continued to watch Ana, knowing it would be neighbourly to go and help, but wondering if, just maybe, the clause had been more than a mere coincidence.

12

Fiesta for life!

It was a clear, chilly night and a big domed sky sprinkled with stars hung above the impressive spires of the church when we arrived in the square humping our own body weight in bags. We'd arrived to check into the B&B that was going to be our home whilst the messiest work to the house was carried out.

It had been a strange feeling leaving Celia's early that morning. By the time I finished restoring my room to the exact way I'd found it when I'd first arrived in Majorca, I had a lump in my throat. As I closed the door for the final time, I was reminded of my very first day with Celia and the fact that I was now moving on to the next stage of my adventure. It was one she figured in, but no doubt a stage that would be very different. I'd looked at Harrisson checking his watch impatiently, his usual signal for me to get a move on.

I was relieved to see the pretty art nouveau building with its lit-up window by the entrance. The French-style bar was empty but welcoming, and the owner, an overly smooth Majorcan, was poised to greet us from his desk at the end of the bar. He spoke almost perfect English and I'd managed to negotiate a good rate for a long out-of-season stay. His cigarette burnt to a butt in an ashtray as he delighted in telling us proudly about the history of the building and the culinary delights his resident chef offered. I nodded and smiled, willing him to hurry up so that we could check in.

It didn't matter that our room was tiny, noisy and freezing cold. It had a heating system that blew out hot air like a hairdryer, and instantly turned itself off when you left the room, and the only channel in English on the TV was the highly repetitive Sky News. Such details seemed unimportant. We were full of excitement about our new life and journey.

The next morning we were up uncharacteristically early. Too early even for breakfast, as we had to be at the house at 7 a.m. to meet our team of Spanish builders.

It was still dark when we left the B&B and I was still wiping sleepy dust from my un-made-up eyes as we negotiated the cobbled streets. The rest of the town, however, was already coming to life. The bars were filled with workmen smoking the first cigarettes of the day with a quick, strong shot of coffee. The smell of freshly baked bread and croissants that emanated from the bakery made my stomach flip. Smart Spaniards heading to the city passed us in suits, and the town's *abuelas* had started to emerge from their front doors in slippers and pinnies, throwing out rugs and *ratero* dogs to start their morning cleaning routine.

We followed the narrow streets that wound out of town and down through the wider tree-lined avenues that led to our small district. Save for a few cars that sped by and the buzz of activity at the local bakery, all was quiet. We had only just opened the front door to the house as the builders arrived, shouting '*Hola!*' behind us.

The guys, dressed in layers of jumpers, hats and heavy work boots, introduced themselves with friendly grins and English handshakes.

'Guten morning,' said the main builder, Poli, with a charismatic twinkle in his eye, rather pleased at having mastered an English greeting. He was a short, stocky man with a mane of curly rock-god hair scraped back into a ponytail.

Introductions over, we showed the men around the house. Harrisson spoke in broken English and reiterated the work that needed to be done in each room by drawing on the walls of the house in pencil. I did my best to translate in terrible Spanish, and asked Poli to speak slower. Already I was worried that things were getting lost in translation as I stammered over my words and checked a pocket dictionary for others.

Yet no words could have prepared us for the first delivery of the day. Just thirty minutes after the guys arrived there was the roar of a rusting dump truck, its engine shuddering right outside the house. Poli excused himself, signalling that he would take care of it.

We followed him downstairs to see a vast pile of what must have been several tons of sand dumped straight into our entrance hall and on to the antique tiled floor we were so keen to preserve. I looked at Harrisson with wide eyes, feeling that already something had gone wrong.

'Ees normal,' Poli said, catching my eye.

'For building?' I asked.

'Oh, to mix cement,' figured Harrisson.

'*Si, en la terraza*,' Poli reiterated.

Before long, Manolo, the heaviest of the three men, with a wobbling paunch, had set up an ancient cement mixer on the terrace. The pile of sand, however, didn't move from the hallway. It was necessary, the men said, to keep it inside, so that it didn't get damp from Sóller's famous *humido* — a fine white haze of damp that lingered across the valley each morning. The guys used small black rubber buckets and long-handled triangular shovels to shift the sand from the entrance to further back in the hallway, beyond the glass and wood partition.

'Where are your tools?' asked Harrisson with precise and slow diction when Manolo had stopped to take a breather. He'd expected the arrival of drills, angle grinders and a stock of power tools along with the team that morning.

'*Es todo!*' replied Manolo with simplicity and a smile. Harrisson cast his eye in disbelief over the small selection of trowels and hammers the men had brought with them.

'This,' he told me, contemplating the idea of three guys in their late thirties doing everything by hand, 'might take longer than has been quoted.'

Outside, on the terrace, Poli, Manolo and their labourer Pepe were unwrapping foil-covered *bocadillos* and chatting, with loud eighties pop blaring from a battery-operated radio in the background. It was nine o'clock. Breakfast time. First break of the day.

★ ★ ★

The street that ran parallel to the rear of the house was the centre of our small district. There was a typically Spanish ratio of two bars to one general store and an old-fashioned tobacconist. One of the bars was already open and a hub of activity. The smoky, simply furnished room was filled with workmen perched on bar stools, and older guys reading newspapers and slipping Soberano brandy into their early-morning coffee, some with dogs at their feet. The barman grunted a '*si*' at us as we sidled up shyly to the freshly scrubbed bar.

We ordered two coffees and two *bocadillos*, which we saw the barman knock up himself, adding olives and capers to our *jamon* and *queso*, even at this early hour. The bread was smothered generously with olive oil, the cheese was rich and delicious and I soon forgot about being the only woman and the only English couple in the bar. It was, I realised, where the older men nipped in before they went to the bakery next door for the fresh *barra* (or baguette) they'd been sent out to collect by their wives. Where men taking their sons to school might dash into to catch a glimpse of the news that blared from the big TV screen, and where workmen came for their first snack of the day. In short, a place for the locals, and that was what I was keen to become.

After a leisurely hour, Harrisson dutifully returned to the house whilst I grabbed another coffee and my wedding notes before starting to carry out my side of the bargain — shopping for materials for the renovation. After a couple of hours, with my mind focused on wedding details whilst the TV blared with the local news and the bar was filled with chatter, my mobile rang. It was Harrisson.

'Izz, I might need you to pop back. Ana's been round.'

'Sure, no problem,' I soothed. I was already relaxing into the *tranquillo* mountain lifestyle. 'Is it about the water?'

'Er, no,' he stammered. 'Not sure *what* to make of it.'

I was intrigued.

'Poli made me understand what she was on about. The guys were taking out those hideous big glass and wooden partition doors in the hallway when she suddenly appeared. She was as friendly as usual, but she told the guys that she had organised to collect the doors later that day in a van, saying that she'd agreed it with us.'

'Really?'

'Yeah. Poli spoke to her. I don't know what

he said, but he asked me afterwards if I was sure we wanted to give them to her. Apparently the doors are valuable. They're antique and something people are often on the look-out for to put into the houses here.'

'And we didn't ever offer them to her, right?'

'Right. But she asked for you, of course.'

I'd already learnt that it was the woman of the house who ruled the roost and made the decisions. To Harrisson's amusement, whenever there was a delivery or the neighbours popped by, they'd always ask *'Donde esta Isobel?'* and he felt slightly put out that they wouldn't talk to him.

'Think I'll call Francisca. Maybe she can help rather than me risk neighbourly relations with my crude Spanish.'

'Well, neighbourly relations don't seem to be what we thought they were,' Harrisson sighed. I hung up the phone and dialled Francisca, asking the estate agent to explain to Ana that there may have been some confusion. After all, I wasn't sure if she was trying to make a bit more money on the house, or if she genuinely thought the doors were hers. All I knew was that in just one morning I'd been constantly surprised.

We had a surprise of a different kind the very next day. We were back at the house at

7 a.m. and trying to get used to the idea of the early start as our daily routine. After all, our builders did it every day. Harrisson was keen to be at the house whenever the builders were, and that meant hours standing around in a dirty, draughty building site as the weather started to take a turn for winter.

'Can't you just brief them and then let them get on with it?' I'd asked that morning.

'Sure,' he mocked. 'Then the moment I'm not there and they don't know where in the bathroom to put the shower, it'll get plumbed in the wrong place.'

I took his point. I fetched him a takeaway coffee from the local café and headed down into the main town square to set up an impromptu desk with my laptop, a notebook full of wedding plans and a cup of thick Spanish hot chocolate. Unlike Starbucks or any London café focused on high turnover, in Sóller the waiters didn't take the least bit of notice if you only ordered one drink and made it last from when they were pressing the local oranges for juice at breakfast time until they were serving lunch. I was engrossed in matching brides to venues, squeezing budgets to accommodate elaborate dreams when Harrisson appeared covered in a thick coating of dust.

'Don't!' he exclaimed, warning against a

comment about his appearance. 'I've come to take a wash. This stuff is itchy.' I stifled my giggles and tried my best to nod sympathetically. The dust made him look like a ghost.

'OK, you get cleaned up, then I'll buy us some lunch,' I offered. 'I've been hearing people talking about grabbing a *menu del dia* at a bar on the other side of the square. Let's try that,' I suggested, before he turned to head for the gents.

The bar that had the simplest frontage and no visible sign of a name was definitely one that was popular with the locals. A small space, with a chequered floor and a deep mahogany bar that stood proudly above several small bistro tables, it was buzzing with the lunchtime rush. Each seat was taken and the bar stools held the overspilling smokers. Glancing around the room for a spot to perch, I recognised the smart *chica* who usually served me in the bank tucking into a tortilla, the manager of the post office slurping on a steaming bowl of soup and a host of workers and older couples out for lunch. We stood clueless at the bar. Harrisson knocked back a bottle of beer in minutes to quench his dusty-throated thirst as we waited for a table to become free. Before long we were seated and ordered a simple lunch. As Harrisson updated me with stories of

Harrisson was in the habit of joining them. During most of the week they'd fetch a simple *boçadillo* from the local bakery to eat with a short strong coffee. On Fridays, however, Harrisson would report, there'd be a cry from Poli of 'Fiesta for life!' and the men would down tools and treat themselves to breakfast in one of the local bars.

At first they'd laughed at Harrisson, who despite the weather would leave the house all excited to join them wearing a faded cashmere jumper, ripped jeans and Havaiana flip-flops. They protested in embarrassment at this *loco extranjero* and insisted he put on his slightly more appropriate Converse before they'd take him with them. At the men-only bar tucked away beside the tram track at the back of our district, the same table would be waiting for them, where they would eat something hot, washed down with a carafe of red wine.

On his first visit, without a menu in sight, Harrisson had suggested that Poli order his breakfast for him. Despite the hour, he'd accepted a glass of wine with gratitude but waited for his food before drinking it. When a sizzling hot earthenware dish arrived, not without ceremony, Harrisson peered into the contents. The dish contained something meaty in a tomato sauce, into which he dipped a slice of bread, gingerly at first. Poli, he said, had stared at him intently as he prodded at the murky contents with a fork before tasting it. The builder's interest had made him wonder exactly what the dish contained. On his fork the meat felt spongy beneath the thick sauce. Poli stared at him some more. Harrisson remembered closing his eyes, bringing the fork to his mouth and popping in a generous mouthful. The taste was deep and richly textured, but not unpleasant. Harrisson smiled at Poli. '*Es bien*', he said, as Poli roared with laughter. When he explained that the tapa was a dish made from pig's tongue dressed with brandy, Harrisson had suddenly found a desperate thirst for red wine.

At a similar hour I'd be focusing on getting simple chores finished before my working day began. I was soon factoring in constant trips to the laundry and trying to explain that Harrisson's battered building jeans didn't need ironing with creases. I also visited the local market, to make sure we ate enough fresh fruit and could make our own *bocadillos* at the house at lunchtime, clearing a little space to make them as best I could without the luxury of water or electricity. The chores slowed life down and brought me back to basics. Although I felt constantly cold and grubby, it was a time that wasn't without humour. I loved to visit the market every day and hear the fishermen's wives burst into song as they gutted the daily catch and set the fish on ice to tempt all who visited. I'd chat to the lady who sold the best local vegetables, grown on her allotment, and say 'hola' to the elegant señora who sliced huge legs of jamon and served the creamiest Spanish cheeses and the sharpest olives from the deli counter laden with tempting Spanish treats. Best of all, I loved visiting the house.

I'd often creep up on the builders belting out Rod Stewart or A-ha at the top of their lisping voices in broken English, their radio forever tuned into Radio Ochenta — a Spanish channel entirely devoted to English eighties pop — as they worked. When I'd arrive, one of the men would always announce 'Isobel aqui' at the top of his voice, and we'd stop to chat in our mix of broken English and rudimentary Spanish. When they were off duty, cleaned up and out with their families in the town, they would always stop to ask how we were. It wasn't long before their wives and children did the same.

As my relationship with the men started to grow, I learnt that Pepe, the slightest of the three, with a long, sad Moorish face, was a fisherman. He always looked so forlorn because he hated the cold winter climate and longed for the summer, when he could be out at sea. Every day he chipped away at the thick, solid stone walls in the main entrance space, making a channel for electricity cabling with a small trowel, his face lighting up at the opportunity to tell me about a particular local fish to look for in the market, and how to select the freshest catch. Manolo, the policeman, always kept us up to date with the fiestas that regularly took place in the town, and we'd often see the guys taking a starring role, beating drums, dressed as devils, running a barbecue or taking part in a religious parade with their children. And on regular days, in such a quiet, calm town, it would always make me smile to spot our favourite policeman looking a little demoted and disillusioned as, dressed in full uniform and sunglasses, he oversaw the children spilling out of school in the afternoon.

As progress was made at the house, Harrisson, I was relieved to hear, bonded more intimately with the builders. His face drawn and tired from the physical exhaustion of long hours in a cold, damp old house, he'd nevertheless recount the stories of the day. Spending so much time together, the men had mastered a way of communicating in a mix of pencil drawings, gestures and single words in Spanish, Catalan and English. They spoke, he told me, about football, music and their children, and of course, each was learning a little of the other's language in the process. Poli would now proudly greet me with a 'Gooood mourning, Isabella', in his best attempt to mock the English upper classes, whilst Harrisson was learning phrases he told me he couldn't repeat, as the men taught him 'the Spanish of the bar, not the school'. Despite not always understanding one another, they'd started to become close, close enough to playfully mock each other, and the men had started to refer to Harrisson as 'Blanco Blanco' because he insisted on painting everything in the house white.

The white, he'd decided, was to extend from the newly plastered walls to the heavy wooden beams that stretched the length of the ceiling in the large entrance hall, in order to lighten up the gloomy, oppressive space. The builders protested endlessly, telling him that it was a tradition to keep the dark Spanish wood. We had, of course, seen evidence of this in many of the local entrance halls in the town, their handsome wooden doors pinned back to let the thin warmth of the midday sun seep through immaculately polished inner glass doors in the winter months. Whilst the men put their hands to their faces in mock horror whenever Harrisson threatened to paint the beams, they couldn't deny that the room appeared both brighter and more contemporary once he had painstakingly given each one several coats of *blanco*. Whilst we imagined that we'd become the talk of the town for doing so, Harrisson had also discovered that unlike the grander townhouses, our beams were in fact a cheap, simple wood, stained to look rich and dark.

As November crept on and the days seemed long and arduous, I juggled looking after the budget for the build, ordering supplies so that the guys could press on at the house and carrying on my work with the weddings. Having spent so much time in Majorca helping other people choose things for their new lives, I now relished buying kitchen appliances, bathroom fittings and lighting with Harrisson for our own new home. He had been more than a little surprised and particularly pleased to discover specialist stores stocking the latest designs on the outskirts of the dusty old town.

'Missoni Home,' he'd coo, or 'Woah, Izzy, look, a whole shop devoted to Porcellanosa. In Sóller, who'd have thought?' Whilst I was more interested in trawling junk shops in search of vintage pieces, he definitely had an eye on the new.

We soon became friendly with many of the local shopkeepers and suppliers, who on hearing that Poli would be collecting the goods would often offer us a discount and insist we pay them only after we'd made sure we were happy with our final, fitted products. It was a million miles away from our experience of shopping in England.

It was on one of these trips, to the local tile centre, where the assistant always greeted me with a smile and never minded me flicking through the never-ending supply of terracotta and ceramic designs, that I received an unexpected call.

'Izzy?' the voice had questioned in a slightly husky tone that I recognised but couldn't quite place. 'Izzy darling, it's Remi.'

My mind whirred back in an instant to my old life in London. 'Rem, how are you?' I squealed excitedly.

'Yeah, good,' she replied in her familiar languid drawl. 'You?'

'I am! Where are you? On location at some swanky fashion shoot, I can imagine,' I continued, answering my own question.

'Izz!' Remi exclaimed, laughing gently. 'One thing at a time! I'm actually in Majorca, which is why I thought I'd call.'

'You are?' I said, my heart racing. 'On the island? When am I going to see you?' My old instincts returned to me in a second and I caught myself checking out my scruffy reflection in the shop window as we chatted. I was speaking to my fashion stylist friend wearing what had become my renovation uniform — my only pair of old jeans that didn't need laundering, tucked into flat leather boots, and layers of long-sleeved T-shirts topped with an oversized chunky sweater and Harrisson's college scarf. My only accessory was a battered leather satchel strapped across my body, which contained my laptop (for work on the weddings and my renovation spreadsheet) and a general day-time survival kit. I turned away from the window, remembering how well groomed Remi always was and knowing that my own face was free of make-up and my unruly hair scraped haphazardly into a knot and held in place with a Bic biro. It was a look that Remi would consider way beyond grunge.

'So where are you staying?' I asked.

'On the Paseo Maritimo,' Remi cooed, rolling the words around her mouth in a self-conscious effort to perfect her accent.

Remi, it transpired, had come back to the island to visit Massoud, the Arab billionaire I'd seen her with at Layla and Max's wedding. When Dan (her on-off boyfriend when we were living in Notting Hill) lost his job in the City's financial crash, Massoud had invited her to come out to his yacht, which he moored in Palma in the winter, before it sailed to more exotic waters at Christmas. Between a fashion shoot in Paris and a series of pre-booked spring campaigns back in London just before December, she'd decided she needed a break and thought the offer sounded like fun.

'And is it?' I asked her as my eyes searched now for the next set of tiles to scrutinise.

'Actually, yes, I'm loving it here,' she said contentedly. 'I'm totally chilling out.' I could hear the gentle cracking sound of liquid hitting ice in a glass as she continued. 'Massoud's always entertaining. Mostly for business. It's been fun, but I told him you were here and he said why not invite you both over for drinks?'

'Sounds great, Rem, but we're right in the middle of the building work on the house.' I wondered if Harrisson would have the energy or the inclination to go. 'Why don't I meet you in town for lunch one day instead?'

'Lunch? Honey, it sounds like you both need to escape for an evening!' she quipped. As usual, Remi was persuasive and keen to get her own way. 'Nothing formal,' she insisted. 'Just come by tomorrow evening, say nine o'clock. Harrisson will love it here,' she gushed. Before I could come up with any more excuses, she added, 'I'll text you the name and location of the yacht . . . see you then!' before hanging up.

Harrisson, although shattered from a day of hard physical labour, sounded keen to go into the city to meet Remi and Massoud when I put it to him that evening. After he'd cleaned himself up, we'd pulled on our only clean clothes and headed out in search of something cheap, hot and filling to eat. The air outside felt chilly and damp against my just-bathed skin, the night sky was clear and the streets were bare, with leafless trees towering above the church and the stillness of the empty square. It was quiet but beautiful. Harrisson put an arm around my shoulder against the chill of the evening as we made our way to one of the local restaurants. I'd assumed that eating out whilst we didn't have a kitchen would be fun and decadent, but the reality, in winter time, when many of the restaurants were closed, was that choice had become limited, the traditional menus rarely changed and our budget was becoming tighter the more we spent on the house.

'A night in Palma sounds good to me,' he announced, pouring himself a second glass of rough red from the half carafe we'd treated ourselves to. 'A few drinks, a bit of luxury.'

He smiled. 'Sounds like the perfect break from the house.'

Later that evening Harrisson lay on his stomach across the bed, flicking through endless Spanish TV channels as I scoured the measly contents of my temporary wardrobe and sighed. Of course, I hadn't factored in something like an evening of cocktails on a billionaire's floating gin palace when I packed for a couple of months of hard graft and keeping warm. And although Remi would, as always, be judging me on my appearance, buying something new when all of our money was being invested in the house seemed like a crazy indulgence. My eyes panned across the row of trashed jeans and worn knits that didn't matter if they got paint-splattered. At the end of the rail was one lonely dress. Plain and black, with a button-down back, one I'd forgotten I'd packed just in case a meeting with Celia, a bride or a wedding venue popped up unexpectedly. I'd have to make a trip to the supermarket for some tights, I thought sleepily, then, with my lone pair of heels, although hardly nautical, it would do. I shut the door on my clothes and went to snuggle up next to Harrisson.

13

Euro terrorista

Harrisson had been driving for over an hour and we were arguing about where to park as we finally reached the port. The small car/van hybrid he had hired for the build was covered in dust and smelt faintly of cement. He frowned as I turned down the stereo to read out the details of how to find the mooring that Remi had sent to me in a text.

'Doesn't really mean a lot right now,' he moaned, having missed the turning for the car park.

'We'll find it,' I sighed, tired of arguing, although my eyes told me a different story. The port, even in November, was bristling with a sea of white masts, clicking as they bobbed on the choppy water.

Harrisson parked the car in silence and grunted at the direction he thought we should head in. The sun was low and pale in the sky and lit up the cathedral behind us with a rich ochre light. I linked my arm through his and we headed off in search of Remi and the yacht. I needn't have worried. At one of the furthest points away, a vast white superyacht, all angular shapes and high-tech design, like a James Bond villain's boat, was emblazoned with the words *Lady Mistral* in gold script. I squinted at it, double-checking the name. It was the very same one that Remi had texted to me.

'H . . . not sure how to tell you this, but I think that's it,' I said, pointing.

'Really?' he said in excitement, unlinking his arm from mine to put his hand up to his eyes against the low glare of the sun. 'Cool!' he exclaimed with schoolboy relish. 'It's huge!'

He took my hand excitedly and we headed out across the pontoons, towards the biggest yacht in the millionaires' liquid playground.

As we approached, I could hear a smooth bossa-nova beat floating out across the sea air, the smell of which was fragrant with scented candles. Two men dressed in waiters' black and whites were busy dressing a long, pristine table on the expanse of deck at the back of the boat, one of then polishing a crystal glass with an immaculate white cloth before placing it down again with painstaking accuracy. I looked up. The boat was enormous, with a generous sun deck, and above that a helipad.

'Check out those tenders!' Harrisson

blurted, unable to curb his boyish glee.

'The what?'

'The speedboats. A tender is what you take to get to shore if you're moored somewhere, but on this beauty they're the very best, some of the largest speedboats I've ever seen . . . not to mention the chopper.'

I looked at him, stifling a giggle. I'd never seen him lose his cool like this before. He was usually so underwhelmed, so restrained and understated.

'Izzzzeeeeeeeee, hi!' I heard Remi's voice before I could see her. My eyes scoured the huge gleaming structure.

A tiny figure stood on the very top deck, swatched in a full-length printed kaftan. The Pucci print in deep blues and jade greens was unmistakable, its fabric just sheer enough to reveal the outline of a matching jewelled bikini beneath. It reminded me of our shopping trip in Selfridges back in London, where I'd caught Remi entwined with a cute guy in a changing room when she had supposedly been there to console me when I'd lost my job at On Fire. It seemed like a lifetime ago now, as she wafted elegantly in impossibly high espadrilles to meet us on terra firma.

'Harrisson,' she cooed, kissing him on each cheek in the Spanish way. 'Izzy!' She embraced me as lightly as possible, a Remi 'hug'. Her arms laden with heavy bangles chinked as her hands rested on my upper arms so that she could take a closer look at me. 'How are you, darling?' she asked, looking directly into my eyes. Hers were sparkling emerald, immaculately made up with just the right amount of smoky shimmer and framed by the sharp fringe of her chic black bob. As I opened my mouth to answer, she loosened her grip on me and turned, signalling for us to follow her aboard. As always with Remi, the answer didn't matter much.

I climbed awkwardly on to the deck behind Harrisson, cursing my silly heels and pencil-tight dress, feeling ridiculously out of place.

'She's something, isn't she?' Remi offered as we all took in the view. It was impossible to deny, *Lady Mistral* was incredible. Her deck was a beautiful deep rich mahogany, topped with luxurious white leather banquettes and sunloungers. At the far end, beneath a wide canopy, the lavish dining table was now laid with pristine white linen and highly polished silver cutlery. A beautiful crystal sphere of white flowers that wouldn't have disappointed any of my brides sat at its centre. Smaller vases of flowers and scented candles filled every surface, including a fully stocked cocktail bar, towards which Harrisson gravitated naturally whilst eyeing the more traditional boating equipment, all finished in gleaming chrome rather than traditional brass.

'Mojito, for old times' sake?' Remi asked, and as I nodded with a smile, a waiter appeared, white cloth draped over his arm, to knock up the drinks with a slick and elaborate display of showmanship.

'So, is Massoud joining us?' I asked, intrigued, as we made our way to the banquettes. I perched on a corner, careful not to mess up the spotless, buttery soft leather as Remi kicked off her rope-wedged shoes and curled up into a sea of Missoni cushions. Harrisson stood at the rear of the boat, his eyes scanning the port, his white cotton shirt billowing slightly in the evening breeze as he knocked back a bottle of Mexican beer.

'He'll be here soon.' She smiled. 'He's had . . . you know, a little business to deal with.'

Harrisson raised an inquisitive eyebrow at the statement. 'What does he do?' he asked, his mind back with us.

'Oh, you know me.' Remi laughed. 'I wouldn't have a clue.' She threw her head back as she said it and then started to talk about her own work at home.

The waiters plied us with endless platters of elegant tapas as we relaxed and exchanged stories. We reminisced about Max and Layla's wedding, as well as old Notting Hill antics, and updated each other on our news. Remi's world of fashion styling, magazines and 'super bitches' seemed a million miles from mine, and my old life suddenly felt like it might even have belonged to another person.

Suddenly Remi was no longer by my side. She was up and at the arm of a handsome but, surprisingly for Remi, overweight and older man. I barely recognised him from the shadowy figure I'd glimpsed Remi draped around at Layla's wedding, but from the cut of his navy blue blazer, the Hermès silk handkerchief tucked into its pocket, the brown manicured feet slipped into suede Gucci loafers, I knew instantly that this had to be Massoud.

Harrisson walked over and held out his hand. The man took it, revealing a huge Joseph watch the size of Big Ben encrusted with diamonds beneath his immaculate cuff. He kissed me lightly on both cheeks, in a haze of strong, musky aftershave, taking my hand in his, his heavy signet ring feeling enormous in my palm.

'*Encantada*, Isabelle,' he greeted me in

Spanish. 'Remi, of course, has told me all about you.' I blushed a little and stood up straight. 'Shall we sit for dinner?' he offered charmingly. 'I'm so sorry to keep you waiting.'

'Not at all,' I replied for all of us, feeling his dark eyes still on me. 'We've really enjoyed being here.'

With the waiters once again at our sides, they pulled out the high-backed, luxurious leather chairs for us. Another of the waiters popped open a bottle of champagne, Cristal, of course. I couldn't help but wonder if this was a nightly occurrence.

Massoud slipped off his jacket to reveal a flawless white shirt and a well-fed stomach.

'I was admiring your blazer,' Harrisson offered, as a waiter took it away.

'Thank you, Harrisson.' Massoud nodded. 'I have a fine tailor in Milan, I will give you the details.' I silently scoffed at the thought of us ever being able to afford such luxury.

Massoud, although flashy, was a gentle-man. As we sipped tall flutes of pink bubbly, he took a polite interest in our renovation and our decision to settle in Sóller. In return he told us how he chose his yacht. Having been aboard one owned by the Russian oligarch Roman Abramovich he had instantly con-tacted the same designer. I only hoped that we'd get a guided tour of the interior after dinner.

'So who were you with today, darling?' Remi asked, moving the conversation on as a towering platter of *fruits de mer* was placed before us.

'Oh, the President of Iceland.' Massoud shrugged nonchalantly. 'Amongst some other clients passing through.'

'I used to shop there before I saw the size of Kerry Katona!' I quipped, trying to catch Remi's eye to share the joke.

'Not the supermarket, the *country*,' she gasped, and I laughed, blushing as Massoud failed to get the joke. I was on my second glass of champagne and feeling deliciously giddy on an empty stomach.

'Just business,' Massoud added coyly, trying the white wine the waiter recommended he serve with the fish.

Unfortunately, the Iceland statement wasn't my only faux pas of the evening. Whilst Remi, Massoud and Harrisson navigated their way delicately through the generous helpings of fresh fish on their plates, I wrestled in an ungainly way with crab claws, nearly choked trying my first oyster and lost control of a piece of lobster I triumphantly extracted after several attempts, only to have it rescued from the opposite end of the table and taken away in a napkin by one of the waiters. I mouthed the poor guy a 'sorry' and a shrug and Remi glared at me disapprovingly in return.

Meanwhile, Harrisson quizzed Massoud further about his meetings and his business ventures. Massoud was polite but vague in response and in moments had turned the conversation around to sport, yachts and travelling, tapping in to passions he shared with Harrisson.

'So, what *does* Massoud do then?' I dared to ask Remi in a whisper, noticing the way he had carefully avoided a direct answer himself. Remi's green eyes sparkled wickedly as she leaned in to gossip in a low voice.

'Well,' she started, 'obviously you don't make the kind of money he has on the stock market any more.' She giggled. 'And of course, I don't know the details, but I *do* know that *Vanity Fair* are investigating him, along with a fleet of other guys like him right now . . . It's so glamorous, Izzy, I mean . . . *Vanity Fair*.'

'Really?' I asked, wide-eyed. 'What do they think he's done?'

'Oh . . . something to do with selling arms and drugs to Iran or Iraq or something like that,' Remi said flippantly, without a care.

I felt myself turn rigid. Then the touch of a large, warm hand on my arm.

'Isabelle?'

It was Massoud, his voice deep and thick like molasses close to my ear. I felt the hairs on my lobe prickle beneath the heat of his breath.

'More wine?' he offered. 'Or a digestif, maybe? I have let the staff take a break whilst we eat dessert.'

Dessert. I hadn't noticed the sparkling crystal dish that had been put in front of me. I just kept running through my head the idea of being on a boat with a man who sold illegal guns and drugs, and gulped.

'Calvados ice cream,' Remi offered in explanation as we all now sat in silence. 'It's Massoud's favourite. They make it on board, along with these.' She artfully twirled a delicate brandy and chocolate biscuit between two perfectly manicured fingers, before enveloping the fine pointy end with her generous rosebud lips. Massoud watched, transfixed, whilst Harrisson gave me a strange look, or at least one that suggested that maybe *I* was acting strangely.

I looked down at the dish and smiled awkwardly. Maybe Remi had been kidding. But then again, she never really did that. For the first time in a long time, dessert seemed completely unappealing, and not long afterwards, having given me another pointed look,

Harrisson made an excuse about having to be up at 7 a.m. for the builders, and we took our cue to leave.

'So do you think she's in some kind of danger?' I asked Harrisson nervously, as he navigated his way through the city in the car, having demanded to know why I had gone 'weird' at the dinner table.

'No, I think you just had way too much to drink and got carried away,' he answered firmly. 'Massoud seemed like a nice guy and you shouldn't believe everything girls like Remi say.' He laughed. 'She's probably just got it all mixed up. You know, if it's not choosing the right belt to go with a Prada jumpsuit for *Pop* magazine . . . '

'Oooh, that's so unfair,' I retorted.

'Is it?' he laughed, rolling his eyes. I let it drop. Maybe Remi *had* got it all mixed up. Besides, she'd also told me she was flying back to London the following day, so the bulk of her stay was thankfully over. Nevertheless I sent her a text message, despite the hour, to thank her for a great time and to tell her to be careful and call me when she was home. My eyes struggled in the darkness to focus on the tiny screen filled with illuminated letters.

'I had fun though, babe,' Harrisson continued, his eyes still on the road as he spoke.

'Really?' I asked, wondering if he was just being kind; after all, it was my friend we'd been visiting.

'God yes,' he stressed. 'I mean, I'm shattered from the house, true. I'm doing my best to hang in there, but I really miss nights out in the city, unwinding a little, eating and drinking . . . We should start to find more friends like those guys, people who are based here full time, don't you think?'

'I wasn't really into it myself,' I admitted. 'It all seemed so, well . . . fake.'

Harrisson looked at me momentarily with surprise and disbelief. 'You'd better not turn into a boring Spanish housewife!' he teased, and I felt my heart sink a little.

He turned up the radio and we both fell silent as the long road led us up through the mountains, home to Sóller.

14

Viva, viva, viva Espana!

'I'm really not *quite* sure how I let you talk me into doing this again,' I panted at Ray. It was only a few hours since I'd been drinking on Massoud's yacht, and now I was reluctantly jogging with the immaculate German running club along the same stretch of the Paseo Maritimo I'd tottered down the previous night.

'Quite simply, Miss Mistry, you need to lose at least a stone before we can even consider a dress fitting for your big day,' Ray said with a wicked grin, before sprinting off ahead.

'Little beetch!' Ramon chided gently, his eyes fixed lovingly on Ray's disappearing form as he jogged by my side.

We were twenty minutes into our run. The routine, set by the impossibly sporty Uli, was a one-mile jog, half-a-mile sprint format that I'd personally reduced to a continuous plod. And whilst she and her entourage seemed to rise to the task with an easy grace and athletic elegance as they disappeared almost out of view, I was literally sweating white wine and feeling twice their age (as well as their weight) as I lagged behind. Ramon, as always, was waiting for me to give up, so that he had an excuse for a cigarette and to moan about Ray to someone who understood him. Today, however, as we inevitably snuck off to grab a coffee and wait to catch up with the team on their return leg, it was my turn to moan about Harrisson.

Ramon sat back in a director's chair, crossed his yellow Lycra-clad legs and puffed pools of smoke into the open blue skies outside as the café filled. He couldn't have seemed less interested, but I was a woman who needed to vent.

'You know, I thought he was ready for a simpler life, a slower pace . . . He said if I wanted to be here, then that was what we'd do. But now, well, maybe I shouldn't have thought it was a decision I could make for both of us.' I was gulping down sips of coffee in an attempt to ease my aching head, but the caffeine only seemed to fuel my paranoia.

'He just seemed to spark to life last night, for the first time in ages, all over a big yacht and some lobster . . . which, incidentally, is *impossible* to eat.' Ramon was staring up at the sky, his eyes chasing his latest smoke ring. 'I mean, should I be worried that the island

199

will eventually bore him? That he still wants a glamorous media lifestyle? One that he can't find on tap here?'

Ramon stayed silent as I ranted on. Intermittently he nodded, his eyes fixed now on the clouds that lingered in big marshmallow shapes above the sea, his cigarette firmly stubbed out in the simple glass dish on the table.

'Darling,' he drawled finally, as my ramblings petered out and my eyes filled with tears, 'you can't expect men and weemen to always want the same things.' I wasn't sure if I was too hung over not to be overemotional, but I had the distinct feeling that my fears were more than a hunch, and Ramon's words only seemed to justify them.

The crisp, sunny winter's morning had given way to a pale-skied afternoon in the mountains when I reached Sóller. Some of the houses close to the square had started to decorate their entrance halls with vast nativity scenes for Christmas. Lights had been rigged through the streets, their unlit bulbs forming huge dot-to-dots of giant snowflakes, lanterns and the words *Bones Festes*. The children playing in the square, wrapped in scarves and woollen pea coats against the damp chill of the fading sun, looked even more animated than usual at the sight.

I stopped in at my favourite deli and marvelled at the huge slices of candied orange peel dipped in chocolate, the glossy jars of jewel-coloured jams and chutneys and the nougatty slabs of *turron* that suddenly adorned the shelves in preparation for Christmas. I ordered some flaky pieces of savoury *coca* for Harrisson and the builders; the pastry bases with a pizza-type topping made the perfect snack to serve with a beer, I figured, as I left the gentle bustle of the square and headed up to the house. When I arrived, there was no one home and I was surprised to see the place deserted. There was no laughter, no banter in Spanish or bad eighties radio, no cement mixer endlessly churning on the terrace.

'H?' I called into the big echoey room. '*Hola!*'

Nothing.

The house felt cold, dusty and unwelcoming; daylight was beginning to fade. With the carrier bag of goodies still looped over my arm, I could only think there must be a fiesta I'd missed and that the men had gone home to join their families. I closed the big heavy wooden door of the house behind me, pulled up the collar of my jacket and trundled over to the bar in the port where I knew the builders drank on their way home, for a final search for Harrisson and the guys.

Before I could reach the bar, I could hear it — football, Majorca style. When Spain played, it was more an event akin to a fiesta rather than a mere match. The owner, a huge supporter, always threatened to close the bar so that he could enjoy the game in peace, but Poli and the boys invariably managed to persuade him to open up for just a small group of them. It was a kind of ritual they played, begging the barman to open when they all knew it was inevitable that they'd be watching the match from the exact spot they always viewed it from, whilst he seemed to put up protest.

With the owner officially off-duty, I walked into a scene I could never imagine in England — although closed, the bar was rammed full of supporters, all helping themselves to bottles of beer, leaving coins behind the bar for every bottle they took, their sea of red and yellow football shirts and scarves vibrant against the simple furnishings. I instantly picked out the builders — Poli, Manolo and Pepe — standing in a row, too excited to sit on bar stools or chairs, beating the drums usually reserved for the religious ceremonies in the square in anticipation of a goal, pounding the skins in time to the chant of the crowd and the feet of the players. When a penalty was awarded to the opposition, they dropped their heads and turned away from the screen, literally unable to watch. It was then that they noticed me, and cheers of '*Isobel, bienvenido*!' followed as they stopped to greet me with big kisses on each cheek and wide smiles, insisting I join them. At the end of the line, Harrisson was in his element. The guys had dressed him in one of their shirts and he watched with his arms thrown in the air in anticipation as Torres neared the goal.

'Babe!' he exclaimed on seeing me. 'Have you ever seen anything like this?'

It was loud and raucous, with brothers Poli and Manolo creating most of the mayhem. Pepe, like several of the men, had brought his kids along. Dressed like mini replicas of their football heroes, they sat on their dad's shoulders, giggling and clapping their tiny hands in time to the drum beats.

'You hungry?' Harrisson asked me, pointing over at a table laden with food. Even whilst watching a game, the Spanish men wouldn't think about drinking without eating. The table was heavy with Serrano ham, a selection of creamy Mahon cheeses and crusty French baguettes.

'Looks pretty good.' I smiled at Harrisson, pleased he was having a good time. From the corner of my eye I saw Poli jump behind the bar and grab several bottles of Mahou beer from the very back of the fridge. I put down the bag of offerings I'd bought and reached out a hand as Poli offered me an ice-cold beer with a grin.

'*Gracias, Poli! Salud!*' I cheered.

He chinked my bottle with his and cried, '*Viva España,*' and the rest of the bar chimed in echo of the cry. I looked back at Poli and saw his face change. At the doorway of the bar stood two policemen in uniform. Young and authoritative, their faces were serious as their eyes surveyed the room. Of course, the place was supposed to be shut. There was no till behind the bar and the noise that eminated from the tiny room was big enough to resonate around the port beyond. From the corner of my eye I saw the owner sink deeply into his chair. Then from my side I heard a big belly laugh. The policemen had thrown their arms in the air with a shrug as they spotted Manolo, their fellow officer, who was now chuckling at being caught causing a disturbance. Jibes were thrown across the room, and before long, Poli had hopped back over the shiny bar and the policemen were slapping their fellow supporters on the back and joining them in drinking a beer.

I caught Harrisson's eye and he gave me a look of disbelief. He seemed relaxed and caught up in the moment, the excitement of the game and his new friends, as they all toasted Spain again.

It was the happiest I'd seen him since he'd arrived, happier, it appeared, than the night before. The look on his face was one of pure, childlike glee, and I only hoped that this was the beginning of him feeling like he belonged.

★ ★ ★

Market day, Sóller. My favourite time of the week. From the tiny double room in our B&B, the square below our tightly shuttered windows came alive early on Saturday mornings. Before sunrise, traders set up their stalls, policemen closed the roads and waiters merrily set their tables and chairs outside their cafés, knowing that in just an hour or two, each seat would be taken as the whole of the town turned out for the weekly event. If the rest of Spain indulged in a *parada* in the early evenings, it was Sóller's turn on Saturday mornings.

Whilst Harrisson pulled a blanket over his head to hide from the hubbub, the noise was one I savoured as I lay still and warm in bed and listened. I wondered if the animated voices I could hear belonged to the beekeeper who made and sold his own local honey on one stand, or the man who specialised in olives on another. I pictured the baker on his way home in the dusk of the early morning as his mother arrived to throw open the metal shutters on the shop and fill the counter with the delicious breads, croissants and *ensaimadas* that he'd spent all night baking. I thought of Pilar, arriving, as she had done for the last twenty years, at the shop where she sold olive- and walnut-wood bowls, souvenirs and fans, and of the fishermen's wives who set up their wet fish stands in the adjoining room to the vegetable, fruit and flower traders in the indoor food market. They were all characters I now knew just well enough to nod a friendly hello to, indulge in a chat and be offered the rates they reserved for the locals. I lay listening, creating my own pictures to the noises I heard below as Harrisson slept through music, laughter and animated chatter, until I could wait no longer.

'H . . . come on, I'll buy you a big breakfast at Bar Central!' I tried, nudging him gently. I knew that although the B&B's offerings were perfectly adequate, they'd become repetitive and far from tempting after several weeks of the same menu.

He murmured something and rolled back over.

'Are you hung over?' I whispered.

No reply.

I guessed that following his big night of football, it was more than likely. I'd left the bar pretty soon after the policemen had arrived. I'd felt tired and cold and was looking forward to a hot bath before devouring the *coca* I'd bought for the boys for supper and snuggling up with my book in bed. The night had been fun, but I was less interested in the final score than the boys were. I was happy to run a big bubble bath, filled with the cheap bath foam that the hotel supplied and leave Harrisson to his fun. With just a bedroom and bathroom to share, there had been little space for either of us to spend time on our own, and this had proved to be the first opportunity.

Harrisson had staggered into the otherwise silent room some time during the early hours of the morning. He'd sweetly removed the trashy chick lit I was reading from my sleepy grip and turned out the light, but as I stirred, he insisted on merrily — and a little too loudly — telling me how Spain had won the game and the policemen had stayed to watch and celebrate.

'The atmosphere, Izz . . . ' he had slurred slightly, smelling of beer and cigarettes 'Immense! And the noise!' He only just found the words to accompany his excitement.

'Neighbours in the port rang the police *three* times,' he emphasised, like a schoolboy proud of a prank. 'They came once, stayed, and when they knew Poli and Manolo were responsible, they didn't bother investigating after that . . . Those two young guys were cool, you know . . . the policemen guys . . . yeah, they even came out on to the streets to celebrate when Spain clinched it . . . '

The conversation flooded back to me now as I spotted a soggy Spanish football shirt thrown in a crumpled heap on the floor by the foot of the bed. I vaguely remembered Harrisson telling me with pride that a neighbour, fed up with being unable to sleep, had finally turned a hose on the supporters as they had drummed and sung triumphantly through the streets.

I looked over at Harrisson now as he had turned in a slumber to face me. His eyes were lightly closed, his face perfectly expressionless and lost to sleep, his breath, catching slightly, repetitive and soft. There was no way he was going to join me in the market and no way that I wanted to miss out, waiting for him to wake up.

I strolled through the streets and dreamt of how it would be when I could fill up my straw basket with fresh vegetables from Teresa's allotment, fruit just picked from the local citrus trees and flowers from the fields, to take back to our new and completed home. But the experience of shopping on a Saturday, was more than enough for now. I loved nothing more than visiting my favourite stalls scattered through the open streets, jumping out of the way when the little wooden train clattered through the square. I nodded my hellos to the traders, whose faces had become familiar. To the man who sold the very best pre-Christmas treats, the lady whose trestles were always stocked with an eclectic array of antiques.

I went in to chat to Pilar, marvelling at the latest fans she had received in stock, thinking of the brides who might like them as favours for their tables, which design matched which wedding scheme. As always, I had to make an excuse to break away after a twenty- or thirty-minute chat. I dawdled through the town, giving a smile to the local postman, to a neighbour dressed up for market day and a young mum I'd met in a supermarket queue. At the Calle de sa Luna, the sleepy shops were alive with trade and tourists, the streets full of pedestrians and a group of school kids who had set up their own stalls, selling home-made cakes. I took a stroll past the bookshop, playing music from speakers rigged up outside, and after buying a newspaper, took a leisurely walk towards the square.

'Izzy!' I heard a very English voice from behind me, and turned around to see Tomas, red-faced, out of breath and smiling. 'I saw you from way back . . . ' He was puffing slightly, having run to catch me up. 'How have you been?' he asked.

'Good!' I replied, still surprised to see him. 'And you? And what about Celia?'

'Yes, all good,' he said, wiping his brow with the back of his hand self-consciously. He looked embarrassed, as if having chased me down the street, he now had no idea why, or what to say. 'It's been a while, hasn't it?' He smiled, his eyes searching mine fleetingly. After an awkward pause he offered, 'So how's the renovation going?'

'It's going well, thanks, taking shape,' I bumbled on autopilot.

Then, something strange happened. I don't know if I was a little tired and overemotional at him asking, if it was that warm familiarity that he had, or if I just wanted some reassurance, but I was soon divulging how I really felt.

'I don't mind the mess and the dust and living in the B&B,' I heard myself say. 'I just hope Harrisson ends up loving the house as much as I do when it's all finished.'

'Oh, I'm sure he will,' Tomas replied politely, 'especially having been so hands-on, surely?'

'I hope so. It's just, I sometimes worry that when it's finished he'll be, you know, bored.' As I said the words, I could feel my throat tighten at the thought. 'He's so used to London and being on shoots, travelling . . . And, well, I just worry that a quiet life in the mountains of a tiny island won't cut it.'

Tomas had his head gently cocked to one side, listening intently.

'You know, I just love it here. I love the people, the market, the simple things.' He nodded as I continued. 'I'm just not sure if Harrisson is going to find all of that enough.'

'Well, has he had a chance to find out?' Tomas asked, his eyes inquisitive behind his glasses. God, he was so sensible. It was a thought that hadn't really crossed my mind.

'Well, he gets on really well with Poli and the builders . . . ' I started.

'I'm sure,' Tomas said warmly, 'but you haven't been here long enough to make your own friends yet, I would imagine. And you've not really had time to, what with the renovation.'

'No, you're right,' I sighed.

'Or to find out more about those simple

things you like, or share them with Harrisson.'

'True.'

Tomas looked thoughtful for a moment.

'Tell you what,' he said, smiling. 'I'm having a lazy Saturday-afternoon lunch with some friends with a place in the mountains next weekend. Why don't you both come along?'

'You can't just invite us!' I teased him.

'Of course I can,' he answered with a grin. 'That's just it. Any friends of mine will be welcome . . . you know the phrase, *mi casa es tu casa.*'

I giggled at the cliché.

'They're having a barbecue.'

'It's winter,' I pointed out. 'Haven't you told them?'

'Everyone barbecues here in the winter!' Tomas laughed. 'They think the English are absolutely insane for lighting fires in the summer, when it's too hot to stand in the full sun toasting your food! I imagine they'll prepare a *lechona*, a delicious roasted pig, or maybe a paella or something similar. Of course the place is pretty basic, but I think it will give you both a bit of an insight into real Majorcan weekends.'

'What do I bring?' I asked.

'Just come along,' Tomas offered kindly.

'Both of you.' And with that, I gratefully accepted and we went our separate ways.

When I reached our favourite café a few moments later, I discovered Harrisson nursing a *café con leche* in the shade. Dressed in long chino shorts with flip-flops and a coral-coloured Smedley sweater, he waved to get my attention.

'Hey,' he offered delicately, his eyes concealed behind mirrored Aviators.

I let out a giggle, surprised to see him. 'How are you feeling?'

'Yeah, well, you know, it was a great night,' he drawled, his face a little pale at the mention of it.

'It's been a great morning too,' I told him excitedly. 'I bumped into Tomas and he was so kind. He knows we don't really know anyone here yet, and his friends are having lunch next Saturday at their mountain house here, and we're invited. Isn't that great?'

Harrisson looked thoughtful for a moment and caught the attention of a passing waiter.

'Apparently it's a place they go to for weekends, although they live in the town. They barbecue and eat outside, in the mountains. Sounds amazing, doesn't it?'

'Yeah.' Harrisson smiled in his usual laid-back way, his hand mussing his already bed-rumpled hair. 'Sounds cool. But look,

I've been meaning to tell you, Iz, I've been booked for a job next weekend.'

'Oh, you have?' I answered, pleased for him and disappointed all at once. 'Where?'

'London. It's an ad campaign. Some new luxury jeans brand. The money is good,' he stressed, 'but I'll be away from Thursday, for the whole weekend.'

'Sounds great.' I smiled, juggling mixed emotions. 'But what about the final push on the house?' I asked tentatively. Harrisson had promised me that we'd be moving in straight after Christmas.

'It's only two days that I won't be on site,' he said, slightly curtly. 'Poli knows what he's doing.'

Of course, we needed the money, not least to put into the house, and I was pleased that Harrisson was still getting called up for work, despite having been out of London for a few months. But at the same time, I couldn't help but feel disappointed at turning down Tomas's offer. It felt like the start of rebuilding a better relationship with him, as well as a chance to meet some new friends.

'You go though, hun,' Harrisson said, stirring at super-slow speed the coffee the waiter had put before him, as the busy market crowd continued to bustle by.

'I might do,' I agreed. 'I might do.'

15

Adios, Harrisson

'Celia?' The line to Andratx was thick with buzz and crackle and I could barely hear the fuzzy voice at the other end of the phone. 'Celia, it's Isabelle,' I repeated.

It was Monday morning, and I was sitting huddled on the bed at the draughty B&B in an oversized sweater of Harrisson's and big knitted socks. Harrisson had left for the house about an hour ago. I'd kept the shutters closed against the cold white skies and the mountains topped with snow and tried to resist the smells of breakfast that crept upstairs from the kitchen below. I was checking in with Celia, having also felt the need to call to explain to Tomas that Harrisson wouldn't be coming to lunch the following weekend. I hadn't yet decided if I felt right going along on my own; I was going to leave that to see how the conversation went, if my mobile behaved itself.

'Isabelle!' Celia exclaimed eventually, cutting in and out. 'How lovely! Now tell me, how is it all going?'

Celia was in a good mood. She'd landed a new client for a winter wedding with a generous budget and just a few guests, to take place a week before Christmas. And she was keen to catch up with my own wedding plans, which, I had to confess, I'd completely neglected.

'They've got their hearts set on the Son Net,' she said. The venue was a five-star hotel. 'And of course at this time of year, the possibilities for exclusivity are good.'

'Sounds perfect,' I chirped, wondering if she'd ask me to help. My mind raced slightly at the thought. With the house still in chaos, my office temporarily located in the local café and my flights already booked to go home to London for Christmas, I wondered how I'd cope.

'Now,' Celia asked thoughtfully, 'is the build going to schedule?'

'Do you know, Celia,' I told her, honestly, 'I think it is! Harrisson and I are still due to move in after Christmas and the builders seem to have everything under control. Seems to me that this *mañana* mentality the Brits keep on talking about is a bit of a myth.'

'You've been lucky so far, my dear,' Celia quipped.

It was good to catch up. I missed Celia and as we caught up on our news, other people's wedding plans and discussed the next time I was coming over to work, I fondly imagined her sitting at her desk immaculately groomed, in some tweed and cashmere number topped with pearls.

'To be honest, Isabelle,' she said with warmth, 'I imagine it must be rather busy for you just now, so I am sure we can wait until the new year to catch up properly, if that would be more convenient. As I've previously warned you, that first week after the New Year's Eve proposals is quite labour intensive on the phones and email. I'm never quite prepared for the flurry!'

'Oh yes, of course,' I agreed. 'Unless of course there's anything you need help with — '

'Don't even think about it.' Celia stopped me midsentence. 'On another note, it would be lovely if you were to come to supper before you go back to England for the festive season.'

'I'd love to, Celia,' I gushed, touched by the invitation. 'Thank you.' I couldn't help but imagine Celia's roaring open fire, her beautiful clean house and delicious home cooking. I pulled my bare knees closer into my chest and hugged them beneath the sweater.

'Tomas and I would enjoy seeing you,' she

replied courteously.

'Oh yes, actually, if we're all done, it would be good to speak to Tomas,' I tried to add naturally.

'Yes, he mentioned that he saw you in Sóller on Saturday,' Celia replied. 'Didn't he tell you that he was flying to Scotland later that day? Something to do with some rare heather and a paper he's researching,' she continued in explanation. 'He won't be back until next Friday evening.'

'Oh, he didn't say, but it's not important,' I added. I'd find another way of letting him know.

'Now, dinner . . . ' Celia continued in her usual organised way.

* * *

The rest of the week seemed to whiz by in a blur. Whilst the town of Sóller got ready for Christmas, there was a final push at the house. The plumber installed the new bathroom, Poli started to build the concrete kitchen that Harrisson had copied from the pages of the Spanish *Architectural Digest* magazine and Pepe, increasingly cold and forlorn, finished digging out the channels for the electricity cables from the two-foot-thick stone walls.

In the town, the nativity scenes in the hallways of the traditional Sóller houses seemed to grow daily in scale, with the most successful and intricate adaptations of biblical stories proudly shot for the cover of the local paper. There were band practices, religious ceremonies and a general feeling of anticipation in the streets illuminated by twinkling lights, as tourists seemed to return and the Spanish began their Christmas shopping, especially for food.

It was soon Thursday and time for Harrisson to get cleaned up and transform himself from dusty builder's mate to edgy London art director.

'You know,' he said from the bathroom, carefully clipping the overgrown stubble he'd cultivated during the last week in the house, 'I'm pretty relaxed about the campaign.'

I'd been quizzing him about how he felt flying back for the job and whether it was strange to think that one day he was painting walls, up to his eyes in dust, and the next talking to a photographer about mood and light and models.

'I've worked with Paolo, the photographer, a million times before,' he said, 'and I know the model they've booked, along with the rest of the creatives, so it should be fun.'

I glanced at the battered leather holdall on

the bed, ready to be filled, with just an hour before Harrisson had to be at the airport.

'Besides,' he grinned, emerging from the bathroom, 'gives me a chance to unveil my new look. What do you think, hey?'

I burst out laughing. Not at his appearance, but at the statement, which, frankly, made him sound more like Ray than a straight guy.

I couldn't deny that he looked good, despite how shallow he sounded. He had deliberately laundered the jeans that had taken the worst battering on the build, added a simple tan Spanish leather belt and a blue checked shirt with the sleeves rolled to the elbows, with a co-ordinating T-shirt beneath, its deep V holding his folded-over mirrored Ray-Bans. On his feet he wore sharp tan Spanish brogues.

'Kind of 'Palma meets London'.' He smiled. 'To show I'm more *tranquillo*.'

I raised my eyebrows skywards, guessing that it was all part of the job. But later that night, as I tried to get comfortable in the B&B alone, I was reminded of all those lonely times that I'd come second to work for Harrisson. I knew it was crazy. Of course he had to go off and work. It was going to be how we'd survive, I told myself. But as I watched Sky News on rotation and picked at a packet of oily Spanish crisps and an apple, I had a sinking feeling of déjà vu. Maybe I was supersensitive because we were so close to moving into the house and yet it seemed so far away from being completed, or because it was almost Christmas and time for us to spend time apart anyway, with our families. Whatever it was, by the morning I'd decided that I wasn't going to spend the next three days feeling paranoid; I was going to go to the mountain house with Tomas.

16

A family affair

I met Tomas in the square that Saturday. I was sitting chatting to Francisca, who was only just containing her children's excitement at seeing all of the shops and market stalls decked out for Christmas.

'*Mama, mira!*' wailed Magda, her smallest, for the umpteenth time, tugging at Francisca's sleeve as we gossiped on the stone seat that circled the fountain at the heart of the square. Bathed in the pale, thin glow of the winter sun, it was the place where all the local children seemed to gather and play happily, as their mothers stood keeping a watchful eye whilst they caught up on each other's news.

'Magda, *no!*' Francisca screamed as she wagged a firm finger, crouching down to the child's height. 'I'm sorry, Isabelle, they get so excited for Reyes,' she apologised at the interruption, 'even when we tell them that the kings only come with gifts for very good children.' I smiled and shrugged sympathetically at Magda. I could only think that Spanish children were good to wait until the sixth of January to open their presents. Even if it was their tradition, it must have seemed like an endless build-up.

I'd bumped into Francisca by chance as I waited for Tomas. He'd sent me a text from Scotland to confirm the date and time to meet him for lunch at the mountain house, and I'd replied in a hurry, pleased to keep the arrangement. Now I waited, my wicker basket brimming with offerings for Tomas's friends — *turron* for the children, a local bottle of rough red wine and a bunch of wild-looking winter flowers from the market.

A cute little Spanish boy threw his ball purposefully in my direction, with gloved hands and a wide, cheeky grin. I bounced it back, as Francisca greeted his mother with gusto.

'Looks like I've come at a bad time,' an English voice said laughing. 'Or do you need me to referee?'

I looked up to see Tomas, his shape clear against the pale blue sky. The little boy, seeing that my attention had been taken by a much bigger playmate, burst into tears. His mother rushed over and swept him up.

'I often have that effect on children.' Tomas shrugged as we said hello. He was clutching a small English Christmas tree in a big pot, covered in a hessian sack. I hadn't seen a single Christmas tree on the island, and I suddenly had a pang for home.

'Don't ask!' he warned, seeing my face change as I wondered how he might have travelled with such a thing from Scotland on a budget airline. 'So, how are you?' he asked politely. 'And Harrisson? Are we waiting for him?'

I'd completely forgotten to tell Tomas that Harrisson wouldn't be coming along to lunch.

'I'm sorry,' I said, feeling the need to apologise. My cheeks flushed. 'Harrisson has had to work, in London.'

'Oh, right, right . . . yes . . . of course,' he mumbled.

There was an awkward pause. Tomas looked uncomfortable and I stared at the crowd of children playing.

'Do you think it matters for the numbers?' I asked, breaking the silence.

'Oh gosh, no, that's no problem,' he assured me, pushing his horn-rimmed glasses up on the bridge of his nose. 'Let's get going,' he said at last, as a group of the children had started to gather and marvel at the Christmas tree.

We took Tomas's car up to the mountain house and I was thankful that someone else was driving. The road was little more than an uneven single gravel track that I never knew existed. It started at the very back of the town and climbed quickly, winding its way around the hairpin bends that edged the steep, staggered terraces of the mountain. My ears popped as we climbed further skywards and my booted feet instinctively glued themselves to the floor.

'Just look at that view,' Tomas enthused, having been silent for most of the journey.

'I can't.' I laughed nervously.

I could feel Tomas turning to look at me, but felt the need to keep my eyes fixed firmly forwards, as we wound our way up more and more steeply.

'Almost there,' he said, chuckling slightly.

'Thank God,' I replied, feeling as green as the luscious pines that peppered the view from the windscreen.

We passed goats teetering on impossible inclines, gnarled old olive trees that seemed to sprout from the rocks that lined the roadside, and tracks edged with wild flowers that meandered down the mountain face. As I contemplated how on earth anyone managed to get electricity, water or even just a weekly shop to such a place, Tomas cried, 'Hang on!' and turned the steering wheel sharply.

I now realised that the gravel path had been relatively safe, as we descended on to a steep incline that clearly wasn't intended for any vehicle that wasn't a Land Rover. I closed my eyes and clung on with one hand to my seat as Tomas wheel-spinned and bumped for a good half-mile in silent concentration before finally reaching an abrupt halt.

I opened my eyes instinctively and turned to look at him. He gave me a wide smile and patted my shoulder.

'All right there old girl?' he asked, unable to contain his laughter.

Before I had the chance to answer, there were children smiling at us through the the car windows.

Tomas opened his door of the car and shot out to hug and kiss a little boy and a little girl, picking up the latter, who must have been only seven or eight, and holding her at his hip as he chatted away to her in Spanish.

'They ran to meet us when they heard the car,' he shouted back to me.

The little boy was already at my side. He must have been around twelve years old.

'Some rescue party!' I quipped, happy to feel the leather sole of my boot hit the dusty gravel.

'*Mucho gusto*,' I said to the boy. '*Como te llamas?*'

'*Soy Juanito*,' he replied shyly, hiding his face from me slightly.

Flamboyantly I stretched out a hand for him to shake. 'Isobel,' I told him, using the Spanish equivalent of my name.

'Tomas!' Juanito yelled, kicking up big swirls of dust as he ran over and jumped up at his friend. After a bear hug Tomas put Juanito down and I saw him mimic me with the handshake. '*Que Ingles!*' he exclaimed to the boy, before giving the small grubby hand an erratic shake like an eel so that it flew up and down, Juanito giggled. I'd never seen Tomas look so natural and animated.

'*Hola!*' other voices chimed. The grown-ups.

Tomas had his head buried in the car, and emerged to everyone's delight with the Christmas tree. He leant down with the children, and I could hear him explaining how English people dressed a tree like the one he'd bought them for Christmas. And how this one, if they kept it in its pot and watered it, would keep year after year.

Meanwhile I introduced myself to the adults. '*Encantada,*' I offered, kissing Juan and Estrella on each cheek and thanking them, in my rudimentary Spanish, for inviting me, a new neighbour, to join them for lunch.

'*De nada!*' they assured me, with shrugs. They were warm, friendly and relaxed. Juan had a rugged, earthy Latino look, mixed with the baggy jeans, worn T-shirt and grown-out haircut of a modern-day hippy.

After we'd made our introductions, we followed the running children. Juan was smoking a roll-up cigarette with the Christmas tree slung over one shoulder, and Estrella was chatting away to Tomas and trying to include me until they spoke so quickly I couldn't understand a word, let alone pause long enough to join in the conversation. At the end of the track everyone stopped, and as soon as I reached the others, I could see why. The view was beautiful. I let out a genuine gasp.

Juan put down the tree and came over to join me, as the others continued on, to proudly show me his little patch of heaven, as he called it. He explained the boundaries of his land, which terraces were his and where the little orange grove, which belonged to his neighbour, started. He told me how he and his brothers had cleared the land to build by hand the little house that was perched on it, exactly how many months it had taken and how many hundreds of years old the olive trees that marked the boundaries of his little part of the mountain were. We paused, both of us, to take it all in. On such a clear day we could see the church that towered above the town square, and the clear swell of fresh blue water, surrounded by low mountains, at the port way beyond it. The grand stone houses that chugged smoke from their chimneys were dotted into the mountains and grew to a dense mass of stone at the centre of the town, which appeared from here to be a thumbnail map of the real-life version I was used to seeing in full scale.

Juan moved on again, without another word, and we followed the sound of laughter and chatter down to the terrace of the house built into the mountainside below.

On seeing us, Tomas beat off Juanito — named, I twigged now, 'Little Juan' — from a play fight and came over. 'Beautiful, isn't it?' he said.

'Amazing!' I replied, enthralled. The house was tiny, barely bigger than a *casita*, and built from the local stone, which, Juan told me in broken English (recognising that my Spanish wasn't all he had initially thought), had been found on the mountainside.

Sitting on mismatched chairs pulled up to a long wooden table outside were extended family and friends. They all greeted me with kisses and such warmth that my own smiles, in return, made my cheeks ache, as if they were forced. I could see Tomas blush and protest as a woman who turned out to be Estrella's sister congratulated him on his *guapisima* girlfriend.

As Juan chuckled and went to fetch Tomas a beer, I followed Estrella inside. The women were all in the kitchen and I was keen to help with lunch. Well, I had been, until I realised exactly what it entailed. They were preparing a whole baby pig, or *lechona*, for roasting. Estrella must have seen my astonishment, and sweetly suggested I wash and peel the muddy potatoes instead.

The kitchen was rudimentary. There was a solid wood floor and some free-standing cupboards, topped with a slab of marble at one end and a vast and historic-looking butcher's block at the other. The cooker itself was little more than a camping stove, fuelled by a huge red gas canister, and piled on a flimsy metal-framed table were huge catering-sized pots and pans, including the largest steel paella pan I'd ever seen. Five litre bottles of water were lined up on the floor, as of course there was no running water; and plates and glasses teetered on the same tabletop, as there was little room for storage. Although it was closer to camping than cooking, the women seemed unfazed. The kitchen banter was fast and furious and I soon lost track of the conversation, even when the women deliberately slowed down for me and those who had slipped into the local dialect reverted back to standard Spanish.

After a while, little Jessica — pronounced with an 'H' — came to tug at the regulation pinny I'd been handed to put on, like the rest of the women, to prepare lunch.

'Isobel, Isobel!' she protested. 'I want to show you my room!' she said in Spanish. As Estrella gave me a wink, I followed her daughter to explore.

There were three bedrooms in the mountain house, each furnished simply and flooded with light from the windows that framed the incredible views. Jessica shared her room with Juanito, with bunk beds, which I watched her climb. She showed me her secret drawer of toys, her prized sticker collection and the Little Mermaid 'perfume' that her *padre* had bought her for her birthday, and which she insisted on spritzing me with generously. Before long, Estrella was at the door.

'I hope she's not tiring you, no?' she said to me sweetly in English.

'No, she's so cute,' I replied genuinely. 'Let's give your mum her presents,' I added to Jessica in Spanish. 'Just a little something to add to the table,' I explained to Estrella.

Jessica ran outside to show the *turrón* to Juanito as Estrella thanked me warmly for the wine and flowers, popping the latter into a rustic white metal jug and placing them in the centre of the wooden table outside, before insisting that I sit down.

I sat in the space next to Tomas, who was engrossed in conversation with the men and drinking beer from plastic cups. It was a relaxed scene. Some of the señoras and teenage señoritas joined the men in chatter.

Juan made a ceremony of serving the red wine, which he explained to me was pressed at St Bartholemew, the local co-operative, from grapes he'd harvested from his brother's vines, which we heartily applauded. Tomas, always the gentleman, introduced me to the rest of the guests, the nieces, nephews, sister and brothers of both Juan and Estrella, whom he'd met, he explained, when he was studying at the botanical gardens and they'd been working in the entrance booth.

Before long the clear mountain air was filled with laughter. Juan's wine was as strong as it was rugged, and the extended family, so obviously comfortable in each other's company, were warm with friendly banter and jokes, whilst the children, who had been playing wildly, were now on their best behaviour. As Estrella put out plates, Jessica appeared at my side with a tiny fold-up chair, to squeeze into the already tight gap between Tomas and I. She shot him a possessive look as she did it, before smiling widely at me.

It was almost 3.30 before Estrella put out little baskets of thickly sliced country bread, shallow earthenware dishes brimming with glossy oil and others laden with small oily brown olives and deep green capers. I was ravenous.

I pulled my cardigan and thick scarf around me as I looked out over the mountains, holding Jessica's tiny hand. One side of the rock face was cast into shadow as the pale sun began to fade, and I regretted my outfit of a white cotton Victorian petticoat that I had found in the *segundo mano*, the second-hand shop in the town, with woollen tights, boots and an oversized cardie. It had been an impulse buy on an urge not to arrive at the lunch in either my painting clothes or my one single black shift, but now I realised, looking at the other women in their jeans and jumpers, how out of place I seemed. But it didn't matter. Tomas caught my eye as I snuggled further into my scarf and looked longingly at the fire, just too far away to bestow its warmth on the table but close enough to fill the air with the wonderful smell of the roasting pig.

'Do you want my jumper, Izzy?' he asked, the wood smoke rising behind him.

'No thanks, I'm fine, the food will warm

me up,' I insisted, smiling at his kindness.

Juan carved the *lechona*, which had been roasting on a spit with an orange in its mouth for several hours, as Estrella served the rich, garlicky local potatoes with pride. It was all delicious, and Jessica, Juanito and the other children were well behaved, devouring the juicy pork and potatoes with their adult-sized cutlery.

After our feast, *crema Catalana* was served, a Spanish crème caramel, which Estrella had also baked in her makeshift kitchen. And before long, piping mocha pots of coffee were on the table, along with bottles of brandy. I hardly noticed daylight disappear from the mountain and the sun, pale and pink, dip behind it, until Tomas pointed it out to me. By now I was engrossed in playing a pencil and paper game with Jessica of 'Oso', a Spanish variation of noughts and crosses, for which she had endless enthusiasm. She kept donating points to me, as my grasp of it seemed so poor, after several glasses of red wine and just one sobering cup of piping-hot black coffee. The wine seemed to have taken effect around the table too, as some of the women burst merrily into song.

Juan, Estrella, Tomas and I moved closer together as the other guests started to thin out later in the evening. The children had gone to bed. Estrella made more coffee, Juan lit another cigarette and we supped the rough local brandy to keep ourselves warm. I was growing sleepy and losing my grip on the conversation. By now the sky had turned the deepest navy, and only the firelight and some church candles in red plastic pots that Estrella lit in a line down the table illuminated the valley. We all seemed to sit instinctively in silence to take in the beauty of it. The clear velvet dome was sprinkled with stars, and the moon was the thinnest slice of a crescent. Before long, my eyes were heavy and I was struggling to keep awake. I wasn't sure if it was the home-made wine or the mountain air that had made me so drowsy.

'Isobel.' Estrella nudged me gently from almost a slumber. 'Why don't you stay? Really, for us it is no *problema*.'

'No, no,' I protested, struggling even in English. 'We should really go. Tomas has the drive to do and it's a tricky road.' My stomach churned a little at the thought of the precarious mountain journey at night.

'Isobel,' Juan said with a serious tone, 'are you sure the driving is a good idea?'

I looked over at Tomas, who until recently had been so chatty, and saw to my amazement that he was now fast asleep. Estrella and Juan laughed at my response.

'I'm so sorry!' I gasped. 'It must be really late. We should get going.'

Juan and Estrella insisted that leaving was a crazy plan, and I had to agree. Navigating the road in a sleepy, wine-hazed stupor, wasn't the best idea I'd ever had. I took up Estrella's offer and went to help her prepare somewhere for us to sleep.

'Maybe Tomas can sleep in the lounge and I'll take the bedroom,' I suggested, reverting to my English primness.

'Lounge?' Estrella asked

'*Perdone, el salon*,' I clarified in apologetic Spanish.

'But we don't have the lounge. This, the outside, is the lounge, right?' Estrella reminded me.

She was standing in the doorway of the only spare room, holding thick woollen blankets and fake fur throws for the beds.

'Of course, no problem,' I said sleepily.

'The *baño*, the bathroom, Isobel,' Estrella, also tired, corrected herself, 'is down at the end. Of course, remember there is no water from the tap, but bottles, OK? The toilet, it can work, but it is chemical. But for shower, we have this outside for tomorrow.'

I nodded and thanked her, kissing her on each cheek. 'I'll get Tomas,' I confirmed and headed outside. At the table under the stars I found Juan sitting up alone, strumming his twelve-string guitar by candlelight, and I assumed Tomas must have made his way to bed.

A single candle from the table burned on the seat of the chair, the only piece of furniture in our room beside the two single beds. It illuminated the space just enough for my eyes to adjust and see that Tomas was already tucked up. His glasses had been placed neatly on the floor and his clothes folded in the haphazard pile of someone who'd had too much to drink. As my eyes adjusted to the dark stillness of the room, I could make out his face by the flickering candlelight. The familiar sprinkling of freckles that had remained even though summer had long passed, the angle of his cheekbone, the fullness of his mouth and the straight line of his brow, softened by that foppish public-schoolboy fringe.

His breathing was shallow and silent. One surprisingly muscular arm, looped over the top of the blankets, clasped them tightly to him. With no one to see me looking, it was difficult not to study Tomas. I thought of the way he'd been earlier that day. How natural and earthy he had acted with the kids and how they loved to clamber all over him. How respectful and gentle he'd been with the other people there and how much more relaxed he seemed than I'd ever seen him with anyone before. And now it occurred to me, for the first time: anyone English. It had been the perfect afternoon and I couldn't help but know that it wasn't one Harrisson would have fitted into. Or would have wanted to.

Tomas rolled over, interrupting my thoughts. I looked away instinctively, and then slowly back again, and stifled a yawn, as if he could see me. I tugged off my boots and placed them by my bed, careful not to make a sound. Then, in case Tomas awoke, I snuck fully clothed beneath the sheets, before wrestling to take off my dress beneath the covers. It was strange, at my age, to be sneaking around and hiding myself from a fully grown sleeping man, I thought with a smile. But there was something very wholesome about the whole scene, I mused, lifting my dress above my head and taking in the sickly-sweet smell of the perfume that Jessica had insisted on drenching me in. Something about being out in a simple cabin at the top of a silent and chilly mountain. Or should that be something romantic? I pondered guiltily, finally turning out the light.

* * *

'Isobel, please, another *ensaimada*!' Estrella encouraged the next morning at breakfast. She had sent Juan down to the nearest baker to fetch fresh *barras*, croissants and, of course, a bundle of the traditional Majorcan flaky pastries, and he had returned with Juanito in tow, carrying paper-wrapped parcels almost the size of himself.

Jessica shot me a satisfied grin as she tucked into a soft *ensaimada*, her mouth covered in icing sugar, while Estrella leant over her to pour me another *cortado* coffee.

The other faces around the table were pale and weary-eyed beneath the clear morning sky. Tomas was chatting merrily in Catalan with Juan, who dug his knife into a round of cheese, taking a creamy chunk to accompany his ham, warm bread and olives, oblivious to Juanito copying him. I blushed a little, remembering how I hadn't been able to resist watching Tomas sleep the night before, and looked out at the view. The pine and olive trees, wild flowers and rugged mountaintops were bathed in the early-morning sunshine, and the scene was no less impressive than when I'd first seen it the previous afternoon.

'*Gracias.*' I nodded to Estrella, taking the coffee and turning back to the table. 'So, what's your plan for today?'

'Work, of course . . . The vacation is only

for the children,' she confirmed with a hint of Spanish pathos. 'I clean the hotel in the port, you know, the big one.'

'Sure, I know it.' I smiled.

'Juan will look after Jessica and Juanito here. They will help him with the work on the house.' She smiled. 'What will you do?' she said, finally sitting down at the table.

'Oh, Harrisson, my boyfriend, is back today. He's been working away,' I replied, suddenly feeling guilty that I'd had such a good time without him.

I saw Estrella glance at Tomas, who was still engrossed in conversation with Juan, and fall silent as she ripped a croissant in half on her plate.

'I could just sit here all day, though,' I confessed. Aside from the tinkling of bells strung around goats' necks, the distant sound of donkeys and the trill of birds, it was almost silent so high up in the mountains. The town seemed a million miles away below, and with it the reality of daily life.

'There is no rush, *chica*,' Estrella soothed. '*Tranquillo*.'

I smiled, feeling perfectly content to sit for a while.

'Actually, Izzy, we should really get going,' Tomas interrupted sensibly from the other end of the table. 'I should get back to Celia, and we'd best leave these people to start their day.'

Estrella protested with a wave of the hand and a few words in Spanish, but Tomas insisted. I got up from the table and started to clear the plates.

'Isobel,' Estrella protested again. 'Jessica will help me.'

Seeing that we were leaving, Jessica licked her sticky fingers before jumping down from her chair. Juan gave me a bear hug of a goodbye. Juanito ran to jump on Tomas, and Jessica gave me a kiss and insisted on patting a pink sparkly sticker firmly on to my cardigan.

'Estrella,' I said, kissing her on both cheeks, 'thank you so much for a wonderful time.'

'*De nada*.' Estrella shrugged, a little embarrassed at my gushing English gratitude, as the rest of the family waved us goodbye.

I felt slightly queasy as Tomas traversed the winding, narrow mountain road back to Sóller. He took the bends quickly, as though he drove the route daily, and I only hoped that it meant we'd arrive back on a straight road sooner.

'I'm so glad you invited me, Tomas,' I managed, feeling green. 'I had the best time.'

'I'm pleased . . . ' he said, staring intently

at the road ahead in concentration and falling silent.

He seemed distant again. I wasn't sure if it was the journey he had to make with a hangover, but the warmth he'd shown me the night before and the little looks I was sure I'd spotted him giving me at the table were gone. Before then, I'd only hoped that we'd get to a place that we didn't feel uncomfortable with each other any more. Now . . . well, I didn't know what I expected, or wanted. But I was obsessing, I realised, as Tomas finally spoke.

'Izzy, I wasn't going to tell you, but I'm a bit worried about Celia,' he said, his voice wavering slightly as we reached flat ground at the bottom of the mountain.

17

The longest journey

'Babe,' Harrisson greeted me, later that evening. He was standing in the large wooden doorway of our room at the B&B, weighed down with luggage and bags loaded with duty-free.

'Hey, how was the shoot?' I asked, walking over to hug him.

'I'm shattered. It was crazy, and there's *such* a story,' he sighed, dropping his battered leather overnight bag and taking off his Ray-Bans. I'll fill you in later, but first, I've got something for you.'

I squealed with childish delight. 'I'll make tea,' I announced, sounding suspiciously like my mother back in England, as Harrisson rummaged through his bags for my goodies.

The afternoon sun had fallen behind the church and was low over the mountains I saw from the window as I filled up the kettle in our tiny room. I thought fleetingly of Juan and Estrella and Tomas at the mountain house and smiled. Dropping tea bags into the cups, I felt a pang of something else.

Harrisson had come back from his trip with gifts, and I was thinking of the night before. Bad Izzy, I scolded myself. Before I could dwell on my thoughts, I heard Harrisson behind me and felt his warm arms wrap themselves around me.

'I'll spill the milk,' I giggled, struggling to open a tiny plastic carton of UHT as he planted a kiss on the nape of my neck, his lips warm and soft against the coolness of my skin.

He spun me around to face him.

'Missed you, you know,' he admitted, in words I knew didn't come easy to him.

Then he knelt down momentarily before announcing, 'Ta da!' and handing me a posh paper bag. I sat on the corner of the bed to check out my prize. *Freedom Jeans*, the bag said, in looped gold letters on thick charcoal paper.

'I haggled with the stylist at the shoot for them. They're sexy.' He smiled.

'Oooh,' I cooed. 'New skinnies, thanks!'

'And then I got you this,' he said softly, passing me this time a duty-free bag. Inside was a jar of Marmite — I'd missed the stuff so much that I'd even dreamt about slathering it on hot buttered toast — along with a box from the London jeweller Theo Fennell.

My heart skipped a beat. I opened it up and peered inside. A solid silver Marmite top was shining back at me. I looked up in amazement.

'I know it's extravagant,' Harrisson justified, 'but you seemed to miss the stuff so much — '

I stopped him mid-sentence, standing up to kiss him. It *was* extravagant and I could think of nothing I needed less, when the jar of the salty brown stuff had been more than enough, but it was so sweet and thoughtful of him.

'And finally . . . '

'What, more?' I laughed with surprise.

'Yes, this,' he said, producing a third and final bag.

Inside was the latest Prada perfume, boxed lavishly in a set with body cream and bubble bath.

'I thought after all the mucky renovation work, and that stuff like Fairy Liquid that you bathe in here . . . '

'I *love* it,' I smiled, tears welling in my eyes. I was overtired, overemotional and Harrisson had been so thoughtful. I couldn't help but feel bad about having such a great time whilst he'd been away, and I wondered why, exactly, I didn't think that I should tell him all about it.

I passed Harrisson his tea and demanded he tell me about the shoot instead.

'You won't believe me if I do,' he teased, propping up the pillows on his side of the bed with one hand to get comfortable.

'Try me,' I said, indulging him.

'OK, so Paolo the photographer arrives the night before the shoot,' he started, kicking off his brogues and letting them drop beyond the bed. 'They put him up in this swanky new boutique hotel in town and he's fine. I speak to him, and you know, Izz, he's one of those guys that when we catch up, it's great, it's like we spoke yesterday,' he said, digressing, 'and I suggest we go out in Soho for supper, and you know, after one bar and another we end up at the Groucho.'

'Of course you do,' I sighed, remembering Harrisson's love of the many private members' clubs around London and how he managed to always get into the best without ever joining one of them.

'So then, the next morning, we're all on set at God knows what hour. But no Paolo.'

'So it was a heavy night?'

'No.' Harrisson laughed a little too quickly. 'But no one could get hold of him.'

'That's weird.'

'Yeah, exactly.'

Harrisson turned on the Sky TV and put it

on mute. It was one of those habits that English men seem to have: not being able to survive ten minutes without television, whether they intend to watch it or not.

'So, we carry on with hair and make-up, get the models ready, and the client goes over to the hotel to try and find him. All the while I'm leaving him messages. Well. In the end, he calls. It's almost lunchtime.'

'So where was he?'

'Locked in his hotel room, refusing to come out, whilst the client is banging on his door.'

'No!' I laughed. 'How come?'

'Well, apparently this client, the creative director at Freedom, who'd schmoozed Paolo, telling him she loved his work so much and couldn't wait to work with him, then called in the early hours of the shoot day to say that she had the shots all worked out and thought she should tell Paolo all about her vision and her storyboard before he arrived on set.'

I looked at Harrisson, puzzled.

'Yeah, she was really specific about it: what she wanted in shot, the props, how the model should pose, how the set would be lit . . . so Paolo went crazy. He didn't think the ideas would work, and even if they did, he'd have no creative input.'

I nodded.

''Why they book *me*?' he demanded when we finally spoke. 'They want a munkeee!' Harrisson mocked in his best Italian accent.

'So what did you do?'

'I had to strike a deal with him. He *had* to come to the studio. We'd mock up the first set the way the client wanted it, but if it didn't work, we'd talk about it.'

'Sounds logical,' I agreed.

'You'd think,' said Harrisson. 'But you should meet this woman. A real piece of work. She was demanding the impossible. Her ideas looked cheap, she had zero style and she wouldn't listen to anyone else's input. I mean, why even have us all there?'

'So what happened?' I asked, intrigued.

'It just took for ever. Paolo was really unhappy and in the end only agreed to take the shots if we took his name off the whole campaign.'

'Jesus,' I said, as Harrisson looked even more tired.

'We didn't wrap until almost midnight. And even then, no one was totally happy with the results.'

'Poor baby,' I soothed, stroking his hair. 'So who is this evil bitch-troll creative director anyway?'

'Your worst nightmare,' he replied convincingly. 'You know what, though?' he asked, with a glint in his tired eyes. 'We came up with a great new nickname for her by the end of it.' He paused for dramatic effect. 'The Devil Wears Zara.'

I rolled around on the bed laughing until Harrisson coaxed me beneath the covers.

★   ★   ★

'Tomas?' I asked. 'I've been so worried. I had to call.'

It was later that week, and I'd spent days worrying about Celia, ever since Tomas had told me that he suspected she wasn't well. With the brides quiet in the run-up to Christmas, and Harrisson making one final push to get the house ready, I'd had little else to occupy my mind, beyond the usual shopping trips for lights and wall sockets.

'How is she?' I asked tentatively.

'Well,' he replied in hushed tones, 'she seems the same to me. Pale, drawn, weak, but putting a brave face on the whole matter, and every time I broach it . . . ' He trailed off.

'Sure, I know, she sticks out that British stiff upper lip and changes the subject,' I helped him, remembering the time when she'd first talked to me about Tomas himself, and how she had been reluctant to express any sign of emotional weakness then. At the time, I hadn't wanted to ask how she'd become estranged from her son since her husband had died. After all, we'd not known each other for long. But even as we'd grown closer, she'd retained a professional distance that let me know that any discussion of emotion was off limits.

'Exactly,' he confirmed.

I sighed, feeling at a loss about what to suggest.

'She's out gardening today, though,' Tomas offered, 'tending the roses. I hope it's a good sign.'

I thought of Celia, immaculate in twinset, headscarf and wellingtons, wielding her pinking shears and pruning her beloved rose bushes. She'd be in her element, with Tomas out in the garden, sharing his vast knowledge of plants. I only hoped that dear old Pep, Celia's long-term gardener, wouldn't feel put out.

'Do you think she'll still be up to supper next week?' I asked. 'She was so sweet to offer, and it will give me a chance to check up on her too, but I hate to think of her struggling to cook if she's not feeling up to it now.'

'Of course,' Tomas interjected. 'She has been talking of little else and has been planning a Wednesday-morning visit to Andratx market especially. Don't worry, she doesn't know it yet, but I'll make sure I'm on hand to help out.'

I thought of Tomas bumbling his way around the kitchen, and smiled.

* * *

Harrisson had promised me a Christmas shopping trip in Palma, and I'd been excited about it for days. I loved living in Sóller, but there were times when a city fix was definitely in order, and Palma never seemed to disappoint. I loved the winding stone streets lined with the kind of individual shops that had long disappeared from London, and the wide, elegant avenues that looked like they belonged in Barcelona rather than to a small Balearic island. It was chic, stylish and filled with lavish stores that I couldn't even contemplate stepping inside on my budget, like the Spanish label Loewe, as well as super-scaled versions of Spanish high-street brands like Mango and Massimo Dutti, which I was itching to raid. However much I'd planned to visit the oldest chocolate shop, the largest department store and the traditional basket-makers for my Christmas gifts, I couldn't help but be seduced by thoughts of 'a gift for you and a gift for me' ratio.

I glanced out of the window of the B&B,

where I'd been sitting in the bar downstairs with my house renovation spreadsheet open on my laptop, totting up the spend and wincing, with a hot chocolate to soften the blow. It was the only palatable way to do accounting. As the afternoon faded to dusk, I took my cue to get ready to go, grabbing my bag, big woollen scarf and pea coat with a shudder, remembering how the mountaintops had been dusted with snow earlier that morning.

The white Christmas lights created pools of shimmering light on the cobbles that lined my festive walk through the town. There was a ceremony taking place and a hubbub outside the church, tourists walking the streets and locals seeking warmth and early-evening tapas in the bars, lit up with fluorescent lights. I followed the row of old-fashioned street lamps, anticipating the pitch darkness that would inevitably follow when they came to an end at the edge of town. My breath made icy, ghostly shapes before me as I walked, picking up my pace as the roads became black and only the lights from a passing car, or a house, illuminated the way. The noise of barking dogs seemed louder than it ever did in daylight. Finally I reached our *camino*. I still had to tell myself that very soon, after all the work, we would actually live here.

The house as I approached was silent. No workmen and no lights behind the shuttered windows. I pulled up the heavy brass knocker at the door and gave it a rap, but I knew already that no one was home. I thought of the night of the football, and wondered for a moment if I should check the bar. But first I checked my phone. I had a missed call and a voicemail from Harrisson, as well as a text that I hadn't picked up. I listened to the message before rummaging in my bag for my house key.

'Babe, it got real cold at the house, so I've sent the boys home and I've come into Palma early to see those guys who sell that great twentieth-century furniture. Why don't you treat yourself to a cab in, and join me? I'll buy you supper after the shops close.'

A cab? From Sóller? I could, of course, order one, but it seemed such a London thing to do and such a waste of cash when we were scrimping every penny to get the renovation finished.

I sat down on the step outside the house and checked the text message whilst I thought about what to do.

Izzy, it read, *we are at the hospital. It's Celia. I thought that you'd want to know. Tomas.*

I sat for a moment in shock, before texting him back to say *I'm on my way* and dialling the taxi number after all. Then I waited, unaware of my bum turning numb on the stone step as the minutes passed. After a while I rang Harrisson. When I heard his voice, I burst into tears.

'It's me,' I said through shaky sobs.

'What on earth's wrong, hon?' Harrisson asked. I could hear him stepping outside, leaving the bustling noise that I assumed was a bar, to find somewhere quiet.

'I can't stop, I have a cab coming.'

'Oh, good,' he said.

'No, I'm not coming into town. I have to go to the hospital. Tomas called . . . it's Celia.'

'Oh Izzy, I'm sorry,' he said sympathetically. 'What happened?'

'I don't know. I'm going to go and find out,' I replied.

The cab drew up, its lights making me squint. I was shaking with cold and apprehension as I held the phone to my ear. It was almost worse not knowing what had happened to Celia than if I had heard more from Tomas, and my mind was stabbing at wild and dramatic guesses.

I gave the driver the name of the hospital. He threw a lighted cigarette butt out of the window and nodded.

'OK, look, you do what you need to do,' Harrisson told me before we said our goodbyes. When he hesitated, I could hear that he wanted to tell me about the great stuff he'd found in town, but had thought better of it.

He didn't offer to come with me, I kept thinking, over and over again as the car raced towards the Sóller tunnel. He didn't offer to come.

* * *

The next half-hour was a blur. A blur of gleaming surfaces, as the bright white lights bounced off the walls and floors that seemed to merge with the ceilings in the never-ending corridors of the hospital. I walked at a pace that teetered on the verge of a run and tried to focus on the ward and room number that the kind-faced receptionist had given me. The voices I heard in Spanish around me felt alien. The patients, wandering the halls in white paper robes, looked ethereal. My Friday night had turned surreal. I took a wrong turn and cussed, then finally stumbled, somehow, upon Celia's room.

The door was ajar and Celia was propped up in bed, with Tomas by her side. He had her hand in his, I could see through the gap in the doorway, and her face was turned towards him as he spoke to her in gentle tones.

'Izzy?' I heard his voice question as he raised his eyes.

'Hi,' I said quietly, finally plucking up the courage to step inside. I realised I'd been standing at the door for some time, as if to brace myself for the reality of the situation, to figure out the best way to address it. 'How's the patient?' I tried to chime merrily.

Celia turned slowly towards me, her face pale and, for the first time I'd seen, completely free of make-up. Her blue eyes were almost opaque with dullness, her cheekbones newly prominent.

'Oh I'm just fine,' she said wearily, despite her appearance. 'I don't know what all the fuss is about.'

She was putting on her usual gung-ho, schoolmarm demeanour, but it wasn't fooling any of us, not even, it seemed from the tone of her voice, herself.

'What happened?' I asked Tomas, pulling a wooden chair up to the bed and gently patting Celia's arm.

'I was reading in the sitting room and Pepillo came in making the most terrible fuss. He just wouldn't leave me alone. I thought he wanted to go out, so I walked towards the kitchen to open the back door, and then I saw her . . . completely out cold on the kitchen floor. It really was quite a shock.'

'Do you remember collapsing, Celia?' I asked her tentatively.

'I don't recall a jot,' she replied frankly. 'I'd gone to make a cup of tea, put the kettle on, and the next thing I knew the ambulancemen were fussing over me,' she said almost crossly.

'They were wonderful with you, though, Mother,' Tomas corrected her. It was the first time I could recall him using the term rather than her name.

'What do the doctors say?' I asked.

'They're running tests,' Tomas replied, clasping Celia's hand again. 'They are going to keep her in until they receive the results.'

Celia made a scoffing noise.

'You need to look after yourself,' I told her with patronising concern.

'Nonsense, dear,' she replied stubbornly. Tomas gave me a sideways glance and raised his brows. 'It was nothing, and now I'm completely fine. But I am glad,' she added, as a hint of sparkle returned to her eyes, 'that Tomas was there with me.'

A Spanish nurse entered the room breezily to see if the patient was comfortable. She checked the clipboard at the end of the bed

257

and started to chat away to Celia in a mix of Spanish and English.

'We're lucky Celia's Spanish is so good,' Tomas said proudly, watching the scene. 'It's never quite as easy when you have to call in a translator.'

I pulled him over towards the window, its blinds drawn back to reveal the twinkling lights outside, as the nurse continued.

'Is it serious?' I asked in a whisper.

'I just don't know,' he said frankly. He looked tired, and of course, concerned. 'I suspect there's more to this than a mere fainting fit. She's not seemed herself for quite a while. Knowing Celia,' he continued, lowering his voice further, 'if there was something wrong, she would keep it to herself and try to hide it for as long as she could.'

I instinctively put a hand on his arm. 'So in a way, this might be a good thing . . . you know, at least now she can be examined.' I wasn't sure, as soon as the words had come from my mouth, if they'd been the right ones to say. 'That didn't sound right, but . . . '

'No, I know what you mean,' Tomas replied, with the first trace of a smile I'd seen all evening.

'And how long do they think they'll keep her here for?'

'They won't commit to saying as yet,'

Tomas replied, before yawning.

'Well you don't need to stay the whole time,' I urged him. 'I can always visit.'

'Look, Izzy,' Tomas said, ignoring my offer, his gaze now fixed intently on mine. 'I've been meaning to . . . try and have a word.'

'*Señor*,' the nurse interrupted, as if on cue, 'the doctor will see you now, before visiting hours are over.'

18

Almost Christmas

Tomas was haggling with a market trader, trying to convince her with his most charming use of the local dialect that he should get the discount that she gave to her regulars, despite the fact that she'd never set eyes on him before. I looked on from the other side of the stall in awe. The woman waved her arms in protest and I saw her finally nod, as the queue behind Tomas grew impatient.

'You're so Majorcan!' I teased him as he wandered towards me, his basket brimming with fresh vegetables and a hefty bag of bright, plump oranges.

'No, if I was quite so Majorcan,' he protested, 'I wouldn't have had to have that particular conversation.' He laughed. 'But I don't think she suspected that I am really a bumbling English fool, as I managed to save at least seven euros,' he added. I eyed him suspiciously, unconvinced by the statement.

We'd decided to cook lunch instead of the supper that Celia had hoped to organise before what everyone referred to now as her 'moment'. After a few days in the ward, the tests remained inconclusive, but Celia had made such a fuss that the Spanish doctors had agreed she was well enough to wait at home for the results. Now she was driving Tomas crazy, as she tried to go about business as usual and wouldn't let him help her, even when she seemed too tired or weak to finish the tasks she'd embarked on.

I'd snuck in some days at the office, whilst Harrisson carried on with the work at the house, so that I could help Tomas out and keep a check on the wily old bird too. But she'd soon seen through my plan. On those mornings she'd emerge, as she always had, immaculately groomed within an inch of her Chanel-clad life, in one of her beautiful tweed suits topped with a cashmere stole, but by mid-morning she was already visibly flagging. After the lightest lunch, she'd take a siesta that would last well into the late afternoon. It was something she'd never done before.

'So, did you pick up lots of *calabathin*?' I asked Tomas as the Christmas shoppers in the market strode by us in their droves. 'You know how she likes them in white sauce,' I said, of the marrow-type vegetable that was popular on the island.

'Of course,' he confirmed. 'Not that I have

the foggiest idea what to do with them.'

I smiled. I was looking forward to cooking for the three of us in Celia's big, familiar kitchen. The day was still young and the skies were bright. The crisp, chilly air reminded me of September's 'back to school' days in England, and the market, though bustling, had a more laid-back vibe than when the tourists swamped it in the summer months. The stalls were heaving with tempting Christmas goodies, and one selling plastic copies of Louis Vuitton handbags played 'Feliz Navidad' on a rickety ghetto-blaster — a terrible Spanish pop song that celebrated the festive season but sounded like it belonged in a club in Benidorm at the turn of the 1980s.

'Just a trip to the butcher's,' Tomas confirmed, 'to pick up my order, and then we're all set.'

* * *

Pepillo was itching to greet us when Tomas's wheels spun on the gravel drive at Celia's.

'It's as if he smelt us pick the meat up from town!' I laughed, as he jumped up and scratched at the plastic bag, giving a low growl. Pep and Tomas had kept Celia's garden immaculate, I noticed as I climbed the

262

stone steps to the back door. The ruby-red hibiscus were in full bloom, pomegranates shone like shiny Christmas decorations from two trees, and the indigenous succulents, with their flowers open to the midday sunshine, lined the way.

Inside, the house was unseasonally warm. Log fires raged in both the sitting room and the dining room, greeting us with the fragrant smell of the olive and walnut wood that crackled in the hearth. A Christmas tree dominated each room, both decorated beautifully with antique baubles and real candles, with small bundles of gifts lavishly wrapped in brightly coloured boxes and tied with wide silk ribbons at their feet.

'Celia,' said Tomas, confirming the name of the creator, 'of course.' I looked at her handiwork in awe. There were dishes teetering with sugared fruits and a mantelpiece dressed with figs, pomegranates and fresh foliage from the garden. In the dining room, she had already dressed the table with her finest linen and polished silver cutlery. Three crystal bowls filled with bright Spanish oranges studded with cloves lined the centre, and foliage from the garden wove a runner knitting them together.

Whilst the trees were, of course, an English tradition, the sun streaming through the windows reminded me that we were in Majorca, with the view of the valley and the goats beyond.

'Izzy!' Celia exclaimed as she made her way to the bottom of the staircase. 'I'm so glad you came.'

I noticed as she kissed me on both cheeks that she was wearing a knee-length crêpe dress in a deep forest green with voluminous sleeves, a wide jewelled cuff and wooden-heeled caramel-coloured YSL courts. A flash of red lipstick and her neat chignon completed the look, and it was impossible to think that just a week ago I'd seen the same lady in a hospital bed.

'You look wonderful, Celia,' I said with a smile, 'and so does the house.'

'Pep came into his own this year,' Celia answered in her unassuming manner, whilst pouring red wine into three delicate glasses from an etched glass decanter. 'The bounty from the garden has never been quite so good. Now, I must get cracking in the kitchen. Let's see what you've brought for me,' she announced.

'Mother, we agreed,' Tomas protested, 'that Izzy and I would take care of lunch.'

But Celia wouldn't hear of it. 'Just keep an eye on the fire, Tomas, and I'll promise to call you if I need a hand. Izzy, you can peel the potatoes, but first you might fetch the candle snuffer from the library, else I fear I'll forget to put out the candles on the tree when the time comes.'

I ventured off to the snug, which Celia always, I thought, named a little grandly, although it was a room I liked, with its dark, cocooning feel, ornate chandelier, bookshelves and nostalgic family photos. I pushed at the heavy wooden door and stepped on to the antique patterned floor tiles. 'Right, candle snuffer,' I said to myself out loud. The room smelt faintly of Celia's favourite Tuberose candles and the slight musty smell that lingers from old books.

The candle snuffer wasn't immediately visible. I scoured the mantelpiece and the window ledge, and finally my eyes settled on Celia's writing desk. By now Pepillo was at my feet and looking up at me inquisitively with his one good eye.

Amidst an old-fashioned set of writing paper and an elaborate assortment of paperweights and bottles of neatly ordered ink was the snuffer. Long, lean and copper, with twists in its handle and a tiny cup at its end.

'Got it,' I said to Pepillo as well as myself. As I lifted the object, my eyes were diverted not to the dog, but to something else. An envelope. In fact a series of envelopes, which had been sitting beneath the snuffer, all identically typed with Celia's name and address and bearing the stamp of Son Dureta, the hospital.

I hesitated as Pepillo brushed against my ankles, a paw scratching for a stroke. I couldn't possibly look at the contents, could I? Tomas had told me that Celia hadn't received her results, but maybe, I pondered, these were something else entirely, and of course, something that wasn't my business.

'Down,' I said gently to Pepillo, without conviction, my mind still on the correspondence.

'Izzy?' I heard from the other room. 'Did you find it?' It was Celia's voice. I turned with the snuffer in my hand and Pepillo in tow, and wandered obediently back to the kitchen.

★   ★   ★

Lunch at Celia's was an afternoon of merriment and simple pleasures. Despite Celia's original objection to help, we all pulled together in the kitchen to prepare a feast for three. Tomas made hilarious work of peeling carrots, creating whittled shapes with endless bumps that Celia dubbed 'totem poles'. Pepillo was driven almost crazy by the smell of roasting pork cooked with lemon and rosemary straight from the garden, as quite by coincidence we could hear the squeals of another pig resonating across the valley, inevitably becoming another festive meal.

I winced. Although I liked a roast as much as anyone, I could never quite get used to the earthy way that the Spanish dealt with catching, preparing and cooking their own meat, even if it was the perfect Jamie Oliver idyll.

We sat down to lunch beside the roaring fire in the dining room and indulged in three lengthy courses, our conversation fuelled by red wine, the ease of each other's company and the notion that Christmas was almost upon us. Tomas, I discovered, was working on a new botany paper, Celia divulged the details of her pre-Christmas wedding and I gave an extensive update on the house renovation. The hours rolled by, and Celia's legendary cheese board, served with grapes that Tomas had pillaged from Marta's vineyard and home-made oatcakes, finished the meal, as dusk seemed to sweep over the valley like a veil.

Finally, Tomas and I cleared the last of the plates, insisting that Celia put her feet up in front of the fire in the sitting room whilst we tackled the dishes.

'Maybe a little brandy?' she asked Tomas, who thought she was pushing her luck.

'I wouldn't have thought that was terribly wise until you're feeling completely yourself, don't you think?' he replied diplomatically, eyeing the empty bottles of red on the table.

At the sink, Tomas grabbed a tea towel as I ran water into the bowl.

'I'm glad to hear that it's going well at the house, Izzy,' he offered politely.

'I can't wait.' I smiled at the thought. 'Just to get in there.'

Tomas was filling Pepillo's bowl with leftover cuts of pork. 'Yes, must be exciting. A shame almost that you have to break the momentum with Christmas,' he said, still kneeling down.

'Well Harrisson is trying to get it together so we can at least check out of the B&B and spend one night there before we go home.'

'So he's looking forward to it as much as you?' Tomas concluded.

I hesitated. I just wasn't sure. Harrisson had spoken about nothing but London since he'd come back from his job with Freedom Jeans, and he seemed to be focusing on his trip home again for Christmas. I wasn't sure if it was to get him through the rest of the build, now that the weather had turned chilly, or if it was more than home comforts that he was craving.

'What about you?' I asked. 'Are you staying here into next year? You've never said.'

'Well, the island *does* feel like home and I *do* want to make sure that Celia is properly on the mend before I even think about what to do. But obviously I can't stay living with my mother for ever.'

I thought I had done a good job of changing the subject, but Tomas looked at me straight on as he stood up.

'I just want to make sure that you're happy, Izzy,' he said seriously, as my hands fumbled for the dishes in the soapy bowl. 'I really do.'

★ ★ ★

I thought about nothing other than Tomas's words for the next few days, and if I was honest with myself, about Tomas in general. I'd seen so many different sides to the man I'd once quickly dismissed as dull and too safe that I'd become quietly intrigued. Or so I had thought.

'This, I told you,' Marta said, just a few minutes into our conversation when we met for a drink before the holidays started, her eyes lighting up with excitement. 'I told you he was a good man.' I was telling her how

269

Tomas had been looking after Celia, and in doing so, realised that it was always these moments — man saving puppy, man holding baby — that made us girls turn a little gooey.

We were sipping *la mumbas*, tall glasses of hot chocolate laced with brandy, at a chic café in Porto Andratx on a clear December morning. Marta was wrapped up in a caramel-coloured chunky knit and scarf over skinny jeans, her face free of make-up as always and her almond-shaped eyes shielded behind sunglasses. The gulls that I'd imagined would have long emigrated circled the mountaintops beyond the water, which shimmered as the soft buttery rays caught the ripples of the waves.

'He *is* a good man,' I agreed, laughing, 'but so is Harrisson . . . Did I tell you that we're staying at the house for the first time tonight?'

'Ah . . . *que romantico*!' Marta sighed.

'He's worked so hard to get it ready,' I confirmed.

'I cannot wait to see too,' Marta said with enthusiasm.

'Of course, you must come over as soon as we're back from Christmas.'

'Yes. Christmas,' she repeated without enthusiasm. 'Isobel, I will be, as you say in England, run off my feets.'

I laughed at her cute lisping plural. 'But at least you will be free for Reyes,' I said, referring to the fiesta that the Spanish celebrated in early January.

'*Claro*, of course, and you too, no?'

'Yes, I've made Harrisson promise that we'll be back here. I've heard all about the parade through Palma and the fiesta.'

'Yes, it is in-cre-di-blay,' Marta announced with Spanish vowels. 'We will go together,' she decided firmly, as she signalled for a waiter, handsome in an immaculate white shirt and floor-length black apron, to get us another drink. 'And I have to get to know this Harrisson,' she smiled, turning back to me.

'Yes, I know, it's been so crazy with the renovation that I haven't had a chance to get you guys together.'

'Of course,' she agreed with a twinkle in her eye, 'but I have to make sure he is the good man for you, *cariño*.'

'Don't say that.' I laughed out loud. 'We're getting married, remember?'

'Yes! But you don't talk about this wedding so much,' she observed, her head now on one side.

'I know,' I confessed, as a small flock of tiny brown birds swooped down to peck at the croissant left on the table next to us. 'Everything has been about the house so far.'

'And the diet?' Marta smirked. She had always thought it was a bad idea. 'It is difficult in Spain, no?'

I told Marta about my gruelling running regime with Ray and Ramon, and she eyed me with curiosity.

'And then there's Christmas,' I moaned, stirring my second boozy hot chocolate. 'I haven't even told you about my mother's cooking.'

Christmas . . . The conversation soon turned to family commitments, traditions, and the many parties that Marta had to organise at the vineyard. At least for now, Surrey and my family seemed a million miles away.

★ ★ ★

Having banned me from entering the house for the last few days, Harrisson was ready to unveil his hard work that evening. It was the final night we'd stay together before going our separate ways to spend Christmas with our families in England, and the first night we'd spend together in our new home. It was a moment I'd looked forward to for months. And although the house was far from finished, with some rooms resembling a building site and all without any form of heating, it had been worth the wait.

That evening, we packed up our belongings at the B&B. We were excited to be finally checking out. When we stumbled down the stairs with our heavy bags, feeling stifled under layers of winter woollens, the owner was just as we'd found him all those months ago, propped up by his makeshift desk at the end of the bar, a cigarette burning away on one side of his laptop as he chatted animatedly to an attractive waitress on the other. I was carrying a case to leave at the house and one to take back to England. The latter was so heavy with gifts that I could barely lift it. I knew it would tip the easyJet scales and cost almost an extra ticket price in excess baggage charges, but I couldn't resist buying a little taste of the island to take home to friends and family.

As we battled with the door, we laughed in relief at leaving the small room we'd been cooped up in for weeks. Our luggage clattered against our ankles as we struggled to reach the street, where we chose a last supper in one of our favourite restaurants.

'Something hot and substantial then, babe,' Harrisson recommended, as we glanced over the familiar menus — as if I needed a reason to indulge in three courses and a bottle of red wine. My conversation with Marta about dieting earlier that day had faded to a memory. 'We're still a long way off from heating and hot water,' he continued. It was a fact he'd repeated several times, as if by saying it, the words would soften the physical impact of the cold.

After supper, we walked home huddled together for warmth against the clear dark skies and the gleaming golden orb of an almost full moon, a little merry from a few festive glasses of red. Harrisson draped an arm around my shoulders and my teeth chattered beneath the cashmere scarf he'd insisted I borrow from him. It smelt musky and sweet, of his cologne.

As we reached the church across the road from our new home, he stopped me, pulling a silk scarf from his pocket like a magician to blindfold me and although I laughed at his sense of fun and the added element of theatre, I hoped for one fleeting, self-consciously English moment that the neighbours didn't see him guiding me, walking with my arms ridiculously outstretched like a bad ghost impersonator, towards our own front door. The clock of the church chimed nine and made me jump and both of us rock with laughter.

'There are no cars coming, right?' I asked him. 'I've just set up the life insurance,' I joked in bad taste, a little nervously, as the sound of the wheels of the cases that Harrisson was single-handedly pulling followed us across the road.

My hands groped out in front of me for the heavy wooden door at the house's entrance. I felt Harrisson move closer and reach an arm forward to turn the key and guide me inside. Still at my back, he slowly removed the blindfold and put it away in his pocket as my eyes adjusted to the soft, low light.

Harrisson had filled the big hallway with candles. A huge hand-tied bouquet of deep red roses had been plunged into a beer glass from the local bar and sat on the only piece of furniture — a workman's table.

'I thought I should at least try to make the place smell and look nice.' He shrugged softly with a smooth smile as we put down our bags and cases to continue the tour.

The candlelight extended to the bathroom, which was now fitted with Harrisson's choice of rainforest shower and a matching suite. I cooed at the results.

Even the tiles had been laid, and when the walls finally got a fresh white coat of paint it would look like a room in a showhome.

'It looks fantastic,' I congratulated him excitedly.

Back outside the door, the candles drew a line that crossed the hallway and climbed the stairs, without a detour into the lounge or kitchen.

'I thought that the warmest place,' Harrisson said, taking my hand softly in his, 'would be in bed.'

Guided by the seemingly endless row of tea lights that flickered delicate shadows on to the walls as we passed, Harrisson led me to our bedroom. It was the one room that he'd managed to paint especially for the occasion. He'd scrubbed the antique tiled floor with a special mix of oils and spirits that Poli's *madre* had written down for him. He'd dusted the emerald-green-painted shutters and shut them tightly against the large single-paned windows, which still let in a draught. In the centre of the room he'd laid a mattress on the floor as a bed, swathed with quilts and blankets that he'd bought or borrowed.

'I can't believe it,' I heard myself say. 'It's like a fairy tale.' I was welling up with emotion on seeing how much care he'd taken and just how much effort he'd put into making everything perfect.

'Well it's finally real, Iz,' he answered, his hands on the tops of my arms as he looked straight at me. 'And you deserve it . . . *we* deserve it,' he said, with a little shake in his voice too.

I'd never known Harrisson throw himself so wholeheartedly into something that wasn't related to work.

'Here,' he said, before we could get too sentimental. 'Climb into bed or you'll get cold. I've organised some entertainment.'

'Entertainment?' I giggled.

We both undressed at lightning speed and threw ourselves under the covers, before Harrisson revealed his plan.

First he unveiled a bottle of Soberano, cheap but very drinkable Spanish brandy, and two Pyrex tumblers.

'That'll keep us warm,' I laughed when I saw the label.

He made a ceremony of opening the bottle as I kept my arms beneath the blankets, shivering despite the layers.

Next he pulled out a laptop case from his side of the bed.

'This, Isabelle,' he announced, 'is what I call 'TV On Demand' . . . well, not TV exactly, as we don't have any yet, but . . . DVDs at least.' During the dramatic pause, he'd fanned several glossy cases in one hand, putting them down on top of the bedclothes to invite me to take a choice. There were some cult English comedies and films ranging from recent thrillers to black and white classics. 'What do you reckon?' he asked

'I think you've planned everything perfectly,' I replied, although I knew he was really asking what I'd like to watch, 'and I can't wait to help you decorate when we get back.'

That night, we watched two movies snuggled up and sipped brandy, our breath clearly visible in the room when we laughed out loud.

'It's funny, isn't it? Getting used to all the new noises of a different room,' I said as the final credits rolled and the laptop signalled that we were close to losing power. I'd heard an owl nearby, kids whizzed along the street below on scooters, and unseen cars washed our darkened room with the low glow of their headlamps.

Harrisson snapped the laptop shut and rolled over to face me.

'Yeah,' he said almost in a whisper, 'you'll soon feel at home.'

'Well this is home now,' I said sleepily. 'After all of this, I don't want to find another one too quickly.'

The room was pitch black without the light of the laptop to illuminate it. I could just make out the shape of Harrisson's arm on top of his pillow. Bent at the elbow as he rested his head in a cupped hand, it was more muscular now, I noticed, from the building work of the last few months. My eyes strained sleepily to make out his features.

'Is it looking how you thought it would?' he asked.

'Better,' I replied honestly, my eyelids getting heavy.

He leant over and kissed me, gently. 'Good,' he murmured, lifting his head to pause a little, his eyes on mine in the darkness. 'It's all for you,' he said, before his lips were on mine once more.

19

London calling

I woke up the next morning with a jolt. With the shutters still tightly bolted at the windows, the room was as dark as it had been all night, making it impossible to know the time. My mouth was dry from the previous evening's cocktail of red wine and brandy and my head was frazzled from the mix. I moved slowly and reached an arm out for Harrisson. His side of the bed was empty, the covers folded back and the soft imprint on his pillow cold.

'Flight,' I mumbled to myself pathetically.

I willed myself to my feet, grabbed last night's clothes to put on in the dark and walked across the cold tiled floor. My fingers fumbled for the shutters, then for the latch. Finally I pushed them open with a creak.

Fresh air and brilliant daylight instantly flooded the room, and the view made me catch my breath. The church and the orange grove opposite, the handsome country houses scattered across the valley, smoke already billowing from the chimneys of some.

Towering way above the gardens and palm trees were the mountains, covered in a low floating band of soft morning mist that the locals called *el humido*.

I stood there for a moment, taking it all in, my head a little better for the air.

'Izz?' I heard Harrisson call from the hallway.

I turned to face the doorway as he walked in.

'Hi,' he said softly.

'The view's amazing, H,' I said, turning back to it. 'How are you? And how are we for time?'

'There's almost an hour before we leave,' he confirmed with a smile, kissing me on the cheek.

I tore myself away from the window and ventured downstairs in search of my case. The floor beneath my bare feet was gritty and cold, and in daylight I could see just how much work was still left to do on the house, as well as all the things I loved about it.

'Looks great,' I said to Harrisson on reaching the hallway. 'It's just so good to finally be here.'

'You might not say that when you try out the shower,' he laughed.

'Yeah, no hot water, I remember,' I chided him.

'It's a bit more than that,' Harrisson laughed. 'The glass hasn't arrived for the window,' he added. 'It's been delayed. Comes tomorrow, when Poli's here.'

I rubbed my still fuzzy bed-head and shuddered at the thought.

'There's only one way to do it,' he advised. 'Turn on the shower, undress, brace yourself and then throw yourself under the water for as little time as possible.'

I peered around the corner of the door to take a look. Harrisson had taped up the window with plastic supermarket bags, to keep out the worst of the draught and give us privacy. The room smelt of new tiles and cement.

I looked back at Harrisson, already dressed and groomed.

'Or you *could* come in with me, to keep me warm?' I said in my best attempt, with a hangover, at being a seductress.

*　*　*

Christmas that year was just like any other. I returned to my parents' house in frosty Surrey, peering through the windows of the front rooms along our familiar terraced street to see each one decorated as if time had stood still since last year's festivities. I knew that the trendy upside-down tree decked with blue baubles and topped with flashing multi-coloured LED lights in the window of number 19 would have my mother and the rest of her 'Stitch and Bitch' group ranting about tradition, and that we were probably due the annual door-to-door carol chorus by the Neighbourhood Watch. Only the air smelt different, I noticed, getting off the overground train alone; damp and faintly industrial, and the light was different too. As our plane had touched down on the runway mid-afternoon, it was if we had swooped down beneath a thick grey blanket of sky the colour of Victorian slate, the grey of grubby London pigeons. It was a sight that Harrisson had greeted with welcome familiarity but which left me feeling a little nostalgic for the big bright skies in Majorca that always seemed to put me in a good mood.

'Great to be home,' Harrisson had chimed eagerly as the wheels hit the runway.

As the Gatwick Express sped through the stations of south London to a loop of piped welcome greetings in every conceivable language, we swapped notes on what the next two weeks would hold. Harrisson reeled off a list of parties he was attending. Christmas drinks and canapés at Vogue's publisher Condé Nast, the annual festive parties of various ad agencies, including Saatchi's, trendy PR companies and design groups, as well as invites to hang out at clubs I'd not even heard of, with the Notting Hill 'it' crowd he always associated with. He was still trying to convince me to come along to the bashes he didn't dismiss as work. But although he obviously was going to be at all of the places to be seen, with all the people of the moment, I wasn't sure that whole scene was for me any more. Or if it ever really had been.

'To be honest,' I smiled sweetly, 'I'm happy just to meet up with you one night for supper in one of our old haunts, or to go ice-skating at Somerset House maybe.' I shared my plans to see my closest friends, chill out with Ray, catch up with Remi and indulge in some girlie nights and lunches discussing wedding plans, when I wasn't needed by my mother to make sausage rolls for my Aunt Sandra's annual knees-up or feed her swaddled Christmas cake with enough brandy that it became a fire hazard. Harrisson looked bored just hearing about my Christmas, but I was happy to slip seamlessly into the routine that we seemed to follow every year and let Harrisson party until he got it out of his system.

To my relief, that was exactly what I did. I met friends for Christmas shopping trips in

Oxford Street and in Surrey pubs with open fires to drink red wine and catch up on the gossip. Only the topics of conversation had really changed. Friends grilled me about my wedding plans, extended aunts expressed concern at what to wear and pack for the big day overseas and my mother warned me against second helpings of the English comfort foods I'd so missed and about how a tightly fitting wedding dress had never been easy to squeeze into after too much figgy pudding. Her obsession about my weight had started when I'd let myself in that first afternoon with my own key.

She'd been sitting with Dad following a complex crochet pattern whilst he nursed a cup of tea and tried to guess the numbers on *Countdown*.

'Hello, dear,' he had greeted me, parting with his tea cup and getting to his slippered feet to give me a bear hug.

'Isabelle!' Mother had said. 'You *do* look well,' she marvelled pointedly at my figure.

'Yes, we've been living out of restaurants for the past few months whilst we do the house,' I explained.

'Sounds awful,' Dad had chipped in. 'All that foreign food.'

The house looked the same, although Mum had splurged on new curtains in the lounge for Christmas, in heavy burgundy velvet, and the central heating felt subtropical, now that I was no longer used to it.

The days felt short and dark and my time in London long. I missed Harrisson, and I missed Majorca. I kept wondering what Celia and Tomas would be up to, if there were street parties and fiestas in Sóller and how Marta's events at the vineyard were going. I met up with Harrisson early one evening, after shopping with Remi, who was out of control on a mission to find a dress for New Year's Eve. She'd dragged me through Dover Street market, Browns and Harvey Nics, tugging my arm as I veered towards gifts and goodies for other people.

'So when are you next *properly* out with Harrisson?' she'd asked. 'I've started to hate this time of year by now . . . party overload,' she added nonchalantly, as though she was the most invited attendee in the city.

'To be honest, I'm giving the parties a miss,' I sighed.

'Completely? Izzy, next you'll be telling me that you've given up drink and . . . oh my God, you're not . . . ?' she exclaimed with wide emerald eyes, her glossy black bob flicking at her cheekbone as she tore her gaze away from an embellished Gucci minidress to look at me.

'No, of course not!' I giggled. 'I'm just really not that fussed about going.'

Remi looked at me curiously. 'Thank God,' she breathed. There wasn't a single thing that Remi got about pregnancy and babies.

'It all seems to be about networking,' I tried to explain, hopelessly.

''Not-working' is much cooler,' she replied flippantly, to my bemusement, 'but that doesn't mean you don't show.'

She was flicking through a rail of Chloé dresses, with price tags that made me baulk. 'Massoud's having a party on the boat for New Year's Eve,' she said. 'You should at least come to that with Harrisson, if you're back in Palma.'

'You know what, Rem,' I smiled gratefully, 'that's the best offer I've had.'

I encouraged her to buy the Gucci to change the subject and to finally get back to what I thought had been the original reason for our shopping mission.

At the end of the afternoon, Remi, clutching a single carrier bag, hauled her tiny frame teetering on six-inch platforms into a cab that disappeared out of the mayhem of Christmas shoppers, congestion-zone traffic and Christmas lights. I was left carrying my own body weight in perfume gift sets, kitchenalia and a jumper for my dad that I only hoped he wouldn't dismiss as 'too racy'. I had struck gold with a silk Liberty scarf for Celia and a Duchy Originals gardening tool set for Tomas, but I still had Harrisson to buy for and was thankful we'd agreed to exchange gifts at Reyes, to bag myself a little more time. He really was the man who had everything.

We met at an understated bar in Soho, where street fashion, I discovered, had moved on cosmically amongst the barflies I'd last seen there. Harrisson was late. I propped myself up at the end of the bar and made my way through a magazine rack full of titles like *Love* and *Tank* while I waited. I ordered a coffee in an attempt to perk myself up and keep warm, and then another. Finally, as I sent Harrisson a third text, he barged through the door.

'Sorry, babe,' he apologised, his face flushed. 'I overslept.'

'Overslept?' I asked with surprise. 'It's almost eight p.m.'

'Yeah, heavy night last night,' he said with a watery smile and eyes that looked like they longed for even more sleep.

Harrisson, I discovered, had reverted to his old city lifestyle. At our only chance to meet before Christmas, he'd invited along four friends, who tripped in an hour later in a similar state. Keshia, an Afro-American model, dragged along Ali, a stylist, and her girlfriend Zena, from the Ukraine, who was apparently doing 'go-sees' and didn't yet have an agent. Then there was a guy called Bo who everyone touted as a genius, but who stayed completely silent throughout the conversation, nodding intermittently, his features buried beneath a battered trilby decorated with a feather. They spoke about the night before — who was who, sleeping with who and doing God knows what — and when the conversation turned to work, they digressed into the same competitive oneupmanship, boasting about working for a brand, an account, a celeb that I remembered from my own days working in TV in Notting Hill. Seeing me look fed up at being gatecrashed, and my face turn to boredom, Harrisson put a hand on my thigh before ordering his third double JD on the rocks.

At the beginning of the evening he'd introduced me as 'Izzy', to which I'd added 'his fiancée' with a friendly smile and seen him visibly wince. After that, no one had spoken to me for the rest of the night and Harrisson had become completely absorbed by his friends.

It was still early when I decided to make an excuse to leave.

'It's a bit rude leaving when I've got everyone here to meet up with you, Iz,' said Harrisson, with a hint of aggression in his voice. He had followed me to the door and had my arm in a gentle grip.

I stood in silence, wide-eyed and almost sober, which he, I presumed, was definitely not. I'd downed two large glasses of red wine just to get through the evening so far, but if for him the previous night was as messy as it seemed, I guessed he was lacing a hair of the dog.

'But I didn't want to have everyone else come here, Harrisson,' I whispered back, trying to avoid a scene. 'I thought it was just going to be you and me.'

'But it's always you and me,' he said in exasperation. His face, rugged and unshaven, was close to mine and he smelt of stale booze and cigarettes.

I felt my eyes well up with tears. 'That's good by me . . . you and me,' I replied softly. 'I thought that was the point. We're not together over Christmas.'

'Only because you don't want to come out and have fun,' he blurted. 'What else can I do but invite you to everything?' he asked, as if it was the most rational question in the world.

'I mean for Christmas Day, Boxing Day . . . you know . . . ' My voice trailed off. 'I just don't think that staying up all night drinking and being false with a load of people you don't know is fun any more,' I said, staring at my feet, willing them to move.

I could feel the warmth of my tears streaming down my face as I stood in the doorway. Outside, the Soho street was grubby, its gutters filled with litter. I saw a seedy-looking guy dive into the lap-dancing club opposite; its pink neon sign promising *Girls* was draped with a thin, tired string of fuchsia tinsel. I opened the door and a gust of cold air whipped inside the now-crowded room. The girl standing nearest to me shot me a dirty look. I didn't shut the door. I decided it was time to leave.

'Well, maybe we want different things,' I said, my voice croaking with sobs as I took my bags of gifts with me, heading through the freezing back streets to the tube. At Tottenham Court Road, I dared to look back. Harrisson hadn't followed me. He'd let me go. As I balanced carrier bags in the creases of my elbows to rummage in my handbag for my phone, I discovered that he hadn't even sent a text.

The underground was heaving with casualties from office parties, half the carriages filled with a rabble singing carols, and the other half filled with those trying to ignore them. I changed at Victoria, battled with the swarms of people crossing London, and caught the line I'd travelled since I was young, back home. I didn't know how I'd explain the hour to Dad, who still waited up in his armchair whenever I stayed, to make sure I was safely home.

When I turned the key gently in the latch, he was snoring, the Christmas lights still blazing on the tree, the glow still on the electric fire in Mum's elaborate grate. There was an empty whisky tumbler perched on a pile of folded newspapers on the coffee table. An open book had dropped on to his chest. I gently lifted it from the loose grip of one hand and picked up the whisky glass.

He opened his eyes slowly, saw me and smiled. 'Hello, love,' he said warmly, woozy from sleep.

'Sorry I'm late, Dad,' I whispered softly to him. 'I had a row with Harrisson in town.'

'Doesn't matter,' he said, clearing his throat. 'You wash that evidence up,' he nodded, referring to the whisky glass, 'and we'll both have a secret to keep.'

20

Merry bloody Christmas

The run-up to Christmas came and went in a flurry of family gatherings and drinks with friends, but it was Christmas Eve with Ray that was most memorable. At his familiar flat in Notting Hill, which he had cautiously kept whilst living with Ramon in Palma, we watched from the windows that overlooked the busy streets as hordes of people scurried below buying last-minute presents and netted bags of fresh Brussels sprouts for the next day. All wrapped up against the cold as daylight faded, their faces became lit up by street lamps and seemed seasonally cheerful in anticipation of Christmas. By late afternoon, the pubs and bars heaved with merry drinkers who spilled out on to the otherwise deserted streets of Portobello.

Inside Ray's flat we drank hot toddies spiced with cardamon and caught up on each other's news, whilst Ray wrapped gifts in vintage saris and tied bows around the glistening parcels with raw silk ribbons. With Bollywood movies playing on the plasma screen in the background, we spoke about his trip to India for New Year, the wedding, of course, and his newly 'open' relationship with Ramon. It was a concept I just couldn't get my head around.

'So, if Ramon has decided he wants to sleep with other guys — '

'People,' Ray corrected me.

'OK, with other people,' I repeated with a raised eyebrow, 'you don't think that . . . how do I put this . . . '

'That he's bored of sex with me? Or that he's being greedy and wants to sleep with every attractive person he meets?'

'You said that, I didn't,' I giggled as Ray danced, his bhangra moves mocking the female lead on screen.

'It's just that we want to have fun, be free and still have some kind of commitment to each other,' he said, his head bobbing in staccato moves between raised arms, his wrists rapping in time to the beat.

I gave him a blank look.

'Monogamy isn't for everyone, Izzy,' he said, before miming seamlessly to the song, his actions a perfect mirror of the beautiful diva he had his back to as she danced through the colourful streets of Mumbai.

'Well, as long as you're happy,' I said, laughing at his impersonation.

'Yeah, I'm not the jealous type,' said Ray, still dancing. 'And we can't all be engaged to marry some cool guy.'

It was my cue to tell him about my row with Harrisson.

'Don't worry about it,' he said seriously, slumping down into a leather chair. 'He's been working hard for months, and now it's Christmas, he's just letting his hair down.'

'Yeah, I guess you're right,' I said.

'Anyway. This new open relationship could be an eye-opener,' said Ray with a twinkle in his eye.

'I really *don't* want to know the details,' I laughed, blushing a little.

'Ramon and I tell each other *everything*,' Ray continued.

'God, really?' I asked with surprise.

'Yes, it's hot!' Ray exclaimed. 'But sometimes the details aren't what you'd expect.'

I mimed putting my hands over my ears, as Ray topped up my toddy from a piping-hot glass jug on the table.

'Not *what*,' he laughed. '*Who*.'

'OK.' I smiled with relief. 'Who?'

'Massoud,' Ray said simply.

'Remi's Massoud?' I shrieked. 'And Ramon?'

Ray nodded his head.

'Poor Remi,' I said softly.

'What?' quizzed Ray with disbelief. 'You

know Rem better than to think she'd care. To her, Massoud's a part-time Father Christmas. You know that,' he said, lighting an expensive-looking cinnamon-scented candle on the mantelpiece.

'Now, more importantly,' he announced with a serious look on his face as he turned to face me, 'let's make bhajis.'

* * *

Dad wore the bright paper hat he'd pulled from a cracker until he fell asleep in his chair, Aunt Sandra drank too many dry sherries and Mum overcatered. Christmas Day was, in short, like any other, the whole event only slightly marred by a single stilted conversation with Harrisson when he called to wish me a merry Christmas without much cheer. The only consolation was how the conversation had ended.

'I really have to see you, Izz . . . what about tomorrow?'

'Tomorrow?' I asked. 'Don't you have lunch at your stepmother's'

'Yes,' he said softly, 'but what about after? I'll come to you. Shall we meet at the Stag's Head?'

'Sure,' I replied, relieved to hear him sound so keen to make things up.

'See you at four,' he confirmed, and I wandered happily back to the kitchen to help Dad, who was up to his elbows in washing-up at the sink, singing along to Nat King Cole.

The Stag was heaving with revellers the next day. As I pushed through the crowded bar, I nodded hello to Sheila. She'd had her name above the door for years and had got many a husband into trouble when they returned home for Christmas lunch full of the roast potatoes that were always free at the bar.

'Never as good as your mother's,' my dad always said, turning his nose up, all those years when we came for a drink on Christmas morning. The words ran through my head, making me smile, as my eyes searched the sea of faces for Harrisson's.

There was something comforting about being in the local pub. I liked the fact that it never changed. That Sheila hadn't been tempted to decorate or give it a TV-style makeover, that the fireplaces in both bars were always roaring with a log fire at this time of year and that so many of the characters that huddled around them were familiar. Not just the people who had been locals for years, but faces I vaguely recognised as bearing the now grown-up features of kids from school.

I spotted the back of Harrisson's head as

he queued at the bar, his long charcoal-grey Jil Sander coat and the cashmere scarf I'd snuggled into that first night we'd stayed at the house familiar. I gently nudged my way through the crowds with polite excuse mes, not needing to see his face to know it was him.

'Hi,' I said finally, tapping him on the arm as I approached him.

'Izzy.' He smiled weakly, kissing me on the cheek. 'What are you drinking?'

I hadn't given it a thought. 'Oh, whatever you are,' I replied without caring, smiling up at him. I'd missed him, and I hadn't enjoyed the last few days, having left things in a row.

'You all right?' he asked, handing me a large glass of red wine.

'Yes thanks,' I said, nodding as I took a sip.

'Over there,' Harrisson said, spotting two chairs coming free at a table, as people stood up to leave. The pub was warm with the heat of so many bodies, and filled with laughter. Sheila had the biggest tree I'd seen, covered in baubles, its fairy just scraping against the low ceiling.

'Do you mind if we join you?' I asked a couple sitting at the other end of the table.

'Course not.' They nodded.

'So, how was lunch?' I asked Harrisson. I assumed that it hadn't gone well. He often rowed with Frances, his stepmother, and he didn't appear to be in a good mood.

'Fine. You know. The usual,' was his reply, as he stared into his glass.

After a pause, he looked up at me, his face serious and grey. Finally, he sighed.

'Izzy, look,' he said quietly. 'I . . . I've got to talk to you.'

'OK,' I answered boldy. It sounded serious. All kinds of scenarios ran through my head. Maybe a family feud had erupted over Christmas; he'd overspent on the house and not told me; he'd landed another job in New York and was going to miss New Year . . .

'I'm not coming back to Sóller with you,' he said plainly.

'Oh, I was just thinking maybe you've got another job lined up. Well done you,' I said enthusiastically. 'Where is it? Here in London? New York?'

'No, no,' he said, 'you're not listening.' He looked tired. More tired even than the day we'd met up in Soho and it had all ended so badly. 'I can't do this,' he muttered, looking down into his glass again.

I felt my heart sink. My throat clammed up and I took a deep breath as my eyes stung with tears. I knew, without him saying another word now, what he meant.

'I'm not ready for this. You know. My life is

here, Iz.' Harrisson looked up at me, his hand reaching across the table for mine. I stayed frozen, my arm glued to the table as he placed his warm palm over my cold fingers.

'I love you, Izzy,' he said softly, not caring now who heard, 'you know that . . . but I'm just not ready for all of this.'

'But I thought . . . ' I started, my voice cracking.

'I know,' Harrisson said, gently rubbing a finger over the back of my hand. 'And I really tried. The house. You know I knocked myself out . . . '

'But it's for us,' I managed, tears blurring my vision of him across from me. From the corner of one eye, I saw the couple we'd joined gather their things to leave.

'I thought that if I did it it would make you happy,' he said, his eyes welling up too. 'But happy for me is in London. I can't be in a quiet town somewhere.'

'We could . . . ' I started without thinking, then stopped myself. Was I ready to give up Majorca?

'It's not just that,' Harrisson said, knowing what I was going to say. After all, in the last few months we'd spent so much time together, we'd already started finishing each other's sentences. 'I'm not ready for any of it.

To be married. To live in one place. Not going out. Not seeing friends, and I know we'd meet people there, but it's just not the same, Iz,' he said, honestly.

'But you can visit London, like we planned,' I heard myself pleading.

'I thought so too,' he said, taking his hand away from mine now, 'but it doesn't work like that. I need to be in the city. Work in the city. Have a social life in the city. I realise that now.'

'It's all familiar when you come back. I know that,' I argued. 'And when it's tough over there, it's bound to feel better here, where you speak the language and you don't need to stand on a building site all day . . . But we've only just started to give our new life a chance. We haven't even moved into the house yet . . . God, the house!' I cried. 'What are we going to do?'

I looked away from him, my eyes sweeping round the bar, the people, the colours, the Christmas lights merging into one messy blur. It was obvious that he'd made up his mind.

'Look. Don't worry about the house,' he said. 'I know it's hard to believe,' he continued, bringing my gaze back to his, 'but I just want us both to be happy. I'm not going to be happy in Sóller . . . but you are,' he said. 'And it's always been your house. We'll sort that out, I promise. I just don't belong there. And I'm really sorry . . . but being here, I just know that it's not right for us to get married. To live the life you want. It's just not me.'

'But you lied to me,' I blurted, suddenly angry. I'd been here before and he'd promised that this time things would be different.

'No. Really, Izzy, I didn't,' he pleaded. 'I thought I wanted the same things you did. I tried so hard to convince myself. And I thought that if you were happy, and we got the house looking cool, then . . . it would all be good.'

'But it isn't good?' I said, wishing I hadn't asked the question.

Harrisson didn't answer. He passed me an envelope, which he told me contained the keys to his car at the airport and his set to the house. I buried it beneath the table. We sat for more than half an hour in silence. I churned over the facts again and again, as if I needed to repeat them in my head, to know they were real, and I wished for the first time that I was somewhere else, somewhere more anony-mous than the Stag's Head. It wasn't that I suddenly felt self-conscious, aware that people were looking as I sobbed into my glass of wine. It was that by being here, where I'd been so many times over so many years, my life didn't just feel like it was standing still, but at that particular moment it had slipped backwards.

21

Alone again

I went back to Sóller alone. I didn't have the heart to tell Mum, Dad or anyone else what had happened. There was part of me that thought, and hoped, that Harrisson would call and say that he'd made another mistake and things would be fine, and I told myself that I didn't want to upset my family unnecessarily. As I took the train towards Gatwick airport, a part of me felt that by telling Ray, or Marta, I would be confirming a truth and somehow making it a certainty. Yet mostly I knew, as I counted the stations that whizzed by, that deep down I was in denial.

I still bought a pile of wedding magazines to read on the plane, kidding myself that they were for Celia, yet still serious about planning my own big day. I still kept my mobile close as I boarded the Gatwick Express, in case Harrisson made a last-minute call to say that he'd be joining me after all. His ticket was nestled in my wallet, with my own.

There was something surreal about landing in Palma that day. The air was soft and warm as the automatic glass doors parted and I stepped out of the airport. The palm trees towered way above the building, their leaves glistening towards the pale blue sky. I clutched my bags of Christmas gifts and a thick jumper that suddenly felt too heavy for the milder climate and took the travellator to the car park, knowing that as I reached the end, I'd have to open the envelope that Harrisson had given me that day at the pub, fish out his car keys and drive myself to our unfinished home. I took my time, drawing in deep breaths, and went through the motions on autopilot, not allowing my emotions to get the better of me.

Harrisson's car smelt faintly of his aftershave, but mostly of building dust. The boot, which he'd cleared out for our luggage, contained one of his battered leather biker's jackets; the CD player held his favourite compilation CD; and a pair of his mirrored Ray-Bans beamed my own reflection back at me from the dashboard.

'Right,' I told myself firmly, adjusting the seat into position. 'You're insured. You've not driven this van thing before, but take it slow and it will be fine.'

I started the engine up and careered around the car park, getting used to the sensitive accelerator, which seemed to pull away at the slightest touch, and the length and height of the car, which was far larger than anything I'd ever driven.

I slowly got the hang of things, crunching through the gears as the engine screamed for me to change them on the dual carriageway that sped around the outskirts of the city, and up through the mountains to Sóller. I concealed the noise by turning up the radio and pretended that the cars that overtook me didn't exist as I fixed my eyes on the road.

'Good to be back,' I said out loud to myself as I wound down the window a little. The island looked beautiful and it was as if, having been away, I appreciated its landscape with fresh eyes.

At the Sóller tunnel, the *chica* I often pulled up to to greet and flash my pass eyed the van, and me driving it, with a raised brow. We bantered our usual friendly exchange about the weather, but she asked several times if I was OK. It wasn't until I caught a glimpse of myself in the rear-view mirror, as I drove my way carefully through the narrow streets of the town, that I saw that my face was wet with tears, and streaked with make-up.

★ ★ ★

The house was desolate, but Poli and his team had pressed ahead the day after we'd left and fitted the glass to the bathroom window, before upping tools to be at home with their families for Christmas. I set down my case in the bedroom, opened the shutters in all the rooms and took a good look around. Harrisson had always planned to decorate himself, with me helping, but alone, I wouldn't know where to start. I didn't even know how many weeks it would be until Poli would be finished and it would be time to pull out the paintbrushes; how I'd ever reach the high-beamed ceilings or restore the faded wooden shutters. My boots echoed on the tiled floor as I walked from room to room.

Outside on the terrace, the mountains hugged the edges of the valley, the *humido* forming a trailing low mist that hovered in the fading light of the afternoon. The neighbourhood seemed particularly quiet. Ana and Paco were away in Madrid for the holidays and the shutters of my other neighbours' homes were tightly shut against the cool air and the onset of evening. I ruefully eyed the gaping mouth of the empty cement mixer, the planks of wood on the tiled floor and the sacks of sand. It was time to try and get cosy.

I walked around the corner to the local

grocer's, buying a fresh *barra*, some of my favourite Manchego cheese, shiny black olives, candles and a bottle of cheap local red. There was something comforting about being back in the place I loved so much, crossing the tracks that the wooden tram rattled down, passing the stone-fronted houses, the familiar gardens. Back at the house I set up a makeshift dining table in the hallway and pulled up an empty wooden crate as a chair. I found the builders' radio and smiled as Radio Ochenta filled the room with the eighties pop that felt so incongruous in my new surroundings. I ripped up chunks of bread and cut a slice of the cheese with the army knife that Harrisson had left in the kitchen. As night fell, I wrapped myself in layers of jumpers and woollen socks, lighting candles as the light began to fade. I took my mobile and slightly wobbly self up to bed early, hoping to feel warm under the blankets and covers we'd left in the bedroom, whilst I read my wedding magazines by candlelight. I'd almost finished the bottle of wine, but didn't feel in the slightest bit drunk. I wasn't sure if it was the crispness of the air and the coldness of the house that was keeping me sober, or the thought that this was really happening and that I had to get through it.

'Isobel?' a voice asked the next morning as

I scrabbled in the dark to answer my mobile. The call had woken me from a deep, heady sleep and brought me back to reality with a thump.

'*Si?*' I answered quietly. As I sat up in bed and cleared my throat, my head thumped in recognition of last night's drinking and my mouth felt coated with a layer of the dust that lay so thickly in the house.

'Isobel, are you OK?' the voice said with concern. 'It's me, Marta.'

Marta had called to see how my time had been at home and to make plans for Reyes, but on hearing my friend's voice, I lost control. The emotions that I'd tried so hard to contain became an outpour, and through a cracking voice and sobs that caught like lumps in my throat that I couldn't quite swallow, I tried to tell her everything. She was patient, listening intently as I tried to recount what had happened, but we both knew that I wasn't making much sense.

'Isobel, I am so sorry,' she sighed with a sadness to her voice as I finally paused to catch my breath. '*Cariño tranquillo*,' she soothed. 'I'm coming right now, to Sóller.'

I didn't argue. I managed to get myself out of bed and dressed in yesterday's clothes, splashed water on my face and found a half-empty bottle of water to swig before

Marta arrived. I was relieved to hear the rap of the brass knocker at the door, and as I opened it, Marta grabbed me in a bear hug, kissing me on both cheeks.

That afternoon she took me to Port Sóller for lunch. She was sweet and kind, taking my arm in hers as we wandered along the water's edge as I tried, more calmly now, to tell her how things had ended with Harrisson. Our walk led us to a family-owned restaurant that was one of my favourites. The food was simple and homemade with fresh local produce and the best of the daily catch that the local fishermen brought into the port. The family who ran it were always welcoming, but best of all was the view. From the plain white plastic chairs and wobbly tables that lined the pavement across the road from the restaurant, the port looked spectacular. On a clear late December's day, the pale blue sky seemed endless and scattered with just a few soft cotton-ball clouds. The mountains guarded the water's edge and the fishing, sailing and motorboats below, bobbed on the glimmering sea.

'*Guapas! Que tal?*' The smiling *madre* of the family greeted us with kisses as she led us to a table. Her face immaculately made up and her smart clothes kept clean behind a pinny, she passed us each a menu as she enthused about the weather, placing a basket of bread and olives on the table. We ordered two glasses of white wine and she shuffled to the next table in the slippers she always wore and playfully scolded a young Spanish couple for leaving small piles of paella on their plates. From the other side of the road, stretched out in the sun, the *madre*'s terrier Chiki looked on, raising an ear or opening an eye from time to time to check on his master. I looked out across the water and sighed.

'Everything is going to be OK,' Marta insisted.

I looked back at her and smiled a watery smile, my eyes puffy with tears and yesterday's smudged make-up behind my largest sunglasses. Remi had talked me into buying large black-framed Pradas for occasions like these; she had always dubbed them 'post-surgery shades'.

'I hope you're right,' I said quietly. 'Everything feels as though it's been turned upside down.'

'*Claro*.' Marta nodded. 'But you know, you take things *poc a poc*, little by little, and . . . ' She stopped midsentence as the lady appeared at our table again, poised with a pad to take our order. Marta spoke to her in Majorcan that I didn't understand, and she smiled sweetly, rubbed a warm, manicured hand on my shoulder and disappeared inside, taking our menus with her.

Moments later, the lady's son, a quiet, polite teenager with regulation black waiter's trousers tucked into oversized trainers, brought a second basket of bread and aioli, along with a deep green wine bottle to top up our glasses. He eyed Marta with big eyes and a slight, blushing embarrassment as she thanked him.

My stomach groaned with hunger as I tucked into the bread. At almost 3 p.m., it was the first thing I'd eaten since my cold pickings the evening before. I sipped my wine as Marta told me tales of her family Christmas so far and the tastings at the vineyard, and tried to make me laugh with stories of her brothers. Our lunch arrived shortly after, with much pomp and ceremony. Marta had asked the lady owner to bring us what was freshest in the kitchen and best for a broken heart, she told me, as the *madre* walked across the road from the restaurant towards us with a blazing smile, clutching a large steel bowl. She didn't fail to deliver. The deep bowl was brimming with seafood and rice, *sopa marinera*, she announced, sailor's soup, 'made freshly by my husband' she said proudly in Spanish with a wink. The man himself had left his kitchen, and was standing in the doorway, waiting to gauge our reaction. Marta waved a '*gracias, señor*' in his direction and he nodded back, wiping a hand across the food-splattered T-shirt that was stretched across his wide belly.

'Pedro cooks like an angel,' Marta said simply, and she was right. Lunch was hearty, warming and delicious. Marta ladled generous portions of soup into our *grexioneras*, or earthenware bowls, which we emptied more times than I could count. By the end of the afternoon, only mussel shells, a few stray clams and sprigs of herbs lay at the bottom of the steel dish, which the *madre* cleared with glee.

As we nursed *café solos*, I had to convince Marta that it wasn't necessary for me to come back to the vineyard and live with her until the house was complete, and that she didn't need to stay the night with me, but I was grateful for her generosity and to still have a friend who I knew I could rely on so far from home.

'Sometimes, just talking helps,' I said to her honestly, still beating off her generous offers with my English reserve and determination to get things sorted. But I wasn't so stubborn to think that I could do everything on my own. I did agree to her offer of coming to the house later that week to tell Poli and the builders in Spanish what had happened so that they would understand, and at her absolute insistence, I reluctantly agreed to her helping me give the house a really good clean.

'But it is going to keep getting dirty every day,' I told her, 'whilst the work is still being done.'

'Of course,' Marta said, but like any Spanish woman, she insisted that it was important to have a very clean *casa* and told me that if we started the process, I could keep it up daily.

* * *

What I didn't know was that Marta also made calls to certain *amigas* in Sóller, asking them to keep an eye on me. When I went to the bank to check that there was enough money to keep the work going at the house, the Majorcan *chica* behind the counter had already prepared papers for me to sign, to open a new account of my own. Ana, my neighbour, arrived on my doorstep the very same day she returned from Madrid with a plate of roasted red peppers and freshly cooked sardines and a sympathetic look in her eye. And when I went to the local garage, the petrol attendant told me that his wife would give me a voucher to have my car cleaned for free.

The next day Marta arrived on my doorstep with her car stuffed full of cleaning products. She humped an industrial hoover from the vineyard into the hallway, along with a vast array of mops, sponges, bleach and sprays, plus vats of olive oil, lemons and other kitchen staples that she assured me had been best for certain jobs for generations. The builders were taken aback at the endless array of trips she made to her car, protesting that she was wasting her time cleaning when they still had so much dirty work to do. Poli stood up straight, brushed the tendrils of wild hair that had fallen loose from his ponytail back into place and puffed out his chest as she spoke to him. It was the smartest I'd seen him try to look. Manolo, his policeman brother, and Pepe, the fisherman, smiled respectfully, though a little goggle-eyed, at Marta as she spoke.

I squirmed as I heard her mention Harrisson's name to Poli. The two men had become good friends, and I was unsure how Poli would react to the news that he wasn't coming back. Their conversation seemed endless. Poli asked questions and shot me several sideways glances. Finally he turned to me.

'Isobel, I am sorry,' he lisped, giving me a smile. I welled up a little and swallowed hard.

'Poli is of course happy to finish the work,' Marta told me. 'He is sorry that it didn't work for you and Harrisson.'

'Is he worried about money?' I asked her. 'I've been to the bank, so I want to let him know that it's all OK.'

'*Chica*, no.' Marta smiled. 'Here, it is not so important between friends. Money comes later.' She saw that I looked uncomfortable. 'But I will tell him anyway.'

Poli shrugged and looked almost embarrassed at the mention of it.

'As long as he can pay his men, he doesn't worry,' Marta told me with a smile.

Later that day, Poli's wife peered through the open door of the house. She had brought her daughter, a bundle of tea towels and a mop, to help us clean.

'Everyone's been so kind,' I weepily told Marta on seeing them.

'It's nothing. I am sure Poli called her. That's what we do here,' she said simply, 'in Majorca.'

22

Nye, Fyi

'Izzy? It's me . . . Arabian Nights, Studio 54 or Casino Night?'

I was sitting alone, having said goodbye to the builders. I had stoked the wood-burning stove before dusk and just closed the wooden shutters at the windows to the world outside when the call had come from Remi.

She had reeled off the list at a million miles an hour, without even a hello, as I closed the door on the stove and waited for the flicker of flames to appear behind the glass.

'Sorry, you've lost me, Rem,' I admitted with a giggle.

'New's Year's Eve, of course,' she said sternly. She sounded impatient.

'Oh that!' I said with realisation, wiping my dusty hands on my jeans. 'The party.' I shuffled across the room in suede-bottomed bed socks to sit on a chair. 'I thought Massoud was taking care of it.'

'He is, but he's delegated the organising to me whilst he gets on with some post-Christmas business. He's given me a budget, use of his staff and is offering to call in the Admirable Crichton . . . '

'Who?' I asked.

'Party planners extraordinaire . . . they throw amazing elaborate events around the world for celebs; they have a By Royal Appointment . . . '

'Blimey, Remi!' I cooed. 'I thought it was going to be fairly low key. How many people are invited?'

'Izzy, you're not helping,' Remi whined, ignoring my question. 'Which theme?'

'Why do you need a theme?' I asked, pulling the chair closer to the fire. I could almost hear her stamping her tiny and immaculately heeled foot.

'Don't all the best parties have a theme? I thought you'd know. You organise weddings!' Remi said with mounting frustration before pausing. 'But then . . . it's not so different. Maybe as you do that so brilliantly, you . . . should take over the planning.'

'Oh no, no, Remi. Look, I'm no match for the Royal Admirables or whoever they are,' I protested.

'But think of the money we'd save Massoud and the fun we can have spending it ourselves,' she gushed.

I finally felt the warmth of the fire, my cheeks prickling with heat, or was it the flush of on-the-spot panic?

'Pleeeease, Izzy, pleeeease?' Remi whined again.

I looked around at my surroundings. I imagined the budget was at least ten times the amount of the entire renovation budget for the house.

'God, Remi, I've got so much to do here, and then there's the rush Celia's warned me we'll get straight after New Year — '

'But it's just what you need to take your mind off Harrisson,' she interrupted.

I had succumbed to telling friends and family, when I realised deep down that however much I'd hoped he would return, Harrisson simply wasn't coming back. Ray and Ramon had been sweet and supportive — although the relief I felt at not having to attend running club any more would have been enough — but Remi had been back on the island for days, and this was the first time she'd been in touch since I called to tell her and got her voicemail. I wasn't upset by it; it was just her, and I'd accepted our friendship for what it was long ago. It was never going to be deep and meaningful.

'Look, Rem, I'd love to help, but it's so close to New Year's Eve already, and I just don't think I can take something else on right now.'

'Sure, you're right,' she said, softening a little. 'I shouldn't have asked you.' Maybe there was a gooey centre behind that fashionista armour that I was finally tapping into after all.

'It's OK,' I said, 'but why not keep it simple? The local council here always put on fireworks so you'll see those anyway; why not have a DJ, some food and drinks . . . '

'You said there's not much time.'

'Well, those themed events with all that detail can take as long as a wedding to plan,' I assured her. 'And if you haven't got the planners booked now, won't they be busy?'

'I guess,' Remi sighed. 'Although I know Massoud pulls strings. I just wanted to do something fabulous for him at the end of my stay. He's been very sweet and generous.'

'Sounds like someone is quite taken,' I teased her in a sing-song voice.

'You know me better than that, Izzy. After this stay we might not even see each other again. I just want to do the right and polite thing,' Remi said. I wondered if it was true. 'Well, best I get on with the damn thing,' she continued, changing the subject, and we said our goodbyes.

I hung up the phone and opened the door of the stove, poking at the dusty logs with a stick to get the fire racing before adding another. As I bent down to the woven basket on the tiled floor, I thought of Ray and how much he'd loved the tiles when he saw them on our first trip to see the house. And then I remembered what he'd told me about Ramon and Massoud, and gulped.

'Remi?' I heard myself say as she answered my speed dial. 'If you don't end up getting the planners and you promise to keep it simple, I'll help.' I'd figured that after all the help the neighbours and Marta had given me, I should really offer.

★ ★ ★

Early the next morning, just as it was growing light and I was sipping my first coffee of the day, Paco rapped on the door. He stood sweetly on the pavement in the peagreen cashmere jumper that usually provoked a quip from Harrisson that our neighbours were spending the money from the house sale, a smile on his face. From his side he stretched out a hand clutching a carrier bag brimming with oranges. The small, plump and brightly coloured fruit that was ripe on the trees in Sóller. He nodded for me to take the bag, insisting that they were all for me, telling me about his trees and declining my offer of coffee and to come inside.

'*Vamos a ir a Palma!*' he said, announcing his trip to the city as Ana pulled up in their new car. She was waving a '*bon dia*' from the driver's seat, signalling Paco's cue to join her.

'*Bon dia, Ana!*' I shouted back. '*Muchas gracias por los naranjas.*'

'*De nada!*' she smiled as Paco climbed obediently into the passenger's seat. I felt guilt for having doubted my neighbours when we'd first taken on the house. They were so generous and kind. I blushed, thinking of the incidents that must have been little more than cultural confusion.

The air outside was deliciously fresh, the weak winter sun straining to warm the valley beneath a clear sky. I stood for a moment and took in the view of the church. As I was about to close the front door, I spotted a familiar figure walking along the roadside towards the house. It was Tomas. He raised one arm and waved.

'Hope you don't mind me arriving unannounced,' he said apologetically as he reached the open door.

'Of course not.' I smiled. 'I hope you don't mind the noise.' Poli and the guys were working one of their few days between now and Reyes, which followed New Year's Eve. I hadn't a clue what they were doing, but I figured it was the last of the heavy-duty work on the top floor.

Tomas pushed his glasses up over the bridge of his nose, the way he did sometimes when he was nervous. He hadn't been to the house before and I wasn't sure if Marta had told him about Harrisson. I'd been waiting to tell Celia myself, when I went back to work in the New Year. She wasn't the long phone-call type.

'So . . . how was your Christmas?' I asked, breaking the silence as I signalled for him to come inside. 'Coffee? Or an orange?' I offered, Paco's bag of fruit still in my hand.

'Izzy, there's no need to pretend,' Tomas said, reaching a hand out and placing it on my arm. 'Marta told me what happened. I thought you might need a bit of help . . . with the builders.'

'Oh,' I said, dropping my gaze, embarrassed. I turned away from him and placed the bag of oranges on the workman's table. 'Well that's really kind, but I think everything's fine. They seem to be on schedule as far as I can tell and doing a good job — '

'I thought you'd insist everything was fine if I called,' Tomas interrupted, 'which is why I thought it best to come in person.' As I turned around again to look at him, a smile had travelled across his face. He knew me better than I'd thought.

I smiled back. 'Sure, but really, Poli's been great, I couldn't trust anyone more . . . '

'Certainly looks impressive,' Tomas said, his eyes wandering around the large entrance hall. 'Handsome house you've got, isn't it?'

'Thanks,' I said sheepishly, 'it is.' It still felt strange someone referring to the house as mine, and although I had calculated that I could finish the work, I doubted that I could afford to live there afterwards.

Poli came downstairs to fill his rubber bucket with water and stopped with a start on seeing Tomas. His body language was uncertain as I introduced the men, and softened only slightly when Tomas spoke to him in Catalan. From understanding nothing, I could just make out when the conversation moved on a few minutes later to a list of jobs that Poli and the team still had to tackle. Finally Poli lead Tomas around the house, to show him proudly what they'd done to date. I wandered through to the kitchen and put a fresh pot of coffee on the stove as I heard work stop on the top floor for the impromptu inspection.

'Poli's certainly got things under control,' Tomas confirmed when all the men re-appeared in the dusty and unfinished kitchen. I passed Poli a cup of coffee, just how I knew he liked it, and gave him an appreciative grin as Tomas translated what he'd said. Poli blushed slightly, bringing the coffee cup to his lips, dry with building dust.

I poured coffee for Manolo and Pepe and finally passed a cup to Tomas, as the others took theirs back upstairs to work. I'd tried to insist they take a break, but Poli wouldn't have it.

As the sound of the men's boots and rowdy banter subsided, Tomas turned to me.

'It's going to be OK, you know,' he said softly. It was a side to him that I'd not seen before and it took me by surprise. 'You've got good people around you, Izzy.'

'I know,' I said honestly. 'If this had all happened in London, things would have been pretty tough and very different . . . '

'Probably just different,' he said. 'You have people who love you there too, remember.' His blue eyes were as soft as his words.

'Look, you're covered in dust!' I said to him, deliberately changing the subject and patting his shirt sleeve. 'Sorry, it's impossible not to get filthy here,' I said apologetically. Closer now, I looked up at his warm, open face.

'I have an overwhelming desire to give you a brotherly hug,' he admitted, and as he wrapped me up in those familiar arms, forearms still lightly tanned from hours in the garden, crisp shirt sleeves pushed up beneath a woollen tank top that felt rich and warm on my cheek, there was a part of me that couldn't help but wish that he hadn't used the word 'brotherly'. I dismissed the feeling as me being overemotional and stood up straight again.

'Thanks,' I said, a little flushed and awkward.

'Gosh, no problem at all,' he said, with a look on his face that seemed to mirror mine. Finally he cleared his throat. 'Poli said that two weeks after Reyes, the guys will just need a few days snagging, you know, doing all the finishing touches. Then you'll be able to start painting.'

'I didn't know you were good with this kind of thing,' I said honestly.

'Well, in the absence of Father, I organised Celia's house renovation when she first came to the island, and before that, her Chelsea flat in London,' Tomas said frankly. 'And I've learnt to be pretty self-sufficient, over the years.'

'So you can give me some painting tips, then?' I smiled.

'Tip number one is that you couldn't possibly do all of this yourself,' Tomas said frankly, looking at the high ceilings. 'These are large rooms and there are too many of them. I would suggest a painting party.'

'Doesn't sound like a great kind of party to me.' I laughed.

'Marta will help us organise it,' he said. 'I'm sure of it.' And with that, I knew it was likely that they'd already discussed it.

'You two are too much.' I smiled. 'More coffee?'

'Thanks, but best I get going. I need to pick up a paper from the botanical gardens before the library closes.'

'OK. It was really sweet of you to drop by,' I said sincerely. 'I appreciate it.'

'You know any time you need me, or Celia, call, or just come over to the house . . . '

'I will, thanks.' I smiled.

'Everything's fine, Izzy,' he said, kissing my cheeks in the Spanish way. 'Everything's fine.'

* * *

'What about that guy over there? The Latino, on the bar stool. He's cute. No, not cute, *hot*. Actually, maybe too hot . . . looks like he's part of my team rather than yours, from the cut of that jacket . . . '

Ray was trying to fix me up in a bar in Palma as we waited for Remi to show. I'd promised her we'd discuss plans for the party and thought it would be good to hook up Remi and Ray again.

'I don't need another guy right now, Ray,' I sighed. 'That's the last thing I need. Something complicated.'

'We could find you English eye candy, if you're worried about the language . . . '

'That's not what I meant.' I laughed. Ray was making eyes at the guy. 'You're unstoppable now you have this open relationship with Ramon,' I teased him.

Ray drew his attention away for long enough to nod to the bartender and place an order for another round of drinks. I leaned back in the red crushed-velvet banquette and stifled a yawn.

'God, Izz,' Ray chided me with a twinkle in his eye. 'Now that you're a sad old spinster in Sóller, you crash before the party's even started.'

I nudged him in the ribs. 'I have to be up to let the builders in at seven every morning,' I protested.

It had just gone nine and the bar, situated in Santa Catalina — the restaurant quarter of the city — was gently simmering with pre-dinner drinkers, Spanish couples meeting before going out to dinner, larger groups of international twenty- and thirty-somethings nibbling tapas, bags of shopping around their feet. The shops outside were full of goodies for Spanish Christmas. Inside, the voices were loud above the music and the decor was cocooning. Deep rich velvets, gilt mirrors and a black floor, with a hint of flamenco to the styling.

'*Gracias.*' I nodded at the waiter, who laid down two serviettes beneath two glasses of wine, and finally a glass dish of cashews.

'Shouldn't we get a bottle?' a voice said from behind him. It was Remi.

'Darling!' Ray announced, standing up to air-kiss.

I confirmed the bottle with the waiter, along with an extra glass, and stood up to give Remi a light hug.

'Dramatic,' Remi said, looking around approvingly. 'Kinda Almodóvar. And cute guy on the bar stool over there.'

'Yes, we've seen him,' we replied, almost in unison.

'And Ray has already added him to his list.' I smiled as the waiter returned with the wine and an ice bucket, and poured Remi a glass.

'So, the party,' Remi started, getting down to business. She was still taking off a pale grey cashmere coat topped with what I thought, with a wince, was probably a real fur collar. Beneath it she was wearing tweed shorts with buff suede peep-toe platform ankle boots and a silk chiffon cream blouse. Her bare mocha legs had a flawless sheen; her signature bob was even more impossibly glossy than I'd remembered it. She held out the coat to the waiter without giving him so much as a glance, and he politely took it.

'Yes, the party,' Ray echoed excitedly. 'Fabulous. Izzy's told me about the yacht, sounds fierce. I love the idea that you have all of this money to lavish . . . '

'Oh, I'm taking it very seriously,' she replied matter-of-factly, and from a cherry-red crocodile Hermès Kelly bag pulled out an artist's sketchpad.

Having studied fashion, Remi could draw. Her pencil sketches for the party were beautiful, although I couldn't help but smirk at how the first five pages had been devoted to drawings of a backless crêpe jumpsuit with a halter neck and wide pants that she was obviously hoping to wear. Ray spotted it instantly.

'Uhhh,' he gasped loudly. 'So seventies Halston. Love it! Are you having it run up?'

'Well, I do have to visit Massoud's tailor for his suit, so I thought, why not?' Remi replied.

Ray nudged me playfully under the table. 'Why don't you have them made for all the waitresses and get them all to wear Remi bob wigs, then you can always be the perfect hostess, tending to everyone's whims?' he suggested lavishly. Despite the nudge, he seemed serious. It was the start of a conversation that grew increasingly elaborate as the wine flowed. Ray encouraged Remi with her wild ideas and elaborate plans, and I found myself being the party-pooper, reining them in, being realistic due to time, logistics and what was physically possible for us to fix in just a few days.

'OK, Izz, so if you're saying it's a fire hazard for us to all light Chinese lanterns and watch them float across the water at midnight, what about fireworks of our own? Maybe in a single chic colour?' Ray said. 'Remi, what's the new black?'

'It's not legal on the island. You have to apply for a licence. And anyway, there will be the ones the council supply over the cathedral and Maritimo, so it would be a waste,' I interrupted.

'How about Cirque de Soleil, dancing from the masts of the yacht whilst the fireworks go off?' he suggested, on a roll.

'Don't you think they'll be booked for New Year's, darling?' Remi quizzed.

'Small point, the boat doesn't have masts,' I reminded them. Ray and I roared with laughter.

By the end of the evening, as Ray turned

our third bottle upside down in the ice bucket, and the bar looked set to close, Remi had a plan.

'Now I'm excited,' she cooed, clapping perfectly manicured hands together, nails painted, I noticed, a matt shade of chinchilla grey. 'Just the guest list to refine and we can get the official invites out. Most people were emailed or Facebooked months ago.'

'So I take it I should keep the evening free?' Ray said hopefully.

'Of course!' Remi confirmed. 'I thought it was a given. And bring whoever you like. Are you seeing someone right now?'

Ray shot me a look and we fell silent. Remi didn't seem to notice and moved on.

'Izzy, I can't thank you enough. So you'll sort the caterers and the florist and the band?'

'Of course, Rem. I do it daily, it's no great shakes to me. And the DJ, really, it's fine. And you'll talk to the bar crew on the yacht about supplies, glasses, plates, ice . . . '

'Yes, seems simplest,' she confirmed.

'So who else is invited?' Ray asked excitedly. 'Celebrities? The rich and famous?'

'If I told you, darling Ray,' said Remi discreetly, 'there would be no surprises to come.'

Ray sighed wistfully. 'Well, if there's

nothing juicy left to discuss, we should settle the bill.'

'I need to get a cab to Sóller,' I agreed. 'It's getting late.'

'I thought you'd want to come clubbing!' Remi said.

'Tempting,' Ray chimed, 'but I have Ramon all to myself tonight at the apartment.'

'Let's save it for the party,' I agreed.

Outside, Ray grabbed my arm in his and took Remi's on his other side. At almost midnight, the restaurants were still busy and European house pumped from a doorway that led to a basement club.

'Ladies, we'll hail a cab for Izzy, then I'll walk you to the boat, Rem.'

We nodded in agreement.

As we turned the corner of the street, a couple up ahead caught my eye. A tall guy, helping a beautiful-looking Spanish girl into a coat as they left a fusion restaurant. I looked again as he put his arm around her shoulders. The hair, the straight-legged jeans, the smart blazer. It was him, I could see as light from a street lamp caught the side of his face. Tomas.

'Isn't that . . . ?' Ray started, as sharp as always.

'Celia's son Tomas, yes,' I told him. 'I think it is. You have a good memory,' I added, remembering a night we'd all gone clubbing last summer.

'But it looks like he's dating a babe,' Ray said with an element of disbelief.

'Yes, it does,' I agreed, unable to take my eyes off them, 'doesn't it?'

In the taxi, the white Christmas lights that decorated the city flashed by my window. I watched the familiar landmarks pass, the shop fronts with their twinkling displays and the Corte Ingles flagship store wrapped in a huge red bow, and told myself it was silly to feel jealous. I was just being overemotional, surely, after everything that had happened with Harrisson. Wasn't I?

23

Omg!

Although Celia and I had agreed that we wouldn't set foot in the office until after the holidays, I found myself at her house the very next day.

'I have gifts from London,' I announced cheerily, as Celia opened the door that morning and Pepillo bolted outside, his tiny body clattering between my legs and the door as he did so. 'I didn't think it would be very English to wait to give them to you at Reyes.' I beamed.

I'd called Celia early, after the builders had arrived, having made myself a simple breakfast of juice, bread and jam, the bread still warm from the store around the corner, the juice from Paco's sweet Sóller *naranjas*. The best thing, I figured, for a mildly fuzzy head.

'I just called to see how you are,' I told Celia. 'I'm sorry I didn't ring as soon as I got back from England, but, well, things have been — '

'Tomas mentioned you've had a difficult

time, but didn't go into detail, of course,' Celia kindly interjected, 'but if you want to talk about it . . . ?'

'Oh no, it's not that, I just wanted to tell you in person and find out about your Christmas . . . and how you are.'

'So how is everything at the house?' she asked, changing the subject expertly away from her health.

'Good, really good, it's taking shape,' I said positively. 'And I have a party to help organise to take my mind off everything else and give some of our contractors extra work.'

'Really? Not moonlighting, Isabelle, I hope!'

'Of course not!' I laughed. 'It's for my friend Remi. She's throwing a big New Year's Eve party on a yacht and has roped me in, no pun intended.'

'Well, dear,' Celia said frankly, 'why don't you come over today? Really this period between Christmas and New Year is just too dull. Tomas is insisting I rest, but it would be lovely to see you and you can use the office to make your calls. I'm sure that kind of thing can't be easy from a building site.'

'I'd love to,' I said excitedly. 'As long as you're sure I'm not interrupting anything?'

'If only, dear,' Celia quipped.

Shortly after putting down the receiver, I

had got myself together and sped over to the other side of the island.

Now I was waiting in Celia's sitting room as she indulged in her elaborate tea-making ritual in the kitchen. As always, the room, like its owner, was immaculate. The only thing that had changed since my last visit was a distinct thinning of the beautifully wrapped gifts beneath the exquisitely decorated tree. I perched slightly awkwardly, as usual, on Celia's spotless cream sofa. A cashmere throw the colour of toffee was folded over the footstool in front of Celia's chair, beside which she carefully placed a tray with bone handles, dressed with a silver tea service and Oriental patterned china.

'Thank goodness for some fresh company,' she sighed, pouring the Darjeeling. 'That's a little naughty of me I suppose, as Tomas has been wonderful,' she added a little guiltily, 'but there's something about female company that you just can't beat.'

'I know what you mean.' I smiled. It was good to see Celia, and this was her way of telling me that she felt the same.

That morning we caught up on our news. I told her about Harrisson, and she nodded her chic blond ponytail in sympathy. She didn't ask questions, she just listened. To lighten the mood we swapped Christmas stories and shared funny tales of disastrous gifts, inedible Christmas dinners and badly behaved relatives from our personal archives. It was only as the light reached the highest point of the day, beaming down across the valley into Celia's windows, that I realised that it must be nearing lunchtime.

'Your gift!' I remembered suddenly. 'Will you open yours now and I'll pop Tomas's under the tree?'

'I'm never one to turn down a generous gesture!' Celia agreed.

The wrapping paper was crumpled from travelling in my suitcase, the bow creased in all of the wrong places, but Celia smiled gratefully as I handed her the present. She unwrapped it slowly and delicately, finally unravelling layers of tissue paper before holding up the delicate scarf to the light.

'Liberty print, how thoughtful,' she said. 'Silk too, that's really very kind.' She tied the scarf in a gentle bow around her neck. The colours were soft against her skin.

'You're welcome, Celia,' I said, delighted that she was so taken with it.

'I really wasn't expecting us to exchange gifts,' she replied, obviously embarrassed that she didn't have something for me in return.

'Oh, you've been so good to me,' I said honestly, 'and it's only a little something.'

There was a moment of awkward silence.

'I've just remembered your calls,' Celia said, getting up from her chair to clear away the tea things. 'Would you like another cup to take up with you?'

'No, I'm fine,' I said watching her move. She still looked a little shaky to me as she carried the tray out to the kitchen, but I knew she wouldn't hear of me helping her or entertain any questions about her health. Maybe it would take a little time for her to get back to being strong again.

Upstairs, the office was bathed in pale, buttery afternoon light. Celia's desk was clear of work and free of clutter, a single item, her leather diary, perfectly centred to the side of her old-fashioned phone. I tried to ignore the computer at my own desk, covered in bright Post-it notes, with memos and messages I'd written to myself, and shuffled the papers I'd left askew, along with the notepads and files, into a single neat pile. I pulled back the familiar chair and sat down, enjoying the quiet and order that I didn't yet have at home.

'Right, Remi,' I mumbled to myself, fishing in my handbag for the notes I'd made.

I looked up at the computer again. What if Harrisson had sent me an email? I dismissed the thought. If he had wanted to get in touch, he would have sent a text, I told myself as my finger hovered momentarily over the start key. I pulled it away.

I rifled through my box file of contact cards for the names and numbers I needed. I called Lorenzo, the florist I had in mind for Remi, and ordered her flowers. She wanted a palette of deep violets, the darkest rouge noir red and other shades that were almost but not quite black. Lorenzo loved the concept.

'My God, darling,' he drawled, 'how chic! Your client sounds very Gothica . . . and with cash too!' I giggled at the thought. Lorenzo had lavish ideas, reeling off designs, the Latin names for the blooms, and assuring me that despite the holiday season, a certain supplier in Germany would have no problem flying everything over. 'We just give him a little extra incentive,' he told me, 'from the budget.' He was excited about his Gothica client, and providing 'something a leetle different', rather than more 'white, white, white flowers for another big boat'.

I thought better of calling Arnaud, the DJ, before much later in the afternoon, but tried the caterers, hoping they wouldn't be working on an event for the season. I heard footsteps coming towards the otherwise silent office as Cati answered the line, and Pepillo came bounding into the office, skidding slightly on the highly polished floor before jumping on to my lap.

When I looked up, Tomas was standing in the doorway. I waved and mouthed a hello and continued with my conversation. He tried to quietly call the dog, but Pepillo had no intention of moving. He had managed to get himself comfortable on my lap and I couldn't protest without sounding unprofessional to Cati. It was as if he knew. Tomas shrugged a sorry and I looked down at my merino wool sweater, already coated in tiny black hairs. He smiled, amused as the dog wriggled, his claws scratching at my jeans to find an even more perfect spot. As I hung up the phone, Tomas let out a laugh.

'You two have always had a love-hate thing going on, haven't you?'

I smiled back, raising my brows, and picked up the mutt by his sausage-shaped body. He made himself heavy and stiff in protest, as I carefully put his paws to the floor.

'Something like that. Hi, Tomas,' I said in mock disdain.

He came over and perched on the corner of my desk.

'I didn't expect to see you,' he said, looking glad that I was there.

'I've promised to help Remi organise a party on her boyfriend's boat for New Year,' I explained. 'Celia insisted I make the calls from here.'

'And you had no intention of checking up on her, of course?' he mocked.

'Wouldn't dream of it.' I smiled innocently.

'Well, it seems like a good time to tell you that she's had the all-clear,' Tomas said, dropping his voice to a near whisper.

'She has?' I asked, feeling my heart swell with relief as I clasped my hands together. 'What did the tests say?'

'That it was a heart murmur,' Tomas continued, his face falling more serious as he drew closer to me, to reduce even the slightest risk of her hearing. 'She's fine, but the doctors have warned that she needs to start seriously looking after herself to avoid any future problems.'

'Well that is good news,' I whispered back with a smile. 'And if there's anything — '

'Well yes, there is,' Tomas interrupted, as though he'd already given it much thought. 'You can help me to keep an eye on her. Make sure she doesn't take on too much with the weddings next season. You know Celia, she won't give in to this. We need to be a team,' he concluded conspiratorially. I looked up at his face full of concern and instinctively reached for his arm to reassure him.

'Of course, it goes without saying,' I told

him, gently rubbing the crisp cotton shirt sleeve, trying to conjure a smile. It didn't work. 'So, team captain,' I announced, back in my normal voice, remembering the purpose of my visit, 'I've brought you a present.'

'Me? Did you?' Tomas said, his blue eyes wide with surprise.

'Yup. I'll get it, it's downstairs under the tree.'

Tomas waited in the office as Pepillo followed me downstairs to the sitting room. With Celia nowhere to be seen, I carefully pulled out the present from beneath the tree and headed back to the office. Tomas had made himself comfortable in Celia's chair. I went over to the desk and handed him the gift.

'Sorry, you can see it travelled from England,' I said apologetically.

Tomas pulled at the paper and smiled widely at seeing the gardening set inside, leaping up to give me a bear hug. I laughed, taken aback by his response, before nestling momentarily in the warmth of it, nuzzling my nose into his chest, breathing in his warm soapy smell.

'Thanks, Izzy,' he said softly. 'For this . . . and you know . . . with Celia.' I looked up at hearing his voice, and his eyes, deep and blue behind his glasses, fixed on mine. He drew closer to me, slowly, as if wanting to study something he couldn't quite focus on. Finally, as his nose softly brushed against mine, I could feel his breath warm on my lips.

As we kissed, Pepillo barked and jumped up at Tomas. I giggled. 'He thinks you're attacking me,' I mumbled after moments of drowning in his pillow-soft mouth.

'Shhh,' Tomas said, his lips only briefly away from mine, his hand at the curve of my lower back. 'Ignore him.'

'Celia will wonder . . . ' I started.

'Celia has gone to visit our neighbour,' Tomas told me with a mischievous twinkle in his eye.

★ ★ ★

'Ray? It's me.'

'Izzy? Are you driving? Hang up, you crazy woman, and call me later.'

'I can't. I'm in shock,' I replied. I was on the Via Cintura, the motorway that was the quickest route away from Celia's house.

'Izzy, pull over. Look, you're not the kind of driver who's adept enough to multitask, shock or no shock.'

I knew Ray was right. I'd been cut up by two drivers whilst attempting to call him and finally swerved at the last minute to take the next exit to the coast. I parked the car where the path descended to the sea. The beach below was deserted. I sat for a minute with my hands on the steering wheel and willed myself to move. I finally shut the car door behind me, pulled up the collar of my jacket against the breeze and took in a gulp of sea air, determined to take a minute to think.

My mobile buzzed in my pocket. It was Ray calling me back.

'OK, Mistry, what's the skinny?'

'Oh, it's silly, you'll laugh,' I said, pausing to look out to sea. 'I kissed Tomas.'

'Really?' Ray squealed. 'Were you starved of sex with Harrisson for months before he left?'

'No,' I giggled. 'It just happened.'

'What? In daylight? Sounds a bit risqué for our botanist. I'd have put money on him being a lights-out, pyjamas-on type, even for a kiss.'

I laughed again nervously.

'OK, just spare me the hetero details, sister. I have a delicate stomach.'

'I know it's nothing really . . . but I don't know what to do,' I said quietly.

'You don't need to do anything,' Ray told me. 'He'll know you're just on the rebound from Harrisson, and in a way it had to happen sooner or later. Anyway, didn't we see him out with another *señorita* last night?' He paused. 'Really, don't worry about it. Look, I've got to go. I'm off to lunch with Ramon's family, we're already late.'

'Of course, sorry, Ray, you should have said.'

'No I shouldn't. Love you, mmmwhaah,' he said, signing off. 'Call later if you need to talk.'

As I put my mobile along with my hand in my pocket, I heard a voice behind me.

'Izzy?' It was Tomas.

'How did you know I was here?' I asked, blushing like a schoolgirl and brushing away the tendrils of hair that had come free from my scraped-back ponytail.

'A hunch,' he said, looking down at me, smiling. 'I thought you might need a drink,' he offered, pulling a pewter hip flask from his jacket.

I took the flask and had a swig. Whisky, warm and smooth.

'I didn't think real people had these,' I said, marvelling at the object as we continued to walk. 'They've always seemed a bit fictional really.'

'Isabelle Mistry,' Tomas said gently, 'stop changing the subject.'

I turned to him and smiled.

'I was worried you might be in a panic,' he said. I looked up at him.

'Me? No, of course not,' I replied, without conviction. 'It was only a kiss . . . '

'Exactly,' said Tomas, 'and I shouldn't have, Izzy, I'm sorry.'

24

Release the stars

'Remi, hi!' I gasped, leaning in to a lithe bare back, a single black pearl clasp holding together the Halston-inspired halterneck jumpsuit at the nape of her neck, just beneath that trademark bob.

'Sorry,' the elegant figure apologised in a thick Spanish accent as she spun around. 'Last time I see Remi, she is at bar, at other end of the boat,' the girl continued in staccato English, pointing with one hand as the other artfully balanced a silver tray of cocktails.

I smiled awkwardly at Ray and Ramon as we each grabbed a martini glass.

Ray was wearing a narrow-cut sixties-style suit and was fussing with the hand-painted McQueen silk scarf that he'd draped across it. It was a piece I'd have dreamt of borrowing constantly back in Notting Hill.

'I suggested that with so many guests, Remi needed an army of mini-Remi hostesses to take care of everyone,' he elaborated proudly to Ramon, our eyes scouring the deck. On closer inspection, we could pick out at least twenty Remi waitresses in identical jumpsuits and black bobbed wigs amongst the hordes.

'And it is deliberate, no, that they are all skinny and beautiful?' Ramon quizzed.

'Of course!' Ray stressed. 'She would *never* have had a fat or acne-ridden Remi-a-like, darling. I'm sure they're all models . . . '

It was still early, and whilst the real Remi was nowhere to be seen, her impeccable New Year's Eve party was already in full swing. We stood for a moment, taking in the scene.

Lady Mistral was looking her finest. The vast swimming pool on one deck had been drained to create a dance floor for later on in the evening, and to warm up the party DJ Arnaud's 'Brazilian Carnival Tunes' floated across the water from his decks. The Remi waitresses weaved through the crowds offering canapés, cocktails and cava. We stood watching them sashay their way from the bar, where a sleight-of-hand magician held guests captivated, to a chill-out area where the seating areas at the back of the boat had been swathed in sequinned cushions. They followed the lanterns that lit the way to a second chill-out zone dominated by a black-framed four-poster bed draped with grape-coloured organza that billowed in the breeze, and then catwalked their way to the sleek black marble bar beyond it, where they restocked their trays as the barmen made an elaborate show of creating the Flame Daquiris, Pomegranates and Oriental Ginger Martinis from Remi's cocktail menu. From the rear of the deck, it was possible to peer into the interior of the boat, where the endless sitting room had been transformed into a cinema filled with floor cushions and silver helium balloons. A vast digital projector was showing a bizarre-looking Andy Warhol movie. Towards the bar at the back, a glamorous croupier entertained a serious-looking set of men smoking fat cigars at a blackjack table. Just as Remi had wanted, each of the areas was lavishly adorned with towering displays of Lorenzo's rouge noir flowers, and candlelight flickered across the black water of the port. Beyond, the cathedral was lit up majestically in golden light, as the trees surrounding it twinkled with simple white bulbs in their branches.

'*Que un fiesta!*' Ramon sighed in awe, breaking our silence and lighting a cigarette. Within seconds a waiter was by his side offering him a small silver ashtray, whilst Ray had already broken away to chase a cuter-looking *camarero* for a second cocktail.

'How did you create so much in just a few days?' Ramon asked.

'Oh, it's easy when you have the contacts

and it's your day job,' I assured him, blushing a little.

Out of habit, I was already running through a mental audit of the details of the party, mesmerised by the beautiful people and straining my eyes to try to spot the authentic Remi in the mêlée.

'Izzy?' a voice asked as Ramon disappeared to find Ray. 'Izzy, I'd like you to meet Inma, Inma, Isabelle.'

I looked up to see Tomas standing next to a girl I recognised as the beautiful Spanish *chica* we'd seen him with in Palma. It took a moment for the realisation to set in. He'd brought a date. A beautiful date. I felt my face spontaneously drop.

'*Encantada.*' Inma smiled with molten chocolate-brown eyes, leaning forward to kiss me on both cheeks. She was even prettier up close than I'd imagined, her graceful frame draped in a simple pewter-grey dress with elegant ruby-red shoes and clutch, her long hair loose around the stole that was draped to reveal a glimpse of lightly tanned shoulders.

I stood silently, stunned and feeling awkward in the heels that Remi had insisted on lending me. They were already pinching and I couldn't help but wish I'd fake-tanned my lily-white and slightly podgy post-Christmas limbs, yet something more than fabulously evil footwear had me glued to the spot. I knew I should be polite, smile and spark up conversation with Inma, but I just couldn't bring myself to do it. I gulped. I was jealous.

'Inma is the new head of the botanical society here,' Tomas explained, breaking the silence, his eyes bright behind his glasses. 'She's been helping me with my paper.'

'*Encantada*, Inma,' I sighed as warmly as I could above the music. Beautiful *botanist* date, I registered inwardly. Great. They'd have so much in common.

'We must get you two a drink,' I offered, looking around for the next waitress, desperate for a distraction that could lead to an excuse to leave.

'Three,' Tomas corrected me.

'Sorry?' I asked, my face still turned away, my eyes still searching the sea of guests for a Remi-a-like.

'Get the three of us a drink, although four if you would like one yourself . . . ' I gave Tomas a quizzical, sideways glance. 'Inma's husband is here somewhere too,' he continued. I turned back to face him, a smile of relief passing uncontrollably across my face. 'He's a keen gardener, just spotted someone he knows in the crowd,' he added, his eyes now looking mischievously into mine.

I felt the colour return to my cheeks and took a deep breath. He knew. It was obvious by the way he smiled back at me. A wide smile that lit up his whole face as he rambled on about how famously he thought Inma's husband and I would get on. He'd caught me out, and despite the polite nonsense he was mumbling, his eyes — intense and never once slipping from peering deeply into mine — seemed to suggest that he was happy that he had. I finally broke his gaze and looked to the floor, then up to a perplexed-looking Inma, before mumbling an embarrassed excuse to leave.

As I walked away, I told myself that I did, after all, still have Remi to find. There were plans to polish and I felt duty-bound to ensure the event went without a hitch. I couldn't imagine how she was coping.

The party was densely packed, perfume heady in the air, the atmosphere already alive with the anticipation of the new year. An older Spanish lady draped in fur and surrounded by Latino boys half her age spilt ash from a foot-long cigarette holder into the cocktail glass of a well-known pop star. Oblivious, the singer knocked back his drink, enthralled by a beautiful girl dressed as a pirate, an African Grey parrot chiding him in Spanish from her shoulder. A girl dancing a salsa in a thigh-skimming minidress with one guy slipped a business card into the jacket of another as the parrot squawked. As I wove past them, holding my drink high in the air, I saw a magician wow a crowd by slicing a melon in two with a carefully thrown playing card. A group of young *señoritas* protested as their party outfits were sprayed with a thin mist of juice from the fruit as the rest of the crowd applauded. Chiselled Latino boys howled with laughter from afar, before becoming enraptured once more by a group of well-known British models languishing on a chill-out bed. Still no Remi! I avoided the offer of a drink from an overly smooth Latino three times my age and ducked past a group of Spanish footballers playing a drinking game at the bar. Finally, exhausted by the scene, I spotted the steps up to the flight deck, and took them, hoping to get a better view from which to spy Remi.

As I reached the top of the steps, I heard laughter and, quite clearly, Massoud's voice.

'Isabelle,' he drawled languidly on seeing me. He was surrounded by a hand-picked crowd that included two well-known Hollywood actresses I had thought were 'frenemies' and a supermodel, along with various impeccably dressed and beautiful people. I could see Massoud making a polite excuse before quickly weaving his way over to kiss me on both cheeks.

'Thank you for helping Remi. The party, it's wonderful.' He smiled, his hand on my waist and his eyes a little hazy. Before I could answer, Remi was by his side.

'Izz,' she cooed, a glass of pink champagne clutched by glittering black nails, 'it's going so well!'

Remi was wearing an almost identical jumpsuit to her clones, yet hers was embellished with an additional string of black pearls that cascaded down her back and ended at hotpants, which she'd teamed with impossibly high peep-toe platforms. Her eyes were framed with the smokiest make-up as she fluttered false lashes from just beneath her fringe.

'You like it?' she laughed, seeing me clock her outfit.

'Fabulous,' I reassured her. 'But I didn't know you'd decided to go with Ray's idea.'

'Why not?' she said, throwing her head back. 'Massoud *loved* the concept when I told him.'

'I can imagine.' I smiled.

'So, you found the VIP area,' she continued. 'It was such a last-minute addition to the plans I didn't get a chance to tell you. I didn't have RSVPs until an hour or two ago from these guys, but thankfully we have two helipads,' she explained. I stood a little dumbfounded. There was a part of me that had a very uncool urge to wave at both Gwyneth and Kate. Recognising them so clearly from the pages of *Grazia* and knowing so many tabloid details about their lives, I almost felt as though I knew them personally.

'Izzy?' Remi asked. I was still staring.

'Uh? Oh, yes, I thought I'd better find you to check everything's OK', I said, pulling myself together.

'You know,' she said, taking the final sip from her glass, 'why don't you join us and just have fun? We've done enough work and I'm over worrying. It's New Year's Eve, for Christ's sake,' she whispered. 'Time to party.'

With the mention of the P word, Ray and Ramon appeared at the top of the steps, Ray's eyes wide like a kid in a candy store as he clocked Remi's hidden-away guests. He dragged Ramon by the arm and marched him over to the seated crowd, who were engrossed in conversation, bursting through the scene with an extraordinarily loud and squealing 'HIIIIIIIIIII!'

I pulled a face at Remi and she shrugged, brushing off his reaction as nonchalantly as her guests. Yet I couldn't help but see the rather awkward look on Massoud's face as

Ramon watched Ray make his introductions and go goey over the girl's shoes. I didn't have the heart to tell Remi the real story about Massoud and Ramon, not on her big night.

'Izzy, the staff have made up the suites. Bono cancelled, so I have one spare, if you want to stay.'

'Me have Bono's suite?' I gasped. 'I couldn't!' Remi's personal waiter came over to top up her glass with Cristal and offer a fresh flute to me. 'That's too much.'

'Rubbish.' Remi smiled. 'It's the least I can do as a thank you . . . What if I tell you that the skylight is retractable? Flick a switch and you can sleep under the stars.'

'Sounds amazing . . . and that's really kind, Rem,' I cooed. 'But I — '

'That's settled then,' she concluded.

The next hour and a half-floated by in a haze. I obeyed Remi's order to go off duty and let the party take care of itself. From the flight deck the Remi clones seemed to be looking after everything perfectly as the party below swelled in size. The security guard at the foot of the boat radioed a second guard, now placed in Remi's VIP area, and within moments an American rapper, draped in a white fur coat, diamonds and an impressive entourage, took over the only remaining space. Ray, Remi and I read that as our cue to head down to the dance floor, leaving Ramon deep in conversation with a fledgling Spanish actress and Massoud engrossed in business banter over a box of Havana cigars.

After a battle to reach it, the dance floor was already heaving. Still clutching our champagne flutes, we shimmied into the middle, brushing past a guy dressed as a Galliano-inspired sailor dancing with a Twiggy lookalike, big sixties earrings swaying as she broke into a go-go, despite the Latin beats. Moments later, Ray and Remi were gone. The crowd seemed to have closed in, and despite the height of my treacherous heels, it was impossible to see which way was out.

Standing alone, just for a moment, as the party continued to spin by, I had an uncontrollable desire to find Tomas. Before I had a chance to think about which direction to start looking in, a Latino guy took my hand unexpectedly to salsa. He was good-looking, smiling, whispering to me in Spanish. It was too much fun not to join in, if only for a second. I tried my best to follow his moves, my hips rocking to the beat, him laughing and leading me to the edge of the floor. At the end of the second track, I took my cue to move on. Without a watch I could only guess that it was close to eleven thirty, and I decided that a good place to start my search for Tomas was the bar.

The first boat in the port let off a flare, and Remi's fire-eater started his routine at the very end of the ship's bow. I studied the figures of the guests as they turned to face the spectacle, in the hope of spying Tomas.

'Just twenty minutes,' an English guy leaned in to tell me as I glanced hopefully into the sea of faces, 'and from here, we'll have the best view of the fireworks across the bay.'

'Girlfriend,' I heard Ray say as he stood before us, 'what happened to you?' He eyed the overfriendly barfly with curiosity, and the guy turned away.

'I lost you,' I said, my eyes still surveying the crowds.

'Looks like I interrupted someone hitting on you. Should I apologise?' Ray fished.

'Of course not,' I laughed, still distracted, 'although I did enjoy a run around the dance floor with a gorgeous Spanish guy a few moments ago.'

'Yeah?' Ray screamed in disbelief.

I had been amazed too. 'Just New Year's excitement,' I explained, looking fleetingly at Ray, then at the faces that passed behind him. 'So, what have you done with Rem?'

'She's gone back to Massoud and the VIP area, of course,' Ray sighed. 'Besides, I wanted to find you.'

I looked up at Ray and melted a little, remembering that he was always there for me, and felt a little guilty at feeling so desperate to find Tomas in time for the countdown.

'And, Miss Mistry, I thought that I had better inform you that I've seen Tomas frantically searching every corner of this vessel for what I can only imagine is yours truly . . . It really is quite pathetic — '

'You have? Where?' I asked, interrupting him.

'Well, around twenty minutes ago . . . ' Ray started, looking over his shoulder in the direction he'd come from, but as he turned back to me he jumped ever so slightly and started to make strange gestures, nodding his head bizzarely to one side like a demented parrot as a Remi-a-like issued each of us with a tiny bag of grapes. I looked at Ray, perplexed. The bag of shiny black grapes in my hand only reminded me that I was running out of time, and whatever it was he was trying to joke or bitch about, I wasn't getting it.

'What you do,' I told him, 'is eat one with each chime of the clock before midnight. It's a custom here.' Ray still didn't stop his strange body-pop.

'Hi,' a breathy, out-of-puff voice said close to my ear, as a warm hand enveloped my arm. It was Tomas. 'I thought I'd never find you,' he continued as I looked up to see him smiling, catching his breath. He was carrying two fresh flutes of champagne in one hand and his grapes in the other.

When I looked back to Ray, to acknowledge what his mime had been about, he'd gone. I turned back to Tomas. The countdown started, and within moments we were joining in the traditional merriment, filling our cheeks like greedy hamsters, sticky grape juice rolling from the corners of our mouths as we giggled and tried to accomplish the almost impossible task of eating one grape per chime. The port was alive with people chanting the countdown in Spanish, yachts let off their flares, and an impressive firework display began above us, shooting stars into the night sky.

On the stroke of midnight, Tomas passed me a glass of champagne with a 'Happy New — ' Before he could finish the phrase, we were kissing. A deep, delicious kiss that seemed to last through the cheers of the crowd, the rendition of 'Auld Lang Syne' and the applause that followed it, until we realised with embarrassment that some of that applause had been directed at us.

25

I did, I did, I did

I couldn't help but think back to New Year's Eve now as I stood at the steps of the altar. I felt that same leap of otherworldly excitement as I did that night. The spectacle of the wedding was even more overwhelming than Remi's party, the faces more familiar than the few in her crowd, the anticipation more thrilling than us spending our first night together in Bono's luxury suite, where we did of course push the button to roll back the skylight and sleep beneath the stars.

My groom squeezed my hands in his as I looked up at him. His face blurry through my eyes filled with tears as I realised that from that night on, for the months that had led up to this day, we had been inseparable.

Father Cooper was still speaking, his warm Irish accent washing over me, although I'd heard very few of his words. He stopped, waiting for me to catch up.

'Do you, Isabelle Mistry,' he began slowly, 'take Tomas Field to be your husband?'

'I do,' I heard myself say softly.

'And do you, Tomas Field, take Isabelle Mistry to be your wife?'

'Yes, I do,' Tomas replied, his eyes bright and fixed intensely on mine.

Tomas glanced over his shoulder at Celia. Team Wedding started a round of applause in the pews that travelled through the congregation as Tomas released my hands from his warm enveloping clasp for us to exchange rings. I looked back at Remi, Marta and the bridesmaids, Mum and Dad in the front row. They were all beaming a smile that I knew must mirror mine.

★ ★ ★

'May I first say a heartfelt thank-you to everyone who has come today.' Celia addressed the guests with sincerity at dinner. She had called for silence with the tap of a silver spoon on the side of her lipstick-smudged champagne flute and now stood before the tables seating almost a hundred people. She pursed her lips slightly, in contemplation of the next line.

Our wedding reception at Marta's vineyard had flashed by in a dreamy haze. We'd swooped up the driveway lined with endless rows of vines in a vintage Mercedes as the guests lined up at the entrance of the historic finca to greet us. Showered in rice and petals, we'd made our way through the line of never-ending handshakes and through the handsome arched entrance to the cool cobbled interior. Marta and her family had decorated the courtyard canopied by the shade of vine leaves in the Moorish-inspired style that was indigenous to the island and the finca. It was all so familiar and felt both wonderfully relaxed and special.

The atmosphere was partly due to the fact that Tomas had insisted on just two details throughout the whole planning. Firstly, that aside from the church ceremony I was so excited about arranging (once Celia had used her impeccable contacts to secure the almost impossible — an English/Majorcan wedding in the cathedral), I was to let Celia, Marta and her family take care of all the details. And secondly, that the details should be simple and uncomplicated. The decision, born partly out of Tomas's desire for a wedding day that was neither pretentious nor showy, had freed me of the planning, of seeking out the best ideas I usually suggested to my brides, and allowed me to step away from the stress.

As Marta's team of waiters circled the courtyard with silver trays brimming with cava and canapés, Ramon, to my happy

364

surprise, serenaded us with traditional Spanish songs on his twelve-string guitar. I worked my way around the courtyard, clutching Tomas's hand in mine and a champagne flute that never seemed to be less than half full in the other, thanking guests for coming, greeting long-lost family members and reuniting with friends I'd not seen for more than a year, as well as those who had become so important to our lives on the island. They cooed over the flowers, which matched my bouquets in the church, the traditional well with its bucket filled with blooms, the elaborate Moroccan cushions that lined the steps, the simple stone bowls brimming with lemons. For once I was pleased not to claim the handiwork as my own. I said a million thank-yous to Marta and her mother for the styling they had taken so much care to perfect that it even impressed Marta's grandmother.

Tomas stole me away for a moment, dragging me into the room that housed the ancient olive oil press. Lit with soft candlelight, it felt like a deliciously cool sanctuary away from the laughter and banter of the main courtyard. I stumbled slightly, wobbly from the cava, my heels pin thin on the cobbled stone floor, and Tomas grabbed me in an embrace, his eyes welling up as he whispered a single 'Thank you . . . for marrying me' into my ear. Then, as fast as we'd disappeared into the room, we were off again, running round the side of the finca to the gardens beyond, where the rest of our guests were soaking up the last of the late-afternoon sun before dinner.

Ray and Remi were busy matchmaking fashionista friends from Notting Hill, Celia was dutifully entertaining Father Cooper, my mother was trying to communicate in pidgin Spanish with Marta as my dad looked on with emotional eyes. Poli, Manolo and Pepe rushed to pat Tomas on the back, smart in their suits as they sipped chilled Spanish beer. Juan, Estrella's husband from the mountain house, came bounding up to congratulate us, with a shy and tired Jessica on his shoulders and Juanito dressed as a mini matador in tow.

Just moments later, as the builders laughed at the notion of 'plastering' my cheeks with kisses, Marta's team escorted the guests to dine on the main terrace. The single banqueting table, dressed in a simple linen cloth topped with candelabra and bowls of lemons, overlooked the mountains and gardens below. When all were seated, Tomas and I had made an embarrassed entrance to rapturous applause, and all the while, I floated, as I had done since the beginning of the day, through my own wedding.

'I also wanted to share with you,' Celia continued, 'my delighted surprise at being here today. Just over two years ago, when Izzy first came to stay with me, and quite literally bumped into Tomas, I could have never imagined that they would marry. Yet today I can wholeheartedly say that I cannot think of a better wife for my son.'

The table cheered and held up their glasses in a toast. Celia, however, was far from finished.

'Having had the pleasure of working with Isabelle and having her stay in our family home, I can say that I have been almost as quietly concerned with her happiness as I have been with my own son's.'

I gulped in recognition of Celia's gentle allusion to Harrisson, the break-up, the pressure of continuing to finish the house and stay strong. I felt my eyes well up again.

'It has been a great joy to me that over the last few months Izzy and Tomas have been so supportive of one another. I cannot think of a day that I have known them be apart.'

I looked at Tomas, sitting next to me, and smiled. I thought of the weeks that followed New Year's Eve, how we'd quickly found that living on opposite sides of the island was impossible, and had rented a little house, basic but ours, perched up on the mountain close to Juan and Estrella's. How he'd taught me about the wild flowers and trees that grew there, how he'd transformed the interior into a cosy log cabin during that winter, with open fires and long evenings entertaining friends. Then, as winter turned to spring, he had concentrated on his botany as I became embroiled in the weddings, and our time, precious as the evenings grew lighter, the weekend days longer, was spent on the fishing boat Tomas rented from Pepe, at fiestas in the town, or in the mountains, eating al fresco.

'And still, I am sure,' Celia continued, 'that they have so much to learn about each other.'

She seemed to stall now, taking a moment to look out at the mountains as the sun started to sink slowly behind them.

'Of course, we all have a lot to learn about each other,' she continued, and I looked at her face now with a little concern. There was something in her voice that wavered, something uncertain. 'I am not getting any younger . . . ' She started again, clearing her throat behind a watery smile. 'You of course have all been so kind in congratulating me on my efforts at organising today, and I must respond in two ways. Firstly of course to say that the lion's share was done by the family here, to whom I would like you to raise your glasses.'

Salut! The guests obeyed, as Marta and her family bowed neatly, forever professional.

'As some of you know,' Celia continued, more seriously, 'my health has not been quite what it once was and I am no longer able to run around planning endless weddings. It is with this realisation that I have decided that my wedding gift to this very special couple should be the company I have built to organise so many happy weddings myself. Something to help guarantee their future.'

I looked at Tomas in shock, before we broke into wide smiles and raced to hug and thank Celia, still standing before the guests.

As the speeches continued and the entrée was served, Tomas rested his hand on my knee beneath the table. 'So, company executive, how does it feel?' he leant in to ask me. I looked across at the view before us, the garden, in which Tomas had first proposed to me at Layla's wedding, bathed in dusky light.

'Nothing,' I told him with some reflection, 'has ever felt so right.'

We do hope that you have enjoyed reading this large print book.

Did you know that all of our titles are available for purchase?

We publish a wide range of high quality large print books including:
Romances, Mysteries, Classics
General Fiction
Non Fiction and Westerns

Special interest titles available in large print are:
The Little Oxford Dictionary
Music Book
Song Book
Hymn Book
Service Book

Also available from us courtesy of Oxford University Press:
Young Readers' Dictionary
(large print edition)
Young Readers' Thesaurus
(large print edition)

For further information or a free brochure, please contact us at:
Ulverscroft Large Print Books Ltd.,
The Green, Bradgate Road, Anstey,
Leicester, LE7 7FU, England.
Tel: (00 44) 0116 236 4325
Fax: (00 44) 0116 234 0205

LIZZY HARRISON
LOSES CONTROL

Pippa Wright

Lizzy Harrison isn't a romantic heroine. She is in no way hopelessly scatty and disorganised — her life is in perfect order. Okay, she hasn't met the right man yet, she's too busy with her job in PR, her packed schedule of improving activities and her diary planned for months in advance. But after her best friend, Lulu, challenges her need for control, it's not long before Lizzy is thrown into the arms of her boss's top client, Randy Jones. Reluctantly, she relaxes her hold on routine and discovers that losing control could win her more than she had ever imagined.

UNLUCKY IN LOVE

Jessica Fox

Libby Forster is a danger to men —
according to the fortune-teller at her
sister Zoe's hen night. True, Libby is the
queen of reckless romances and disastrous dating, so it's probably best she
temporarily puts blokes on the back
burner. But when Libby escapes to an
exotic Thai island to do the on-location
casting for a romance-slash-action film,
she's soon tangled up in a love story of
her own. Has Libby met her match with
dishy martial arts instructor Craig? She
may think she needs to keep away from
men, but it seems that men can't keep
away from her . . .

THE DEATH OF BRIDEZILLA

Laurie Brown

When Caroline Tucker's wedding-planning business goes bust, she gets sucked into organising her cousin Barbara's nuptials, in Haven, New Mexico. But Barbara turns out to be a Queen Bride — a Frankenbride — Bridezilla even — and driving Caroline round the bend. And when Barbara's car crashes, Caroline is accused of her murder! Luckily, the arrestingly handsome Sheriff, Travis Beaumont, is on the case — not so luckily, he's also Caroline's ex-husband. She's not impressed with this unwanted blast from the past, but she will have to work closely with him if she wants to avoid a future behind bars.

Tia C
great
maga
high
wasn'
schoo
weigh
fashi
mass
abou
Julie
exist
and
Julie
agai